Diamonds & Dust

A Victorian Murder Mystery

Carol Hedges

First Blue Line Edition, Crooked Cat Publishing Ltd. 2013

Discover us online:
www.crookedcatbooks.com

Join us on facebook:
www.facebook.com/crookedcatpublishing

Tweet a photo of yourself holding
this book to **@crookedcatbooks**
and something nice will happen.

For Martyn, Hannah and Archie

The Author

Carol Hedges is the successful British author of 11 books for teenagers and young adults. Her writing has received much critical acclaim, and her novel Jigsaw was shortlisted for the Angus Book Award and longlisted for the Carnegie Medal.

Carol was born in Hertfordshire, and after university, where she gained a BA (Hons.) in English Literature & Archaeology, she trained as a children's librarian. She worked for the London Borough of Camden for many years,subsequently re-training as a secondary school teacher when her daughter was born.

Carol still lives and writes in Hertfordshire. She is a local activist and green campaigner,and the proud owner of a customized 1988 pink 2CV. Diamonds & Dust, A Victorian Murder Mystery is her first adult novel and her first novel for Crooked Cat Publishing.

Acknowledgements

I owe a debt of gratitude to Laurence and Steph Patterson, of Crooked Cat Publishing, and to my editor Sue Barnard, who edited this book so sensitively and well. Also to David Baird for the brilliant cover.

To the following people, who always encourage and support me: Juliet, Lynn, Hap, Francis, the 2 Sues, Richard, Ros, Val, Jo, Ann, Brenda and Sheila, not forgetting numerous friends on Twitter and Facebook ... many thanks.

Most of all, I owe a debt that is un-payable to all those wonderful Victorian authors whose work I have shamelessly plundered, paraphrased and pastiched. Without them, this book would never have been written. I thank them, albeit posthumously.

Diamonds & Dust

A Victorian Murder Mystery

"I behold London: a Human awful wonder of God."

Wm. Blake, Albion

London, 1860. Dream world of pain and pleasure, of fantasy and phantom. It is midnight, a full moon and a cold mist rising up from the river. Mist ghosts the masts of the sloops and Russian brigs waiting to unload their cargo. Mist curls itself possessively around sooty chimneys and rooftops. Mist gently fingers its way into fetid courts and alleyways, and the crammed tenements where myriad Londoners toss and turn in troubled sleep.

Not everyone is sleeping, though, in this vast city of many million souls. Strange shapes of men and women drift through the misty streets like ghostly apparitions. They gather outside dim gaslit haunts. Street corners are beset by night prowlers. The devil slips a diamond ring on his taloned finger, sticks a pin in his shirt-front, and steps out to take the air.

Look more closely. A solitary man is crossing Westminster Bridge. Tall and broad-shouldered, he wears a top hat, and an overcoat with wide lapels and a velvet collar. It is buttoned up against the chill night air.

The man walks with purpose, as if on his way to an important rendezvous. A gas lamp throws its shifting radiance upon the upper planes of his face. The lower part of his face is covered by a knitted scarf, protection from the stinking miasma that rises from the oozing mud.

Footsteps approach from behind him. Someone else is also crossing the bridge, moving with incredible speed. Darkness clings to a misty outline, pooling around feet that step from shadow into light and back into shadow. The figure stretches out a black-gloved hand. Touches the man upon the left shoulder.

He turns. Freezes. Then cowers back, uttering a low cry of

horror and covering his face with his arms. There is the sound of blows being struck, the ripping of flesh, the thud of something heavy hitting the ground. Then silence.

Running steps re-cross the bridge and echo into the distance. The man remains, lying motionless in the gutter, blood pooling beneath his head. A gas lamp flickers momentarily overhead, and goes out.

***

Morning arrives, bringing smoggy clouds that envelop the city like a grey shroud. In a house in St John's Wood, a young woman descends the stairs and enters the morning room. Her name is Josephine King. She is eighteen years old and stands upon the threshold of life. Her whole future lies before her. And so, currently, does her breakfast.

Filling her plate with bacon and scrambled eggs, she carries it to the dining table, where she sits down and unfolds a starched white linen napkin. As if on cue, a prim white-aproned maid knocks and enters, carrying a shiny silver coffee pot. Steam curls fragrantly from its spout.

"Coffee, miss?" she inquires.

"Yes please, Annie."

Josephine King begins eating her breakfast with relish. Breakfast at the Bertha Helstone Institute for Orphaned Clergy Daughters had consisted of a bowl of porridge and a mug of watered-down milk. At the Bertha Helstone Institute for Orphaned Clergy Daughters, feeding the soul was considered far more important than feeding the body. In winter, the milk had lumps of ice floating in it. The porridge was frequently burnt, but they were still expected to eat it. Now she bites into thickly-buttered toast, and recalls the many times she had lain awake in the cold dark dormitory, shivering under her thin blanket, and dreaming about hot roast potatoes and white bread.

She'd probably still be there, learning plain sewing and passages from the Bible in preparation for life as a governess, or a lady's companion, had it not been for Uncle Herbert King. Wonderful Uncle Herbert King, who had run away from England to seek his fortune, and having found it, had come back and rescued her.

Josephine finishes her breakfast and returns to her room. She can still scarcely believe she actually possesses a whole room of her own. It is furnished in the most delightful fashion. There is a writing-desk, a dressing-table with a looking-glass, and a bright chintz-covered sofa.

The walls are painted soft dove-grey, and the floor is spread with Indian matting in maize colour and red. Patterned chintz curtains frame the windows, and on the walls there are crayon sketches of exotic foreign scenes.

She opens the top drawer of her writing-desk and takes out a faded leather- covered book. It is her childhood diary, given to her by Mrs Sams, the woman she met on board the coach taking her to the Bertha Helstone Institute for Orphaned Clergy Daughters.

She recalls Mrs Sams saying to her that a diary was exactly like a best friend. Back then, she had badly needed a best friend. She had lost both her beloved missionary parents to Indian cholera. Barely understanding the implications of what had happened, and only seven years old, she'd been thrust, alone and bewildered, into a world that did not know what to do with her. And did not very much care.

Turning to the first page, she reads the familiar words:

"Arrived at my new school."

So few words for such a momentous event that began with a slow, backside-numbing journey that seemed to go on forever, night and day blurring into one, until the coach ceased to rattle over stony town streets, entering instead a strange landscape of great black hills heaving up to the horizon, with dark woods and deep valleys.

Once more, as if in a waking dream, she hears the wild wind rushing among the trees, sees herself set down from the carriage, her little tin trunk at her feet. She is utterly alone, standing in front of the iron gates of the austere grey building that housed the Bertha Helstone Institute for Orphaned Clergy Daughters.

She turns the page.

I HATE THIS PLACE

is scrawled in big capital letters.
Followed by:

> *Ran away. Had to learn chapter of Leviticus by HART as punishment.*

Ah yes. The punishments. They were very good at punishments at the Bertha Helstone Institute, she remembers. Learning passages of scripture was a favourite, closely followed by being slapped or beaten with a birch-twig rod.

When she was older, the favoured method of punishment was the application of the backboard – a complicated wooden contraption with leather straps. Wearing it felt like being pressed between two tables.

Over the years she was incarcerated, Josephine spent so much time strapped into a backboard that it has left her with a way of standing very upright, with her chin sticking out and a thousand-yards stare, so that when she first arrived at her uncle's house, she had overheard Annie the parlour maid referring to her as a "hoity-toity, arrogant young miss."

She has contemplated throwing the diary away, but she won't, because it is a witness of important things that she needs to remember. She reads on for a while, then replaces it in the desk drawer. Later this morning she will meet her uncle at his office for a discussion about her future. She has already decided that the words *governess* and *lady's companion* are not going to be part of that discussion.

Josephine King sits back and thinks about her wonderful future. The house is very quiet. The only noise is that of the rooks in the trees outside her window. Suddenly the peace is shattered by the urgent ringing of the front doorbell. It goes on sounding throughout the house, as if made by some desperate hand. There is a pause. Then footsteps hurry up the stairs and Annie the maid knocks on her door.

"You must come down at once, miss," she says, her eyes wide. "There are two men from the detective police in the drawing room."

Josephine descends the stairs and enters the drawing room. The two men from the detective police are standing in front of the fireplace. One is middle-aged, with a greying moustache and pouchy, unslept eyes. The other, who is slightly younger, is clean-shaven but for a pair of side-whiskers.

Both are staring silently at the hearthrug. They look up as she enters, and exchange a quick, significant glance. She feels her breath catch in her throat. Something bright blooms in her chest.

"You are Miss Josephine King?" the older man asks.

"Yes, I am."

"I am Detective Inspector Leo Stride from Scotland Yard. This is my colleague, Detective Sergeant Jack Cully."

He gestures towards the sofa.

"Perhaps you would like to sit down, Miss King?"

Every fibre of her being is shrieking out that this man is not bringing glad tidings. She clasps her hands behind her back, and draws herself very upright.

"I think I will remain standing, if you don't mind."

"Very well."

The Detective Inspector draws a small notebook from his coat pocket.

"I regret I am the bearer of bad news, Miss King," he says.

She digs her nails hard into the palms of her hands. It is a trick she taught herself while at the Bertha Helstone Institute. You concentrate upon the pain, thus blotting out everything else.

The Detective Inspector opens the notebook and reads:

"In the early hours of this morning, one of my night-officers discovered a male person lying in the gutter upon Westminster Bridge. Thinking at first that he was under the influence of strong drink, my officer attempted to revive him.

"When he received no response, he proceeded to make a closer examination, and discovered that the man had suffered a brutal attack, which sadly had proved fatal. That man, I have to inform you, was Mr Herbert King."

Josephine knows she is listening, but the words aren't making any sense. Then a spark ignites in her brain.

"I think there must be a mistake, Detective Inspector. My uncle left for work early this morning, so the poor unfortunate man on the bridge couldn't possibly be him."

He bats the suggestion away.

"I have had a brief word with the staff. Your cook never saw Mr King leave the house this morning. The maid says that she recalls him leaving the house last night, but she did not hear him return, and his bed has not been slept in all night."

"But she might have been mistaken. He could have got up very early," she presses on, clutching at the suggestions as a drowning man might grasp a passing branch. "And then maybe he—"

"Miss King," Detective Inspector Stride cuts in firmly, "the man on the bridge was wearing an expensive suit from Moses and Son of Holborn. Also a navy woollen overcoat. I visited the shop this morning, and Mr Moses confirmed that both items were ordered several months ago by Mr King, and delivered to this address last Thursday. He described his client as a tall man with broad shoulders. Mr Moses also furnished us with the measurements he took from your uncle before making the suit. The measurements tallied exactly with those of the man found on the bridge. I am sorry, but there is no doubt whatsoever in my mind as to his identity."

She feels the air around her beginning to freeze. Small ornaments upon the mantelpiece suddenly take on a strange intensity.

"Why would anybody want to kill my uncle?"

"It's too early to determine, although we are not discounting the possibility that robbery may have played a part in the initial motive. Did your uncle possess anything of value that he might have had about his person?"

"He had a gold watch, and a gold signet ring."

The Detective Inspector makes a note.

"Ah. Then it is as I suspected: the motive was robbery. There was nothing of value found upon the body. His wallet was also taken. He must have been picked clean by his attackers after he'd been struck down."

Words swim in her brain like fish under thick ice. She struggles to bring them to the surface.

"Where is my uncle now?"

"My officers have taken his body to the nearest police mortuary."

"I should like to see him."

Detective Inspector Stride shakes his head.

"Your uncle was the victim of a violent attack, Miss King. There are aspects of his death that you, as a young woman, may find shocking."

Briefly, she resurrects a mental picture of searing white heat, and a filth-encrusted bed upon which lies a gasping, terrifyingly blue-faced couple, barely recognisable as her beloved mother and father. They have cholera and are dying. She is seven years old. She reminds herself that death holds no shocks for her any more.

"I wish to see him."

He sighs resignedly.

"Very well then. If you will permit us, we shall accompany you."

Outside, a dun-coloured veil hangs over the housetops, looking like a reflection of the mud-coloured streets below. Josephine is ushered into a waiting four-wheeler, and borne swiftly away.

***

The police mortuary is a windowless white-tiled room in a basement. There are medical instruments laid out upon a counter. The air smells cold and unhappy. On a wooden table is something covered in a dark cloth.

Josephine takes deep breaths to steady herself for the ordeal ahead. Overlap is the last thing she needs. No spilling of memory from one death to another.

The police surgeon removes the cloth.

For a split second she is confused. The dead body lying upon the table has a shock of snow-white hair. Its head lies at an awkward angle, the throat a gaping grin of torn flesh. This is not Uncle Herbert, cannot be Uncle Herbert. Uncle Herbert has red hair, the same colour as her own. Clearly, this man is someone else. A terrible mistake has been made.

Then she recognises the navy woollen topcoat, trousers and high-collared shirt. It is indeed her uncle's body, but terribly altered. His hands are tightly clenched, as if his death struggle has been intense and agonising. His mouth gapes, his eyes are fixed and staring, his rigid face bears an expression of intense horror.

The police surgeon steps forward.

"There is evidence of strangulation," he says in a calm, matter-of-fact voice. "The neck has been broken, and here, at the side of the skull, the bone has been driven in. There has been an attempt to tear out the throat. However I do not think that these injuries, horrific and violent as they are, were what caused this man's death."

He pauses.

"What killed him was something else. Something so unusual that I don't think I have ever seen anything like it before."

He turns to face her.

"Miss King, it is my belief, from a preliminary examination of his body, that your uncle, Mr Herbert King, was killed by fear. The sort of fear that can make a heart suddenly stop beating. In my opinion, he was frightened to death."

***

Some time later, a cab rattles its way through the London streets. The lamps have been lit, giving out misty splotches of glimmering light. The yellow glare from shop windows streams into the steamy, vaporous air, throwing a shifting radiance upon the slimy pavements.

Josephine sits in the rear of the cab, trying to stare a hole through the floor. She feels like a stranger in her own life. Faces pass by in an eerie and ghostlike procession, unaware that just a short distance away, someone's world has been overturned.

Memories come flooding back. She recalls the first time she met Uncle Herbert. She'd been sitting at the back of the sewing class, hemming sheets – she seemed to be always hemming sheets in those days – when the door had opened to admit a small, scared maid who had scuttled across the room and whispered something in the ear of Miss Daemon, the sewing teacher. Whereupon Miss Daemon had raised her eyes and stared hard through her pince-nez, before saying in a sepulchral tone:

"Josephine King. You are to report to the Headmistress's parlour. At once!"

There was only one reason this summons was ever issued, so a score of curious eyes had followed her as she slowly rose, and crossed the length of the room. But upon entering the parlour, the first thing she'd seen was a tall red-haired man standing in front of the fireplace. She had stared at him. The man had stared back. Then his eyes had lit up, and his face broke into a smile.

"Hello Josie," he'd said. "I'm your Uncle Herbert – your father's brother. I've come to take you home."

She recalls placing her small pathetic bundle of possessions into the hired carriage, and then asking for it to stop just as it had left the Bertha Helstone Institute. She'd got down, walked back through the grim iron gates, picked up a large stone from the rockery and hurled it with all her might at one of the latticed windows, shattering the glass into a thousand pieces. It had been a glorious moment. A final gesture of defiance.

Now the cab drops her outside her uncle's house. The questions in her head are like birds beating against the bars of a cage. Inside the house, the air is steamy and acrid. On the first floor landing, she encounters Annie. The parlour maid is carrying an armful of dresses. She recognises them instantly: her lovely new dresses, bought when she first arrived in London. Most of them have never been worn.

"I'm taking these downstairs to Mrs Hudson," Annie sniffs. "She is going to boil them up with some black dye. You won't be wearing colour for a long while. I laid out your other black dress for you."

Her other black dress?

She hurries to her room. On her bed is the itchy, ill-fitting woollen dress she used to wear at the Bertha Helstone Institute. She had thrown it out the moment she arrived at the house. The servants must have kept it. She stares at the hated garment, and a shiver runs down her spine.

Her life has gone round in a complete circle. Only this morning she was a carefree, happy young woman in a secure loving home, contemplating the prospect of a delightful future. Now, she knows without a shadow of doubt that she will never be that person again.

***

It is the following morning. Dark columns of smoke rise from a million massed chimneys, for London in 1860 is a filthy, stinking city. There are too many people, too much coal dust, too many horses, and too many cowsheds and abattoirs. There is smoke in the streets, in the air, in the river, in the clothes people wear as they go about their daily business.

Smoke turns clean washing brown in a few hours, and covers the trees with soot. It enters the nostrils and penetrates the lungs. In Winter, the city is frequently almost pitch dark in the middle of the day, everything visible turning the colour of brown paper or pea-soup.

The offices of King & Co are located on the second floor of a tall smoke-grey building at the far end of a narrow smoky Holborn street. Access is under a sooty brick archway and across a cobbled square, where a stone entrance leads to a flight of dusty stone steps, reminding the visitor of the entrance to some ancient church. The impression is reinforced by the view, from the open half-landing, of the ruins of a burial ground, where ivy-covered gravestones lean against crumbling cloisters.

Josephine climbs the steps to the second floor. She is not sure what her uncle's business was exactly, she only knows he will not be doing it any more, and it is now her painful duty to break the sad news of his death to the clerk.

She enters the outer office. There are invoices impaled on a lethal-looking spike, calendars, and bundles of papers held together by pegs. Picture pages cut out from newspapers are pasted onto the walls. There is a tall wooden desk with a high wooden stool, and a smoky fire in the grate.

There is also a thin young man with a pale bony face, a pale bony nose and pale bony fingers stained with black ink. This is Trafalgar Moggs, her uncle's clerk. She has encountered him a couple of times when he called at her uncle's house to deliver some papers.

"Oh, Miss King – it is you!" he stammers, getting to his feet, and sticking the pen awkwardly behind one ear. "I have just read the tragic news about Mr King on my way to work."

"Read?"

He places a copy of the *Illustrated London News* upon the desk.

"It is in all the newspapers."

She picks up the newspaper. Under a large headline stating MIDNIGHT ASSASSINATION! is a drawing of a smartly-dressed City man being struck about the head by several rough-looking individuals. His top hat has fallen off, his mouth is open in a silent scream, and his hands are raised in mute protest. The drawing bears absolutely no resemblance whatsoever to her uncle.

"*The detective police are baffled by the senselessness of such a brutal killing carried out at night on an innocent member of the general public going about his lawful business,*" she reads.

"The newspaper quotes a Detective Inspector Stride of the detective police, based at Great Scotland Yard," the clerk observes. "He says that Mr King's death was '*act of meaningless violence*'."

Josephine puts the newspaper down.

"I came to inform you of my uncle's death, Mr Moggs, but clearly you know of it already."

"I only know what I have read in the newspaper. I should be grateful for anything else that you care to tell me, Miss King. I have been employed in this office for some time, and Mr King was a man I held in the highest regard."

She waits while he fetches a chair from the inner office. Then she tells him everything that has happened since the visit of the two detectives. The clerk listens attentively until she has finished speaking.

"This is very strange. I cannot imagine that Mr King could

ever be so terrified of anything that his hair would turn white."

He scratches his head with the end of the quill.

"I have been going over and over the day he died in my mind, trying to find something unusual that happened, but there was nothing. In the morning, your uncle dealt with the post, did some correspondence, and saw clients. At three, I put the afternoon post on his desk. A short while later, he came out of his office. He'd got on his ulster and top hat. *I'm just stepping out for a while, Moggs,'* he said. *'I'll be back before the end of the day.'* That was the last time I saw him, for he never returned."

He regards her thoughtfully.

"You are very alone, Miss King ... if you don't mind my observing. Is there nobody ... I mean a lady of course ... whom you could consult about all this?"

"No one," she replies. "But that is perfectly fine, Mr Moggs. The detective police are investigating my uncle's murder. And I can look after myself."

The clerk's face radiates doubt on both counts.

She hurries on.

"I will let you know when my uncle's funeral is to be."

"Thank you, Miss King. I should like to pay my respects. In the meantime, if I can be of any help in any way?"

Caught unaware by the kindness, her eyes blur with tears. She casts a glance around the office.

"Could you continue to run my uncle's business?"

The clerk draws himself up.

"Of course I will, Miss King. Have no worries about that. None whatsoever. It is only what Mr King would expect."

***

Leaving her uncle's office, Josephine catches an omnibus, which drops her at the north side of Westminster Bridge. Detective Inspector Stride had described the exact spot where her uncle's body was discovered. Now she has come to see for herself. She walks to the edge of the pavement. There are bloodstains on the cobbles. The scarlet threads of murder.

She tries to picture the scene. The dark, the gang, the brutal attack, so terrifying that her poor uncle's hair turns white with shock. Everything seems so normal now. Thin grey rain is falling. Foul-smelling water oozes under the bridge. Hurrying passers-by jostle for space on the pavement.

Suddenly she hears a husky voice.

"You come to see where the swell woz murdered?"

Startled, she looks around, but cannot locate who has just spoken.

"Down 'ere."

There is a bundle of rags at her feet. She has not noticed it. The bundle gets up, turning itself into a filthy dirty small boy with strangely intense light blue eyes. He is wearing a man's body-coat, the tails of which are dragging on the ground, and trousers tied up with fraying string instead of braces. His feet are clad in broken boots. In one hand, he grasps a battered broom.

"Who are you?" she asks.

"Oo wants ter know?"

"I do."

"An' who are you?"

"The one asking the questions."

A vaguely thoughtful expression crosses the boy's face. He feels around in his matted hair, eventually removing something tiny which he cracks between finger and thumb.

"Give us a penny? I'll show yer ezackly where it 'appened. Blood an' all."

"I'm looking at it right now, blood and all, for free."

The boy gives her a resentful stare.

"Well, I might be able ter tell you somefink else abaht it, if you likes."

"Really? What?"

"Wot's yer name?"

"Josephine King."

The boy's blue eyes sparkle.

"Josephine King," he chuckles hoarsely. "Jo King. Hohoho. Joking ... Geddit?"

Josephine brings her face as close to him as her sense of smell will allow.

"Where I used to live," she remarks quietly, "there was a girl who made fun of my name. Do you know what happened to her?"

"No."

"She died."

This is partly true. A haemorrhagic fever may have also contributed.

The boy takes a step back.

"Coo ... scary ain't yer?"

"Very. So what can you tell me?"

He rolls his eyes.

"Hard to fink straight when your belly's empty."

She feels in her pocket and holds out a few small coins.

"'Ere. Hold the broom."

The boy runs over to a nearby coffee stall, returning shortly with a white china cup and a thick doorstep of bread-and-butter, which he consumes with alarming speed.

"My eye! That was good," he says, wiping the last crumbs from his mouth.

"So, tell me everything you know."

He shoots her a cunning look.

"Well ... all I can tell you is ... I don't know nuffink. Wasn't there. Didn't see a fing. Hahaha, only joking, Jo King." He waves a grubby finger. "Gotcha!"

A hot tidal wave of anger rises up inside her.

"You nasty little ragamuffin!" she exclaims. "The man was my uncle. The only relation I had left in the world! Now he's dead and I am all on my own. And you think it's funny?"

19

She turns her head away, too proud to let the dirty small boy see her cry. There is a brief silence, followed by a strange scritch-scratching noise. The boy is carefully sweeping a circle around her. He looks suitably contrite.

"Didn't know," he mutters. "Sorry, miss."

She struggles to master her feelings.

"Maybe I could ask round for you," he suggests. "See wot I can find out."

"Friends in low places?"

He ignores this.

"Be back 'ere in a couple of days. I might really 'ave somefink to tell you then. And if I ain't here, ask at the coffee stall – they'll know where I am."

"Who should I ask for?"

"Don't 'ave a name as sich."

"So what should I call you?"

A well-dressed City man arrives at the opposite kerb. He glances in their direction, then shouts,

"Oi! Crossing-sweeper!"

The boy rolls his eyes.

"Call me Oi," he says, picking up his broom. "Why not? Everybody else does."

***

On her return to St John's Wood, Josephine sees that the small silver dish on the hall table has filled up with cards. Since she has been out, half of London's carriages appear to have rolled up at the door.

Who on earth *are* all these people, she thinks. Several of the cards have the top right-hand corner turned down, indicating that the unknown caller brought her equally-unknown grown-up daughter with her.

She tries to recall what Uncle Herbert said about calling cards.

"You just concentrate on settling in, Josie. Go shopping, see the sights. Once you're ready to launch yourself upon London society, I'll find you some jolly girls to run around with and have fun."

Too late, she thinks grimly. She stares at the neat copperplate writing, wondering which turned-down edge might represent a "jolly girl to run around with."

Annie bustles into the hallway, her face wearing a smug, triumphant smile.

"Mrs Thorpe and Miss Isabella Thorpe are waiting in the drawing-room," she announces. "They have come about the arrangements."

The arrangements?

Josephine unties her bonnet strings and pins up some wayward strands of hair. Then, adjusting her facial expression to what she hopes is suitably welcoming, she opens the drawing room door.

A large florid-faced woman in an elegant tight dark blue silk dress and an elaborately-trimmed purple hat is sitting on the sofa. A young woman, equally elegantly-clad, lounges in one of the wing chairs.

"My dear, dear child!" Mrs Thorpe intones in a sepulchral voice, as she heaves herself upright. "What a tragedy! What a disaster! As soon as I heard, I said to Mr Thorpe: *'I must go to her, poor orphaned lamb, and see what I can do.'* You know, of course, that your poor dear uncle was at school with my husband? And then at the university? In fact, if it wasn't for Mr Thorpe's help and advice, your dear uncle might not have had the success in business that he had."

Mrs Thorpe extracts a tiny lace handkerchief from an equally tiny glass-beaded reticule, and dabs at her eyes. She pats the sofa space next to her.

"Sit, sit."

Obediently, Josephine sits.

"Now my dear, call me an interfering old woman if you will, but I was wondering: have you begun to think about the arrangements?"

She waits for Mrs Thorpe to clarify.

"For the burial, I mean. Mr Leverton, the undertaker, should be instructed to see to the finer details. The mourning coaches will need to be secured at the earliest opportunity. And of course the actual internment has to be at Kensal Green. It is the only place for a man of his standing in the business community to be buried."

Mrs Thorpe's corsets creak, as she leans forward and lowers her voice.

"The Duke of Sussex and Princess Sophia are buried there, you know."

She sighs and lays a plump, heavily-beringed hand upon Josephine's knee.

"Do not worry my dear. We are here, and we shall take care of everything. You must leave it all to us."

"Mama is very good at organising things," Isabella Thorpe remarks acidly.

Josephine glances at Isabella. She has a pale prettiness. Her grey eyes are the colour of river-washed pebbles, and her chestnut hair curls in tight ringlets on either side of her face. Her pink striped silk dress, which does not suit her pale colouring and chestnut hair, looks very expensive, as do her spotless grey kid boots.

Looking at her, Josephine becomes painfully aware that her black dress is too tight, rather damp under the arms, and very frayed around the hem. Also, that frizzy orange snakes have once again escaped from the combs and chignon. And that Isabella has noted it.

Isabella reads her glance and smoothes down her dress with a dainty kid-gloved hand.

"I shall take personal charge of your mourning dress and bonnet, of course," she says, studying Josephine with a practised eye.

"Bella is such a dear caring girl," Mrs Thorpe coos.

She hauls herself creakily upright, patting Josephine's shoulder as she rises.

"Now do not fret, poor dear child. Everything is in our hands. Come, Bella my love, we have other calls to make."

Isabella gathers her pretty pink paisley shawl around her sloping shoulders.

"I shall write to you in a day or so. I'm sure Papa will let me have the brougham for our shopping trip."

She gives Josephine a further careful scrutiny from under her eyelashes and sighs sadly.

"Black is a terribly unfortunate colour," she murmurs. "It drains the complexion badly. And of course you will have to wear it for at least three months before you can go into the tiniest bit of colour. I am *so* sorry for you."

Annie is hovering in the hallway, holding Mrs Thorpe's mantle ready. Josephine suspects that she has probably been standing outside the drawing room door, listening to every word.

Elaborate farewells are exchanged upon the doorstep. The Thorpes enter a very smart carriage that has drawn up outside and are whisked away.

As the front door closes, Josephine notices that another visiting card has been pushed through the letterbox, and is lying on the floor, ungathered. She bends down and picks it up.

"Who is Mrs Lilith Marks?" she asks.

The parlour-maid's face freezes. Next second, she snatches the little pasteboard square out of Josephine's hand, and tears it in two.

"Nobody, miss," she says abruptly. "Nobody and nothing."

***

Upon Westminster Bridge the rush hour is in full swing. A steady stream of young clerks in dark suits and bright waistcoats jostle for pavement space with shop-workers and factory drudges.

Cabs weave a precarious path across the bridge, for there is no right of way, no drive-on-the-left rule. It is every man for himself here, and devil take the hindmost.

Horse-drawn omnibuses, their knife-boards packed, rattle to a halt on the south side, and disgorge their passengers, who join the vast swarm eagerly rushing across the bridge, to be swallowed up by offices, banks and shops, just like every other morning. And just like every other morning, the elderly couple running the coffee stall are doing a brisk trade in hot drinks, bread-and-butter, and ham sandwiches.

Eventually the crowd around the stall thins, until there remains only a young woman in an ill-fitting black dress, black coat, and plain black straw bonnet. Her eyes are dark smudges in her pale face, and her bright copper-coloured hair is coming down at the back.

Scrag and bone, the coffee stall owner thinks, wondering whether she has seen her here before.

"Cuppa luverly hot coffee, m'duck ?" she asks, holding her coffee pot aloft over a tray of stained china mugs.

"No thank you," the young woman says firmly, her head held high. "I'm looking for the boy who sweeps the crossing. Do you know where I might find him?"

"What boy?" the coffee stall owner asks innocently. Because you never know, do you?

The young woman frowns.

"He told me his name was Oi."

"Did he now. Well, he ain't here."

"Do you know where he has gone?"

The coffee stall owner shrugs.

"Couldn't say, I'm sure."

"He's gone to buy a new broom," her husband interjects. "He should be back soon enough, if you cares to wait."

"Cuppa hot coffee to pass the time, maybe?" his wife suggests meaningfully.

24

The young woman takes the hint. She digs in her pocket for some coins.

"A cup of coffee would be lovely. Thank you. Yes – and maybe one of those nice slices of bread-and-butter to go with it?"

The coffee stall owner pours coffee into a mug, and hands her the platter. The young woman selects a thickly-buttered slice, then carries both items the short distance to the parapet of the bridge.

"Now, watcher make of that?" the coffee stall owner exclaims. "We dresses like one of them street gels, but ain't we got the airs and graces of a duchess!"

Josephine leans upon the parapet, sipping the bitter black coffee. She watches the light catching the water, turning it chemical-silver. Her head is spinning with cards and coffins, coaches and cemeteries. There is so much to do to arrange a funeral, and Mrs Thorpe is grimly determined that all shall not only be done, but be done properly.

Later, Josephine has go shopping with Isabella Thorpe for some proper mourning clothes. Mrs Hudson's home-dyed offerings have been viewed, and rejected out of hand.

She looks down at her shabby, mud-splattered black frock and recollects reading somewhere that the main reason people wear black is to stop the dead from returning. By veiling and cloaking themselves in black, the living somehow render themselves invisible to the dead.

If she believed this (which she does not), she would wear the brightest colours she could find. She'd give anything to see her uncle again. And her beloved parents, whose dear faces she now sees only in rare dreams.

She is roused from her sad reverie by a shuffling sound, punctuated by a wheezy cough that sounds like a bag of bricks being thrown against a wall. The crossing-sweeper in his broken boots is making his way along the pavement towards her.

"'Ello Jo King. Here you are agin. Thruppence halfpenny,

this broom cost," he grumbles. "Last month, it was only thruppence. Bleedin' daylight robbery."

His bright eyes travel to the half-drunk cup of coffee, then to the untasted slice of bread-and-butter. There is an expectant pause. Silently, she hands them over. He wolfs down the bread, and drinks off the coffee in one slurping gulp, before running a filthy finger round the inside of the cup and sucking it noisily.

She bites back the temptation to comment, reminding herself that it was not so long ago when she herself had been so hungry that the last shreds of rancid meat served up in a thin watery stew were as precious as the finest gold.

Suddenly the boy spots a well-dressed couple waiting at the kerb. He sets down the cup on the pavement and darts out into the road, where he begins assiduously sweeping a path in front of them. Though Josephine observes that he is not so much as sweeping as moving the dirt around, to give it a change of scenery.

Eventually he crosses back, jingling some coins.

"Look! Tuppence!" He grins. "Took pity on me 'cos I was so poor and ragged. Who says dirt don't pay?"

He thrusts the money into some hidden pocket inside his ragged, filthy coat. Then leans his broom against the bridge, and begins to remove the thick half-moons of dirt from under his nails.

"I've 'ad all sorts of people on my crossing, Jo King," he boasts. "You wouldn't believe it. Lords and ladies, famous theatricals, Members of Parliament. I had the Prime Minister on my crossing just the other day. I crossed the Queen once."

"You're right. I don't believe it."

"You wasn't there."

She decides to change the subject.

"So, what did you find out about my uncle's murder?"

"The only one wot remembers anyfink woz Jim Jarndyce – an old soldger from the Crimean War. Sometimes he sleeps in the first doorway on t'other side of the bridge. Heard noises in the middle of the night – said it woke 'im up, so it must've been loud, coz once he's off, he don't come round easy. Blood-curdling screams, he said. Reminded 'im of when he woz on the battlefield. Soon after that, he sez he heard footsteps running. Couldn't tell me much more on account of the mist and the dark, and the amount of drink he'd taken."

"Has he spoken to the police?"

Oi gives a rusty laugh.

"We don't speak to the ecipol round 'ere."

"The ecip— oh, I see. However, I should like to speak to him, if I may."

"Best of luck wiv that."

Ignoring him, she walks briskly over the bridge until she reaches the first doorway on the far side. It is tantalisingly empty, though a broken bottle, a few fishbones, and a puddle of something she doesn't want to think about, all bear witness to the previous night's occupant.

Disappointed, she retraces her steps.

"He's not there."

The boy nods.

"Gone on the tramp. Does that. Says he can't breathe right in Lunnon. Comes back though, regular as clockwork. I can let you know when he does."

She tells him her address. Then she turns to go.

"Hey, Jo King," the crossing-sweeper calls out after her, "I heard as 'ow if you look into a dead man's eyes, there'll be a little pitcher of the last thing he saw. That's what you oughter do. Look into your uncle's eyes, and p'raps you'll see the face of his murderer."

***

Later that same afternoon, a shiny cherry-coloured brougham draws up outside a fashionable West End salon whose shiny plate-glass windows are full of richly-coloured velvet mantles, glacé silk and moiré, all artistically arranged. The Thorpes' coachman descends from the box and opens the coach door.

"Come," Isabella says to Josephine, waving a languid hand.

She glides into the store, immediately securing the services of a couple of showroom women, who usher the two girls to a side-room. Big looking-glasses are set in handsome carved-gilt frames, and a richly-patterned violet carpet covers the floor. Isabella explains carefully what Josephine needs, then sinks onto a small chintz-patterned sofa, while the two women, one of whom is French, bustle around selecting patterns, rolls of black cloth, and trimmings.

"When I was fifteen and still at school, we made it our aim reduce our waists by one inch per month," Isabella says, as the saleswomen begin to divest Josephine of her outer garments. "By the time I left, my waist measured thirteen inches."

The saleswomen look impressed. Josephine, however, is horrified. Isabella is much too thin even now. So what must she have looked like then? What on earth did she eat? Did she eat?

Isabella rolls her eyes.

"Mama makes me lace to nineteen now. She says that less than that is not conducive to my health. Apparently our vicar has also told her that tight lacing is immoral and opposed to all the laws of religion."

She eyes Josephine's maladroitly-laced waist.

"New stays?"

"Oh no, I really don't—"

"We 'ave some delightful articles in scarlet, Mademoiselle," the French woman says. "Front fastening too, for ease of dressing. Zey came in last week, fresh from Par-ee."

Isabella nods her approval.

"We shall take them. It means you won't be entirely in black, which will be *such* a relief, won't it?"

Eventually, after much debate between Isabella and the French sales assistant (a debate in which Josephine plays no significant part whatsoever), two mourning dresses are commissioned: a showy one for the upcoming funeral, and an everyday dress for other occasions.

Then it is Josephine's turn to sit patiently while Isabella chooses a new evening dress for herself, matching it with a bonnet and evening gloves, and commanding, with an imperious wave of her hand, that the entire order of three outfits must be delivered tomorrow.

Of course Isabella does not know (and probably would not care either) that the sewing women in the salon workroom will now have to sit up all night to finish the dresses. Some are no older than herself, and will toil for twenty hours or more without a break.

She certainly does not know that the job of sewing the underskirts will be given to a thinly-clad young woman in a slum attic in Carnaby Street. They will be carefully checked for bugs and fleas upon delivery.

"And now," Isabella declares, "I shall take you to tea!"

Josephine feels her spirits sink. She is a headache on feet. All she wants to do is go home and lie down with a cold cloth over her eyes and the curtains closed.

Nevertheless, rules have to be followed, so she agrees politely that "a cup of tea would be quite delightful indeed."

The brougham drops them outside one of the newly-opened little tea rooms in Jermyn Street. Isabella takes Josephine's arm and steers her into the brightly-lit place, where the air is filled with chatter and light feminine laughter, mingling with the clatter of cups and saucers. She glances quickly round.

"Aha – I see him!" she exclaims, waving a gloved hand.

Josephine follows the direction of the wave, and sees a heavily-set young man in military uniform rising to his feet. He has a chestnut moustache, and long, fashionable side-whiskers, and is watching their progress across the room with some apprehension.

"*There* you are Gussy, you *bad* boy!" Isabella says in a

scolding tone.

"Don't know what you mean, Bella. I've been waitin' for you for ages," the Bad Boy responds, his face flushing. He pulls crossly at his side-whisker.

"Now Gussy, no sulking – it don't suit you," Isabella chides, lowering herself elegantly onto a chair. "See, I have brought my new friend Miss Josephine King to meet you. Josephine, this is Augustus Thorpe, my brother. Gussy is in the Dragoon Guards," she says, adding slyly, "Ain't he handsome?"

"Aw, Bella."

Isabella ignores his protest.

"Tea, I think," she says, addressing a white-aproned waiter who has hurried over to serve them. "Indian tea? Yes. And some bread-and-butter, thinly-cut. Maybe a selection of nice cakes?"

The waiter glides away. Isabella removes her gloves and blows into the fingers to straighten them. Josephine stares down at her lap, trying not to notice that Augustus Thorpe's eyes, which are the same pebble-washed grey colour as his sister's, are looking her up and down with speculative interest, as if she were a prize pig at Smithfield market.

"So Gussy, what have you been up to recently?" Isabella inquires briskly, having finally arranged her gloves to her satisfaction. "Mama complains that you've not been near the house for days."

Gussy pulls at his whiskers again, and mutters something about being on parade (only he pronounces it "pawade").

"Oh, you always use that as an excuse," his sister says dismissively.

The waiter arrives, bearing a loaded silver tray. Despite her headache, Josephine feels her mouth water as plates of food, and delicate china cups and saucers, are placed upon the table. She realises she is ravenous. And the cakes look delicious.

As soon as the waiter leaves, Josephine helps herself to bread-and-butter and begins to eat hungrily. In contrast, Isabella nibbles a slice of bread, crumbling most of it on her plate, before lifting the cup to her mouth and taking a tiny sip.

"Now Gussy, don't you want to know what I bought today?" she asks. "Look! Is it not the most delightful bonnet you have ever seen?"

"Ain't you got any number of bonnets?" Gussy asks, his mouth full of bread. (He pronounces it "bunnits.")

"Silly boy!" Isabella leans across the table and taps him playfully on the arm. "Don't you know a girl can never have too many bonnets. Or shawls. Or lace collars and cuffs." She moves closer to Josephine. "Isn't he a total *scream*!" she whispers loudly, crumbling the remainder of her bread upon her plate.

Josephine forces herself to smile. The Total Scream fixes his pebbly eyes upon her face again. To her horror, she feels her cheeks reddening under his gaze.

"So how long have you and my sister been friends, Miss ...?" he asks. He pronounces it "fwends."

Isabella rolls her eyes.

"Oh Gussy, I explained it all to you, you know I did. Josephine is the niece of Mr Herbert King, late of St John's Wood. Her dearest uncle was at school with Papa, only he died, very tragically and quite quite suddenly, and now she is all alone in the world."

"Rich, was he, this nuncle?" Gussy asks, trying to extract a fat finger from the delicate teacup handle, wherein it has got itself trapped.

Isabella gives a shocked little gasp.

"Gussy! Really! You mustn't ask such things!"

"No, but was he though?" Gussy persists, eyeing Josephine thoughtfully.

"I'm afraid I could not say," Josephine replies coldly, appropriating the last slice of bread-and-butter. She demolishes it in two bites. Then, ignoring Isabella's delicately raised eyebrows, she helps herself to a slice of sponge cake, followed by a fruit tart, both of which she eats in silence.

Eventually the tea is consumed and paid for, and the

Thorpes' carriage returns Josephine to the house in St John's Wood, which, in keeping with the arrangements, is now swathed in deepest black. Straw has also been laid in the street, and the blinds are drawn down.

Letting herself into the house, she discovers that her uncle's coffin has been delivered. It lies open upon the parlour table, which itself is covered with a black cloth. The undertaker has done his best, turning the rigid expression of horror into one of mild perplexity, and folding her uncle's arms upon his breast in an attitude of piety. Wrapped in his shroud, his eyes are open and unblinking, as if he is watching clouds. Josephine stares into her uncle's eyes, fearful lest the image of some nightmarish figure is about to stare back. But there is nothing reflected in the opaque eyeballs. Whoever – or whatever – it was that he saw on that fateful night, Herbert King is taking the identity of his murderer to the grave.

***

The day of the funeral dawns. Josephine rises from her bed and ventures out into the garden. The air is crisp and bright, the sky pearly and cloudless. Birds sing, and there are sparkles upon the grass and trees, as if Nature, hushed in sleep during the still night, has awoken with a determination to crown the day with a special glory, in defiance of the sad events that are shortly to take place.

By ten o'clock the procession of carriages, blinds pulled down, is drawn up outside the house. Horses stamp their feet and toss their heads. A large crowd has assembled to witness the last journey of the brutally-murdered man, and to catch a glimpse of the grieving niece, so young, so alone, so orphaned.

This heart-rending depiction has been dreamed up by several newspapers, who have seized upon the story as an example of how law-abiding citizens are not safe on the streets anymore because criminals are allowed to flourish. This, the newspapers claim, is due entirely to the ineffectual police force, who could not catch a cold, let alone a gang of vicious thugs.

Eventually the front door opens. The coffin, brass-handled and draped in a black cloth, is carried solemnly out of the house by the pallbearers. It is placed in the glass-sided hearse, and surrounded by flowers and black ostrich plumes. The tragic grieving niece appears in the doorway, her face veiled under a black crêpe bonnet.

A murmur of sympathy arises as she climbs into the second carriage accompanied by her supportive friends. The two undertaker's mutes take their position at the head of the procession, which then sets off at walking pace towards Kensal Green cemetery.

Josephine sits between Mrs Thorpe and Isabella. She feels like a prisoner being transported to an execution. Mrs Thorpe keeps dabbing her dry eyes with a black-bordered handkerchief. Isabella Thorpe, after informing her in a loud whisper that her brother *so* wanted to come to the funeral but was prevented by important military duties, sits playing with the tassels of her shawl, humming under her breath.

Mr Thorpe, a large balding man with nothing to say for himself, is sitting opposite, puffing silently upon a cigar and filling the confined space with foul-smelling smoke. By the time the carriage draws up in front of the chapel, Josephine's head feels like a ball of cotton wool into which someone has inserted a needle.

As soon as the service has droned to an end, Josephine rises and slips out by a side door. She wants to catch a few moments of solitude before the next ordeal of the day: the burial feast at the Thorpes' Hampstead mansion. She has just completed the circular walk at the centre of the gardens when the noise of carriage wheels makes her glance to her left.

Beyond the stone statue of a veiled angel that marks the tomb of Ann Gardner (d.1846), she sees a closed carriage travelling along one of the broad gravel paths leading to the gates. Both horses and coach are midnight-black, and there is a black plume at each corner of the coach. The window-blinds of the carriage are down, yet Josephine has the distinct feeling that there are eyes watching her from within. By the way it moves swiftly over the gravel, the coach is travelling light, and yet somehow darkness accompanies it.

***

The Thorpes' house stands at the point where the bricks-and-mortar London landscape gives way to the vast expanse of green wooded Hampstead Heath. It is a large house, supported by ornate pillars and surrounded by ornate wrought-iron fencing.

The first things that strike the visitor's eye, upon entering the dark maroon-and-gold-papered hallway, are the paintings. Every square inch of wall space is hung with paintings, their frames glowing softly in the dim light. The Thorpes intend their guests to be perfectly clear that here is a family with the resources (though not necessarily the taste) to be collectors of Art.

Josephine hovers awkwardly in the over-paintinged hallway, waiting for the Thorpes' stiff-backed manservant to announce her. Even though it is her uncle's post-funeral gathering, it is not her house, and so the rigid formalities have to be observed. Eventually she is announced and shown into the big reception room overlooking the garden, where Mrs Thorpe greets her effusively, as if she is a stranger who has just arrived back from some far-flung land. Mr Thorpe greets her as if he has not got a clue who she is.

Upon an ornate mahogany sideboard is laid a cold collation of hams, chickens, salads and various cakes, all awaiting consumption. The amount of food seems to suggest that the mourners will be in a state of semi-starvation.

Josephine eyes the groaning board with approbation. Funerals always make her hungry, and she has attended many funerals. The Bertha Helstone Institute for Orphaned Clergy Daughters was low-lying and damp, and girls were always succumbing to some sort of fever, and dying or being taken home to die.

On those occasions, all she was given to eat was a slice of bread and a bowl of weak cabbage soup, if she was lucky. Now she places herself strategically close to the side table and awaits the signal to begin. More guests arrive. They line up in the hallway, and hover with fixed expressions of solemnity. Those who have already been greeted circle the room, locating familiar faces, singling out old acquaintances. They acknowledge Josephine, then move away from her with elaborate care, as if she might be breakable, or possibly infectious.

The female mourners gradually congregate in one corner, in a tight little group. She knows none of them, so she cannot join them. Mrs Thorpe is too busy greeting to effect introductions, and Isabella has disappeared completely.

Josephine stands alone. All around her, conversations continue apace. She overhears little snippets: *"Wonder where all his money will go ... Not short of a guinea or two, old Herbert ... Red hair, my dear - most unfortunate! ... Odd the way this gel just shows up before ... You don't think ... No, surely not?"*

Her fingers clench into tight fists. Who do these people think they are? What do they think she is? They have not come to honour the dead, but to gossip, and to slander the living. She moves swiftly towards the French window to cool her hot cheeks.

On the other side of the window she sees a winding brick path leading to the far end of the garden, beyond which stretch the broad green acres of Hampstead Heath. For a brief moment she hesitates. She is very hungry. But she is also very angry, and just at this moment, anger seems more important than food. Josephine casts a quick glance over her shoulder at the room full of strangers. Nobody is paying her the slightest attention. Nobody cares whether she is present or absent. So she might as well be absent. She eases the French window open and slips quietly out.

***

The following morning finds Detective Inspector Leo Stride sitting at his desk in his office at the headquarters of the detective police, attempting to eat breakfast without dropping it on the report he is reading.

Paperwork. There is always paperwork. Lots and lots of it, and it all has to be read and signed off by him. At this rate, he'll soon be spending more time catching up on paperwork than catching criminals.

There is a knock at the door. A young police constable enters.

"Beg pardon sir, but Detective Sergeant Cully says, could you come quick. There's been an incident at Kensal Green cemetery."

Stride feels his heart sink. The word "incident" combined with the word "cemetery" can only mean one thing: a body has been taken. Body-snatchers are pretty near the top of his list of vile scum.

Not only does the filthy nature of the crime revolt him, but there is then the ghastly business of having to inform some grieving family that their loved one's remains have been dug up, and possibly sold for medical dissection.

If he had his way, Stride thinks darkly, he'd hang every bloody resurrectionist from the highest gallows in the land. He abandons breakfast and paperwork, reaches for his hat, and orders the young constable to whistle up a cab.

Alighting some time later at Kensal Green, Detective Inspector Stride passes through the ornate entrance of the cemetery. He follows the young constable along one of the wide gravel paths, reflecting gloomily that no matter how much you dress it up with trees and flowerbeds and landscaping and fine

36

fancy colonnades, a cemetery is not a public park; it is a place to bury the dead.

Stride's sensation of gloom is compounded by the thin mist hanging in the cold damp air, and smell of rotting vegetation, plus the knowledge of what he is probably about to see as he turns a corner, and spots Detective Sergeant Jack Cully standing at the head of an opened grave, surrounded by piles of newly-dug earth.

A group of four constables loiter nearby, smoking. Stride nods them a greeting, then joins his colleague. He looks down into the grave. The coffin is empty, its lid askew.

"Apparently it happened last night," Cully tells him.

"Found any evidence?"

"Footprints."

"A man's or a woman's?"

Cully looks at him strangely for an instant, then lowers his voice.

"It looks like the footprints of a gigantic hound," he murmurs.

He conducts Stride over to one of the piles of earth, and points down.

"See. Quite clear. Must've rained in the night."

Stride stares at the footprints in silence. They are exactly as Cully has described them. He reminds himself that detection work involves logic and rationality, and that what he is looking at now does not come into either category. He waves a dismissive hand.

"This is the nineteenth century, Jack. Not some fictional dark age."

"So what are these then?"

"I don't know. But I do know gigantic animals are the stuff of fairy tales."

"How about those gigantic black pigs that live in the Hampstead sewers?" suggests one of the constables. "I read about them in the newspaper. Running wild all over Highgate, they say. People get woken up by their fearsome grunting."

Stride glares at him.

"*As I said*, there is a completely ordinary explanation for this."

"One of my neighbours grew a gigantic marrow once," another constable remarks innocently.

Stride decides to ignore them all, and strike out for reality.

"Two of you nip round to the medical schools. Ask to see the dissecting rooms. Don't take no for an answer. The rest of you round up the usual suspects. By the bye, do we know the name of the deceased?"

Cully tells him.

Stride breathes in sharply.

"In that case, nobody – I repeat, *nobody* – is to talk to the newspapers. Do I make myself quite clear?"

***

As Stride's men begin their frantic search of the medical establishments, Mr Septimus Able, of Willing and Able, Solicitors, of Gray's Inn Square, is awaiting his first client of the day. Mr Able is an elderly grizzle-haired man, dressed in good black, with a high white cravat. His lean face is parchment-coloured, with skin as dry as the legal tomes that line the walls of his office.

His steely-grey eyes survey the world from under deeply-hooded lids. He resembles one of the birds of prey at the Zoological Gardens, an impression reinforced by his beak-shaped nose and claw-like bony fingers.

Of his client, who is even now approaching the door of his chambers, he knows very little. Not that he knows much of any of his clients, in the personal or societal sense. Of their financial and legal business – that is quite another matter, of course. Of that, he is intimate with every last detail.

He hears a knocker sound in the street, followed by the

familiar tread of his legal clerk in the outer office, and pulls a sheaf of documents towards him. Under the desk, his boots creak gently. The clock on the wall ticks. Steepling his fingers, he sits and waits.

Over the years, Mr Septimus Able has observed many individuals, young and old, male and female, sitting in the brown leather chair that is placed directly in front of his desk. He has witnessed their varying reactions as he reads the Last Will and Testament of their recently-deceased relatives, and they hear the news (good or bad) about the provisions made for their future. Now here he is again. And here, if he is not very much mistaken, is his client.

The door is opened by his legal clerk, who ushers in a young woman dressed in elegant mourning garb. Mr Able observes the straight set of her shoulders, the upright carriage of her head, the halo of bright red hair barely contained by the sombre crêpe bonnet.

He wonders what she is thinking as she advances towards him. He doubts that she has any idea that her life (which, in his limited knowledge of young women, has probably been pretty uneventful) is about to change beyond all recognition.

"Miss King?"

He rises, extending the hooked fingers of his claw-like hand.

Her black-gloved handshake is firm. He approves it. He indicates the vacant leather chair. She sits down gracefully. He notices that her back does not touch the chair.

"I am your late uncle's solicitor and his executor. I have here his final wishes, as set down in his latest Will. With your permission, I shall proceed to read them to you."

Mr Able clears his throat, and begins to read in a businesslike voice. It is not a long document. When he has finished reading, he glances up. The young woman is giving him a long, clear look. Her hands are tightly-clasped.

"Is there anything you wish to ask me?"

An imperceptible shake of the head.

"Then I shall arrange for a regular sum of money to be supplied to you from your inheritance. I shall also arrange to pay the other legatees, as per your uncle's instructions.

"As I am appointed your legal guardian, I shall also arrange for the interest from the stocks and shares you have been left, and the profits from your late uncle's business to be paid into a bank account in your name, which I will open. The money will be held in trust until you come of age. It will provide you with a tidy sum of money. A very tidy sum indeed.

"You are of course, quite free to make whatever arrangements you wish in the future. Until you indicate otherwise, I shall act for you, and in your best interests. If you choose to sell your late uncle's business, I shall be happy to act upon your instructions, if and when you should reach that decision."

He shuffles the papers on his desk. Pauses. Clears his throat once more.

"'There is one final clause. It relates to certain items brought back by your uncle from his travels abroad, namely, a small collection of precious stones, which I believe were given to him by someone he met out there. The collection consists of five emeralds, two balas rubies, four amethysts, and a large diamond known as the Eye of the Khan."

His voice is monotonous, as if he is reading a laundry list. He is aware that stones like these create a deadliness in humanity, a morality whereby they are valued above life. But to him the stones are just fragments of rock and carbon. The avidity and violence they inspire is as much of a mystery as their beauty.

"The two rubies," Mr Able reads on, "are to be handed to a Mrs Lilith Marks, of 3 Endell Terrace, Maida Vale, as a gift."

The client makes a sudden alert movement of her head. Almost as if she has heard the name before. Surely not, he thinks. She is young and very innocent. Lilith Marks and her gay sisterhood would be utterly beyond her limited knowledge of the world.

"The rest of the collection is yours to keep, or dispose of, as you please," he continues. "I believe that your uncle, for reasons of his own, kept the jewels in his safe. But I would strongly advise you, particularly as the diamond is of high price, if not priceless, that they should be deposited as soon as possible in a banker's or a jeweller's strong-room. I can arrange for the two rubies to be delivered to the named recipient, if you would care to have them conveyed to my office."

He puts down the Will.

His client says nothing. She does not move.

Tick, tock. Creak, creak.

"Do you have any further questions?"

A slight shake of the head.

He steals a glance at the clock. His next client is due at any minute. An important City man, coming to consult him on important City business. He does not wish to keep him waiting. He rises.

"Then allow me to bid you a very good-day, Miss King. My clerk will show you out."

Josephine quits the lawyer's chambers. It has started raining, but she is barely conscious of the water draggling the hem of her black dress and seeping into her boots. A cart has overturned in the street, and she has to pick her way between hoof-smashed cabbages and upside-down crates of hysterical chickens. She does not notice.

My allowance. My bank account. My diamond, she thinks. *My life.* She has always felt in want of a life. Now that she has found her status elevated to that of a single young woman in possession of a good fortune, it looks as if she is finally going to have one. Or at least, she will, once she manages to open her uncle's safe. She walks on. The streets glitter. If she half-closes her eyes, she sees diamonds.

***

Sally's Chop House is a dark, low-ceilinged place off Fleet Street. Customers sit either at long tables or in booths to eat their meal. Sawdust on the floor is patterned by the tread of boots. A massive man in dark sleeves and a gravy-stained apron carries big plates of steaming food from table to table.

The massive man (in reality, he is the eponymous Sally) has shoulders broad as a barrel. His nose has been broken so many times it has developed an elbow. The air is hot and steamy, and smells of smoke, greasy cooked meat and cabbage, with a side order of drains.

Detective Inspector Stride is sitting on his own in one of the back booths. He always sits on his own, as he exudes an invisible aura of policeman. He is loitering over a plate of mutton chops and potato, washed down with a half-pint of porter. Spread out on the table in front of him is a copy of a newspaper.

The massive man appears at his elbow.

"Everything to your satisfaction, Mr Stride, sir? Only you don't seem to be enjoying your food like wot you usually does?"

He gives Stride a wide disingenuous smile. It is a smile that hints that here is someone who would never ever stab you in the back, though they might tell someone else where the knives are kept.

Stride waves him away without replying. He stares gloomily down at the front-page headline of *The Standard* which announces in big black letters:

FEROCIOUS GRAVE-ROBBING MONSTER HOUND STALKS KENSAL GREEN CEMETERY!

How did this happen? After all his careful instructions? He reads on in disbelief. Hell and damnation – if this story **has** come from one of his own men, that man should be punished not just for disobeying orders, but for having a mind bordering on the criminally insane.

Why, Stride muses, does the imagination keep peopling the dank city with terrible apparitions? Giant black pigs, the Twickenham vampire, rats that come out of the sewers at night and steal children from their cribs, beggars who grow fish-scales on their skin.

Then he remembers the huge distinctive paw-prints in the mud. Is it worse knowing that Nature might have done an even better job? His appetite suddenly deserting him, Detective Inspector Stride pushes his plate away.

Right now he'd rather be somewhere else, but he has an unpleasant duty to perform. One that he has been putting off all day, but cannot put off any longer. He sighs and checks his pocket watch. Reminding himself that the somewhere else will involve paperwork and shouting at people, he sets off to round up Jack Cully.

***

Mid-afternoon finds Josephine sitting at her uncle's desk in the book-lined study, a pile of correspondence in front of her. There are letters of condolence to be read. There are cards of inquiry, with the words *"To inquire"* written on the top, that have to be replied to by cards with *"Thanks for kind inquiries"*.

Thankfully nobody is calling round, because mourning etiquette dictates that one does not intrude until such time as the mourner decides they are ready to re-enter society. All this she has learned from Mrs Thorpe, who **has** called round, to make sure that the post-funeral arrangements are being carried out to her satisfaction.

However, Josephine is not dealing with the voluminous correspondence. Instead she is sitting, chin in hands, staring into the middle distance. She has other things upon her mind. She is following yet again the train of events that unfolded from the moment she left the lawyer's chambers.

She remembers rushing up the dusty stone stairs of King &

Co, running into the outer office and stammering out the story of the jewels to an astonished Trafalgar Moggs. Then she recalls the heart-stopping moment of taking her uncle's key from Moggs's hand, entering her uncle's private office and breathlessly unlocking his safe.

And discovering that it was totally empty.

***

Meanwhile back in his office at Scotland Yard, Detective Inspector Stride and his colleague are reading copies of the early evening papers. Every one carries some front-page variant of the **"FEARFUL MONSTER CORPSE-EATING HOUND STRIKES TERROR IN HEARTS OF LAW-ABIDING CITIZENS"** headline. Over the course of the day, the story has grown legs and run round the entire city.

"Bit of a nightmare," remarks Detective Sergeant Jack Cully, in his role as master of the understatement. "I gather from the lads it was one of the gravediggers who tipped off the press."

Stride growls.

"That's supposed to make me feel better, is it?"

Cully shrugs. Years of working with his boss has taught him the value of discretion. Stride in this mood is like a thunderstorm. Lightning could strike at any time. Best to lie low and wait for the storm to blow over.

Stride stabs a finger at *The Globe*.

"And what the hell is ***that*** supposed to be?"

"I think it is an artist's impression of the giant hound."

"It's got bloody *flames* coming out of its mouth!" Stride shouts. "They'll be saying it has horns and flashing eyes next!"

Cully murmurs something noncommittal. Stride clearly hasn't seen the picture in *The Sun* yet.

"I tell you, Jack, paperwork and the press: compared to them, catching criminals is a picnic in the park."

"So what now?"

Stride gets up and reaches for his hat and overcoat.

"Now we have to go and inform an innocent young woman, who knows nothing of the world and its wicked ways, that her uncle's body has disappeared from its final resting place."

"Are we going to mention the gigantic hound?"

Stride rolls his eyes.

"Well," Cully persists, "how do you explain the footsteps? You saw them. We all saw them. And none of the medical schools says they have taken in any male bodies matching Mr King's description."

Stride shrugs him off with a wave of his hand. He walks firmly out of the office and heads for the front door of the police station, his voice echoing back along the empty corridor.

"There's no such thing as gigantic hounds, Jack. Never was. Never will be."

"So what made those footprints then, tell me that?" Cully mutters under his breath. But his question falls upon empty air.

***

Studiously avoiding the shouted comments from the little knot of journalists gathered outside the Yard, Stride picks up a cab and directs the man to take him and Cully to an address in St John's Wood.

Arriving at their destination, he alights, ordering the driver to wait. The detectives are shown into the drawing room where they study the carpet until Josephine enters, her face pale, but her expression hopeful.

Stride's heart sinks. There are many aspects of his job that he does not enjoy, and this one comes pretty near the top of the pile.

"Miss King. I hope you are well."

"I believe I am well, Detective Inspector, thank you. Have you brought me some news about the men who murdered my uncle? Are they now apprehended?"

"Not yet."

Her expression unbrightens.

Strenuously avoiding eye contact, Stride addresses his next remark at a spot just over her left shoulder.

"There has, however, been a development. Of sorts."

"Yes?"

She clasps her hands behind her back, and waits silently for him to continue.

Stride clears his throat.

"The body of your late uncle, Mr Herbert King, appears to have been removed from its resting place overnight."

A leaden silence descends.

"*Appears* to have been removed?"

"It has been removed."

"Removed by whom?"

"We do not know as yet. We have inquired at the usual locations."

"What are the usual locations?"

"Err ... certain medical establishments."

"Why?"

Just the sort of question Stride dreads being asked. He pauses, finding himself upon the horns of a dilemma. His mind flails around helplessly. Then decides to take the easy route out.

"With respect, Miss King," he replies, "I'm afraid it is not a subject suitable for an impressionable young female mind."

The words rattle out fast, as if he has lined them up and fired them all in one go, before they have time to wander off.

She stands utterly still, and remains uncannily silent.

"Let me assure you, Miss King, that we are investigating what has occurred. Fully and comprehensively investigating it."

The silence continues.

"My highly-trained officers will leave no stone unturned."

Still she says nothing.

"Do you have anything you wish to ask me?" Stride asks.

She gives him a cool stare that continues for a couple of

seconds beyond the comfort barrier.

"I have many things I wish to ask you, Detective Inspector. But apparently I am unable to do so, as the subject is not suitable for my impressionable young female mind."

Stride feels he is climbing up a tilting slope. He is used to the sort of young women who sell violets, or alcohol, or themselves. The sort you chuck under the chin, and call *Now then, my girl*, in a kindly but superior way. He is most definitely not used to the sort who hit you round the ear with difficult questions, and then use silence as a blunt instrument.

"I hope to bring you better news soon," he concludes lamely.

She inclines her head.

"I hope so too," she murmurs.

The cab is still waiting outside the house. Stride and Cully clamber aboard, and the driver whips up the horse. Only when they are approaching Whitehall Place does Stride rouse himself from the brown study that has fallen upon him ever since leaving the house.

"Murder, Cully. Then bodysnatching. What the hell is going on?"

Not to mention a gigantic hound, Cully thinks. But as this is a topic upon which his boss has refused to engage, he does not mention it.

***

Night falls. Under a black sky so full of diamond stars that it looks as if somebody has thrown jewels up to God, the City sleeps. Listen. You can almost hear the deep rhythmic breathing of the prosperous and the sin-free, safe in their warm cosy beds in their stout brick houses, the last embers still glowing in the hearth. No night terrors assail their slumbers. No opium-fuelled, gin-soaked horrors disturb their peaceful rest.

Far from these opulent dwellings, the flickering glow of streetlamps barely lights the way for the late ones staggering home from an evening's debauchery, pausing only to spew the contents of their last meal onto the already damp and slimy cobbles.

The rough sleepers in Regent's Park huddle cold in their ragged clothing, and wait for the first limpid streaks of dawn to herald another hopeless day, which some will never wake to see. A dog howls. Voices are raised momentarily in angry debate, then mutter away into silence.

Time wears on. In the bedroom in St John's Wood, Josephine opens her eyes. She has been dreaming. Not the dream where she is standing by a crumpled, filthy bed in a hot white room, looking on the faces of two dead strangers who once were her beloved parents. Thankfully, since she arrived in London that dream has no longer troubled her. This is a dream whose details disperse on the instant of waking, leaving a luminal atmosphere behind it. A feeling of menace, a sense of evil, the impression of a shapeless form being dragged across damp ground into a grey mist.

The house is very quiet. She lies in the ashy light of the breaking day feeling as if the small piece of solid ground upon which she stands has broken away from the shore, and she is drifting alone out to the infinite sea.

She tries to fold the events of the previous day, and the memory of what Detective Inspector Stride told her, into smaller and smaller squares, as if it were a sheet of paper, until it is tiny enough to hide in a crease of her hand, tiny enough to imagine that none of it has happened.

Some time later there is a knock at the door and Annie enters.

"Good morning, miss. Another rainy day, I'm afraid."

She crosses to the wardrobe.

"Which dress shall I lay out?"

"The black one," Josephine says, without thinking.

The maid purses her lips and looks at her disapprovingly.

"Are you staying in or going out today, miss?"

Josephine sighs. Where should she go? Her uncle's body has been stolen; the jewels left to her in his Will have mysteriously disappeared, and there is nobody in this great city she can confide in. Then, suddenly, a name comes unbidden into her mind. She sits upright.

"I think I shall wear my best black dress today, Annie," she says. "I will be going out later."

***

Meanwhile, in a different bedroom in another part of the city, Isabella Thorpe is also getting ready for the day ahead. She sits at her dressing table, languidly ignoring a cup of weak tea, while Withers, the lady's maid, brushes and curls her hair.

Isabella Thorpe's bedroom is decked out in frills. The dressing table, the chair, the bed, the canopy, the curtains, even the over-mantel are all covered in white lace frills. It is a bit like stepping into a giant white wedding cake.

Isabella peers at her reflection in the frilled looking glass and sighs. She turns over in her mind the first of numerous arduous decisions she will have to make today, namely, which colour dress is she going to wear? She is just about to issue her final instructions , when there is a light knock at the door and Mrs Thorpe sails in, trailing an aura of lavender water in her wake.

Unsmiling, Isabella regards her in the mirror.

"Well, Mama, how are you?"

Mrs Thorpe raises an eyebrow.

"Still not dressed, my sweet?"

She rustles to the dressing table, and lifts a lock of the chestnut hair.

"How nicely your hair curls today."

Isabella's expression changes from weary to wary. A compliment from her mother, especially first thing in the morning, is usually the precursor to a commandment.

"I really think you should wear the pink shot silk taffeta, my angel. You always look so pretty in pink, you know. And that paisley shawl your dear generous brother gave you would set it off just perfectly."

Isabella goes on looking into the mirror, staring at vacancy. She does not think pink suits her at all, but when Mama is present, she has learned to acquiesce. There are always those times when she is absent.

The little pendule on the frilly mantelpiece strikes the half-hour.

Her mother continues,

"A hot breakfast is waiting for you in the dining-room, when you are ready for it. And after, I wish you to accompany me on some calls. Mrs Carlyle is returned to town, and you know how she delights to see you, and hear all about your school in France."

"Where I picked up so many airs and graces," Isabella says languidly, "but now I don't know my longitude from my latitude. And as for my French... I can't recall a single word."

"You are being whimsical, my love. I am sure there is not a better-educated girl in the whole of London."

"Oh Mama – you mustn't take me *au grand serieux!* I'm sure if I only apply myself to my books, I'll turn out to be an excellent bluestocking by-and-by."

Mrs Thorpe draws herself up.

"Indeed I hope you will not, my love. Gentlemen don't like that sort of woman at all."

"I see. Thank you for telling me."

Her Mama gives an artificial little laugh.

"You are such a droll girl! I do not understand you at times. And afterwards, we must call upon poor little Josephine King. Your father and I are delighted that you both are becoming such fast friends. She is such a dear girl, isn't she? So childish and innocent."

"And she has such a **huge** private fortune," Isabella murmurs, *sotto voce,* but not quite *sotto voce* enough.

"Well, that is true," Mrs Thorpe inclines her head. "And since you mention it, that brings me to another matter which I need to speak to you about."

Isabella bites her lips. She has an inkling of what is coming.

"You know that your father and I only want the best for you?"

Isabella nods.

"We want you to be happy."

"I am happy," Isabella says, through gritted teeth.

"For now, Bella dear, perhaps you are. But this carefree, girlish existence of calls and shopping and pleasure cannot continue indefinitely."

"Can it not?"

Mrs Thorpe shakes her head playfully.

"Indeed no. We must start making plans for your future. And that is why we are going to call upon Mrs Carlyle. She knows the right people, the ones it would be good for you to meet. After all—"

"After all, when you were my age, you were already engaged to Papa, and all the men in London were in mourning," Isabella intones dully.

Mrs Thorpe gives a tinkly laugh,

"Well, maybe not *all* the men in London," she simpers.

Nobody will be wearing black armbands when I get engaged, Isabella thinks gloomily. *Except perhaps me.*

Mrs Thorpe pats her daughter's shoulder.

"And now I shall leave you to complete your *toilette*, my love," she says.

Isabella regards her mother's stout departing back in the mirror, trying to imagine her as young and slender and attractive. It cannot be done.

She turns to the waiting lady's maid.

"I shall wear the green tartan today, Withers. And you can lace me to sixteen inches. I shan't be having any breakfast."

***

Endell Terrace, Maida Vale, is located off the main Marylebone Road. A row of modern whitewashed villas, with black wrought-iron railings at the front. Several villas have canopied walkways that lead from the front door to the gate, discreetly screening visitors from prying eyes.

The morning rain has ceased, and the air is fresh and chilled as Josephine walks slowly along the pavement peering at house numbers. She sees a canary in a cage, a Wardian case on a window ledge, the flick of a feather duster behind a net curtain. A couple of sparrows are hopping to and fro in the gutter.

Two shouting children bowl an iron hoop. A man in a well-brushed top hat comes out of one of the houses, glances quickly up and down the street, then sets off briskly in a northerly direction.

There is very little to distinguish Number 3 Endell Terrace from the rest of the street. A glossy black front door, a brass knocker in the shape of a serpent, a decorative fan in the parlour window, dark red velvet curtains. The steps are newly scrubbed.

Josephine stops outside. So this is where Mrs Lilith Marks lives, the woman whose visiting card was abruptly torn up by Annie. The woman who must have been very important to her uncle; so important that he left her two rubies in his Will.

Suddenly she sees a curtain twitch, catches the blurred outline of a face. Shocked at being caught staring so openly at the house, she turns and hurries away. But she has barely gone a few yards when she hears footsteps hurrying up behind her. Next moment, a hand is laid lightly on her shoulder.

Josephine turns. A woman is standing in the middle of the pavement. She wears a vividly-coloured red-and-blue-check dress with wide pagoda sleeves. Thick coal-black hair is piled on top of her head in a series of twists, held in place by a number of jewelled combs. Her tight bodice clearly outlines the swell of her bosom above a slender waist. Her large dark eyes are fixed inquiringly upon Josephine's face.

The woman is clear-complexioned, with arched black brows, and a full red mouth. She exudes a strange exoticness. She could be the daughter of foreign royalty. She could equally well be something quite different.

"Please excuse the liberty," she says, "but am I addressing Miss King – Miss Josephine King?"

"Yes," Josephine nods.

"I thought so. Forgive me for accosting you in the open street like this, Miss King. My name is Mrs Lilith Marks. I was acquainted with your late uncle Mr Herbert King."

There is a momentary pause before the word "acquainted," as if the woman has carefully selected it from other words she might have chosen to say, but didn't. She produces a tiny silver watch from her pocket, and glances at it.

"I regret that I was not at home when you called. But if you do not have another pressing engagement elsewhere, perhaps you might like to return with me?"

It is an invitation Josephine cannot refuse, and so she follows Lilith Marks, and a short while later finds herself in a small elegant parlour with a richly-patterned Oriental carpet on the floor. The carpet is identical to the one in her uncle's drawing room. Indeed, if she kept her eyes fixed firmly on the floor, she could almost be back there. But she is not. Her uncle's taste in paintings does not run to racehorses, fashion prints, and ladies in various states of undress.

"I see that you received my calling card," Lilith Marks says, after the preliminary rituals of greeting and seating have been completed. "I thought that your maid would tear it in two."

"She did."

Lilith Marks throws back her head and laughs.

"Ah, the redoubtable Annie. Guardian of all that is prim and proper. But nevertheless, you are here."

"I ... wanted to see you."

"And I want to see you, too."

Lilith smiles.

"Herbert – your uncle – spoke of you often," she continues. "It was a hard blow for him to return from his travels to find that both his parents – your grandparents – were dead, and then soon afterwards, to learn of the deaths of your father and mother in India. He thought you had died also. He was overjoyed when he discovered, quite by chance, that you had not."

Josephine stares hard at the intricate pattern of the carpet, feeling a pain behind her eyes in the place that only exists before tears come.

"If you can bear it," Lilith Marks says gently, "I should very much like to hear what happened that fateful night. I only know what I have read in the papers."

Josephine relates everything, including yesterday's visit of Detective Inspector Stride. Lilith sits very still, listening intently. When all has been told, she rises swiftly and walks to the small bow window, where she stands staring out into the street, her shoulders stiff, her back ramrod-straight.

Some minutes pass until Lilith turns from the window. Her expression has changed. Her high colour is gone, and a light has died at the back of her eyes. She sinks into a chair, clasping her hands in her lap.

"Ah, I must have been the last person to see him alive," she murmurs. "He called on me that night. It was late, and I was preparing to go out. I was not expecting him. I may have been a little... but I did not know what was going to happen, or I might have paid more attention. I might have cancelled my engagement, and pressed him to stay."

"It was not your fault," Josephine says.

Lilith sighs.

"Yes, perhaps you are right, and in any case it is too late to regret my actions," she says. "The police have no idea who murdered your uncle, nor where his body has been taken?"

"None whatsoever."

"The vile people who did this must not go unpunished!" Lilith exclaims, the colour rising to her cheeks. There is a brief pause before she continues, more calmly, "I shall fetch some tea; I am sure you must be in need of refreshment. And there is some fruitcake of my own baking. Your uncle was particularly partial to it."

Over tea and cake, Josephine plucks up courage to ask the question that has been burning a hole in her brain since she arrived.

"I have just learned from his lawyer that my uncle had a small collection of precious jewels. Do you know anything about them?"

Lilith stirs her tea thoughtfully for a second.

"I know of their existence. And I know the story of how he came by them, although I have never actually set eyes upon them. It happened while Herbert was staying in Kabul in Afghanistan. He'd been there for some years, but when war broke out between the rulers of the country and the British Army, he was forced to flee from the city.

"He told me that he'd lost all his possessions, and seen the family he lived with put to the sword and their home burned to the ground by the army, who behaved with great brutality towards the poor people of that city.

"Your uncle had taken to wearing native dress. It was in these clothes that he fled into the hills, and it was there that he encountered a young man who'd been badly wounded and left to die by his fleeing companions. Herbert managed to remove a bullet lodged in the man's side, and dress his wounds. Then he put him on his horse and took him back to his home village.

"He did not know that the young man was the only son of one of the most powerful warlords in the area. The father was so grateful for what he had done in saving his son's life that he gave your uncle the jewels. He said that they were very old, that the diamond had been won in battle by his ancestor, Ghengis

Khan, but as Herbert had given him back the most priceless jewel in the world, the jewels were now his, a gift to express his gratitude. I always thought it was a beautiful story, like something out of the Arabian Nights."

Josephine sits quietly, wishing she'd had more time to find all this out for herself. Mr Able the lawyer, and now Lilith Marks, have opened a door into a world she knew nothing about.

There is a pause. Then Lilith breaks the silence.

"There is a small personal matter that I should like to mention, if I may," she says. "Your uncle has some letters of mine. If it wouldn't trouble you overmuch, I should be grateful for their return."

"Oh. Yes, of course," Josephine says. "But I do not know where they might be," she admits.

"He told me that he kept them in a safe in his room."

Josephine stares at Lilith, recalling the lawyer's words: *I believe that your uncle kept the jewels in his safe.* She had thought he meant the safe in his office. She had been mistaken. She rises to her feet, hastily reaching for her bonnet.

"I shall find your letters, and return them to you as soon as possible," she says.

***

A short while later, Josephine arrives back at the St John's Wood house, where she spies a small crowd standing outside on the pavement. Her heart starts hammering in her chest. Now what has happened?

As she draws nearer, one man separates himself from the rest and approaches her. He wears tweed trousers, a gaudy waistcoat, and his brightly-coloured necktie is fastened with a large jewelled pin, in defiance of fashion. His face has a beery appearance, with sharp, eager little eyes.

"Miss King?"

She stops.

"My name is Dionysius Clout. I represent *The Morning Post*." The man gestures at the rest of the crowd. "These, my companions, are all reporters from other newspapers. We are here to express our sympathy towards you in the light of the terrible events that have recently befallen you."

"I see. Thank—"

But before she has time to continue, the man whips a notebook from his overcoat pocket.

"So, Miss King, what is your opinion of the detective police? Are you satisfied with the way they are conducting the enquiry into the murder of Mr King, your beloved relative? What are your thoughts about those who took his body from its resting place?"

Josephine gapes at him. Why are these matters any of his business? Her eyes travel to the men standing behind him. They are all staring at her expectantly, pencils poised over notebooks. One man is actually drawing a picture of her! She grabs the ends of her shawl and holds it up in front of her face.

"I am so sorry... please excuse me," she says, making a run for the steps.

The sound of the front door closing brings Annie the maid scurrying into the hallway.

"Ah, there you are, miss. Mrs Thorpe and Miss Isabella Thorpe called. They left cards."

"There are people from the newspapers outside the house!" Josephine exclaims.

"Oh, are they still here?"

The maid half-opens the door.

"No, no! Do not let them see you. And you must not speak to them."

The expression upon Annie's face indicates that this might just be a command too late. Josephine stares at her accusingly.

"I was only coming up the area steps," Annie replies defensively. "A very polite man asked where you were, but I said I didn't know."

"Well, please do not speak to them again. Ever."

"If you say so, miss," the maid replies sullenly. "Mrs Thorpe and Miss Isabella also asked where you were."

"I was calling upon an old friend of my uncle's."

"Yes, miss?"

Annie folds her arms and stares at her, waiting for further enlightenment.

Guardian of all that is prim and proper, Josephine thinks, recalling Lilith's description of the snooty parlour maid.

"Her name is Mrs Lilith Marks," she says, assuming an innocent expression. "I believe she left a calling card some time ago, did she not?"

Instantly Annie's eyes harden, her mouth sets in a straight line of disapproval.

"She is **not** a suitable person for you to be visiting, miss, if you don't mind me saying so."

Josephine maintains the innocent expression.

"Why isn't she?"

There is a pause. Then the maid says stiffly,

"There are those that say she is no better than she should be."

"But surely, isn't that true of all of us?"

Annie tosses her head.

"And she is a *Jew*!" she spits, as if it were some contagious disease.

"I see. And wasn't Jesus Christ also a Jew?"

The maid stares at her in wide-eyed horror.

"Certainly not!" she exclaims indignantly. "How can you say that, miss? Jesus Christ was British, and a good Christian, just like our beloved Queen."

Josephine relinquishes the unequal struggle.

"I am going to my room to change," she says.

She climbs the stairs to the first floor. But instead of going to her bedroom, she crosses the landing and opens the door to her uncle's bedchamber. She stands in the doorway, looking slowly all round the room, trying to think where her uncle's safe might be located.

Eventually her gaze settles on the wall opposite the bed, where there is a painting of Kabul. Gold minarets and ochre-tiled roofs glow in the pale afternoon sunlight. She lifts the painting off the wall and places it gently upon the bed, her heart leaping as she spies a small metal door in the wall.

Climbing onto a chair, Josephine stands in front of the safe, wondering how on earth she is going to open it without a key. Then she notices that the door is not completely flush with the wall, as if it has been quickly or carelessly shut. She looks around the room, seeking inspiration. There is a brass shoe-horn lying on the floor by the dressing table. She fetches it and inserts it into the crack.

The door opens, revealing a packet of letters tied up in red ribbon, and behind them, a small leather bag. Leaving the letters for the time being, she takes out the bag, feeling the scurry of objects within. She shuts the safe, and, excitement mounting, carries the bag to her room and closes the door. Then she upends the bag onto her writing-desk.

Jewels roll onto the polished wood surface, winking and glittering. Green snake-eyed emeralds. Amethysts, purple like old ice. Two rubies, thick red like clots of blood, and a large colourless diamond. Her hand hovers over them, then picks up the diamond. The Eye of the Khan. It feels solid and cold.

She polishes it upon her sleeve and holds it up. And suddenly, something extraordinary happens. The diamond catches the afternoon light and releases it brighter than it had been before. As if it has swallowed the sun, it throws out rainbows.

The jewel gleams and phosphoresces, filling the room with its brilliance. It is the most beautiful thing she has ever seen. The shock of it grabs hold of something inside her, and tears it open. She cannot breathe.

Still holding the diamond, she goes to the window, and lifts the edge of the curtain. The street below seems empty. Setting aside the two rubies, she replaces the rest of the jewels in the bag and hides them in a drawer. She picks up the two rubies, placing them in her reticule. She will deliver them and the letters to Lilith Marks as instructed. Then she will go to Holborn, and break the good news to her uncle's clerk.

A short while later, Josephine tiptoes downstairs, quietly lifting her coat and bonnet from the stand. At the end of the street she hails a cab. All the way to Endell Terrace, Maida Vale, the diamond burns invisibly in her brain.

**

London in 1860 is notorious for filth and obscenity. There are, as nearly as can be ascertained, nine thousand, four hundred and nine prostitutes, if you believe the Return of the Number of Brothels and Prostitutes within the Metropolitan Police Area. (Sadly, though, statistics can be misleading. The police are notorious for turning a blind eye in return for a quick fuck against a shop door. And of course the figures do not include the under-thirteens.)

Lilith Marks, seated in her well-furnished drawing room, knows nothing of these statistics. She only knows she is eternally grateful to a certain redheaded gentleman, just returned from abroad and desperate for a bit of female company, who had picked her up in the gallery of the Alhambra Music Hall, bought her supper, then taken her back to his hotel room for the night. That one night had turned into more nights, and then had ended up here, in this small but very discreet house tucked away from prying eyes.

Without Herbert King, she'd still be slaving away in some sweatshop in the East End, stitching shirts and trousers by candlelight, until her eyesight failed and her striking dark looks faded. Or she'd be wearing herself out raising a brood of demanding children, sired by a husband who was growing ever more tired of her. Eventually she'd end up like one of those poor ragged creatures sleeping rough in St James' Park, selling herself for a shilling to some filthy, louse-ridden, homeless man.

Instead, she is here, mistress of her own domain. She has beautiful gowns, and jewels worth over two thousand pounds. She has a client list that includes some of the richest men in London; men whose wives would be scandalised if they knew their husbands were paying twenty-five pounds for twenty minutes of her time.

Lilith rolls the blood-red rubies in the palm of her hand, uttering a silent thank-you to Herbert King. She has a good business brain, and she has no intention of spending the rest of her life upon her back, servicing the needs of the sex-starved aristocracy.

Now she and her best friend Kitty Spencer, who lives two doors down and is in the same line of work, will finally be able to rent the little tea-room in Hampstead. This is the future she has set her sights on. A nice elegant place that ladies can patronise after a busy afternoon shopping.

Lilith carries the rubies to her writing desk and seals them in an envelope. Tomorrow morning, bright and early, she will take the envelope Up West, and sell the jewels for as high a price as she can get. She reaches for paper and pen, and writes a quick note to Kitty.

Once she has sold the rubies, she will call upon the landlord of the tea-room, and drive another hard bargain. A lick of paint, and the place will be ready in a jiffy. They will call it the Lily Lounge. A respectable name. Kitty has some foolish notion of calling it after their combined surnames. Lilith does not think that is a good idea.

**

Night falls, quiet as a ghost, upon the city. Snug in their silent houses, the inhabitants find solace in the arms of Morpheus. But not all are peacefully sleeping. In the green wooded hills of Hampstead, Mrs Thorpe is wide awake. She is following a train of thought, and until it runs into the buffers, Mr Thorpe is also wide awake, albeit reluctantly.

"So, what do you think?" Mrs Thorpe asks.

Mr Thorpe sighs. He has had a long day in the City, eaten a big dinner, indulged in a post-prandial snooze behind the evening papers, and now, just as he is on the point of dropping off into a deep and well-earned sleep, he is being asked to think. It isn't fair.

"Wha' about?" he asks muzzily.

"You know quite well what about," Mrs Thorpe says briskly. "We spoke of it earlier."

But he doesn't know. In all the years of their marriage, he has never understood why his wife will suddenly return to a conversation they had in the past, but which he is supposed to remember in the present.

"Bella? Mrs Carlyle's? This afternoon?"

"Mnnh. Yersss ..."

He waits for further clues.

"As I told you, Bella is not like other girls."

He is puzzled. His daughter seems to possess the same number of arms and legs as other girls, as far as he knows. Though obviously, now she is grown into womanhood, he can no longer be sure about the latter, legs being a dangerous area of contemplation for the male sex.

"I don't just mean her French education, for which I blame your Mama – I'd have been quite happy for her to continue at Miss Harbottle's Select Seminary for Elegant and Well-Bred Young Ladies."

Mr Thorpe tactfully says nothing. His French mother is the only woman who can reduce his wife to a quivering mouse merely by the lift of a supercilious elderly eyebrow. This is a trick which he, sadly, has never mastered.

"Bella has whims."

"Whims?"

"She has *fancies*."

"She does?"

"She told me only this morning that she wanted to be a *bluestocking*!"

"Oh?"

"And she eats like a bird – which is no bad thing; eating in public is difficult to accomplish well at the best of times – but Withers tells me she is lacing her smaller and smaller."

Mr Thorpe does not comment. This is mainly because the word "stocking" has led his thoughts temporarily astray.

"It is Mrs Carlyle's view, and I agree with her, that the sooner Bella finds a suitable husband, the better. Marriage will put a swift end to all this fancy nonsense."

"Quite right," Mr Thorpe mumbles.

"The only question is: how is it to be brought about?"

Ah. Mr Thorpe recognises what is happening. He is being taken down an already-prepared path. All he has to do is follow meekly, and all will be well.

"We have the dinner party, of course. Isabella has such pretty table manners. I'm sure she will attract much attention. But I was also thinking that our dear boy Gussy might be called upon. After all, I'm sure he must know many nice young officers from well-connected families."

"Good idea."

"You agree?"

"Oh yes. Gussy is the man for it. Definitely."

Mrs Thorpe sighs contentedly.

"Then I shall proceed accordingly."

"Do so, dear."

Mr Thorpe closes his eyes. He waits. After a few minutes of silence, he allows himself to drift off into a delightful dream, in which he is pursuing ladies with stockinged legs down various unexpected and winding paths.

Mrs Thorpe, however, remains awake, planning and scheming. Once Bella's future is settled, it will be Gussy's turn.

Though that is not going to be nearly such a problem. She has already picked out the lucky girl.

***

Dawn arrives, bringing with it rain. Milk-carts begin their rounds, the red newspaper expresses tear through the streets to catch the early trains. Riverboats get ready to receive the first passengers of the day. And in his cramped office at the detective division of the Metropolitan Police, Detective Inspector Stride has just finished reading through the night patrol reports.

Nearly every report contains a sighting of a "gigantic hound." It has been spotted in Paddington, in Clerkenwell, in Willesden (where it was accompanied by a second "gigantic hound"), and in Islington, where its howling has kept various respectable citizens awake all night.

In Highgate, a "gigantic hound" removed and seemingly ate a line of washing. It was also blamed for the digging up of a flowerbed, the loss of a pet cat, and the disappearance of a ham left by an open larder window. All these events took place at roughly the same time, bestowing upon the animal super-canine powers quite unheard-of ever before.

Stride is just thinking where to file these reports – his first choice being the nearest wastepaper basket – when Detective Sergeant Jack Cully enters.

"We've had a runner from one of the constables patrolling High Holborn," he says.

Stride raises a weary hand.

"No more gigantic hounds, Jack. Please. Spare me that."

Cully bites his lower lip.

"Actually, this might be ... err ... hound-related. Possibly. But whatever it is, I thought I'd better come straight to you, given where the incident has taken place."

Stride looks up.

"Oh, and where's that?"

Cully tells him.

For a second, Stride stares at him in blank amazement. Then he leaps from his seat.

"Hell and damnation. I don't believe it."

***

Josephine has just sat down to a plate of bacon and eggs when Annie enters the breakfast-room with a piece of paper and an important expression.

"A telegram has arrived for you, miss."

Josephine slits open the thin paper and reads:

URGENT STOP PLEASE COME AT ONCE STOP
T MOGGS

She pushes back her chair.

"I have to go out."

"But you haven't had your breakfast," the maid protests.

"Tell Mrs Hudson, I'm sorry, no time."

Josephine takes her shawl, her bonnet and a pair of gloves, and hurries out of the front door.

When she reaches Holborn, she discovers a nervous young police constable standing guard under the brick archway. There is also a small crowd of people waiting patiently on the pavement, because the sight of a nervous young policeman standing guard anywhere suggests something juicy and sensational may have occurred, possibly involving weltering in gore, or death by murder.

Trafalgar Moggs greets her at the bottom of the stairs, his expression anxious.

"Thank you for coming so promptly, Miss King," he says. "The discovery was made this morning by one of the cleaning women."

There are cleaning women? Josephine is astounded. She

follows him up the stairs.

"This was what she discovered," Moggs says, pointing.

A series of deep parallel grooves run from top to bottom of the outer door. It is as if some immense clawed beast has tried to tear its way in.

Josephine feels the blood beating upwards from her heart. Voices sound in the stairwell. Footsteps hurry up the stairs, and the next minute Detective Inspector Stride and Detective Sergeant Cully appear on the landing.

At the sight of her, the Detective Inspector's face falls.

"Ah. Miss King. So you are here," he says, in a tone of voice that clearly indicates he wishes she was not.

"Where else should I be, Detective Inspector?" she replies tartly. "This is – or rather it was – my uncle's place of work."

"Yes. Yes indeed."

Stride glances past her.

"By Christ," he exclaims.

He gets out a small memorandum book and begins scribbling furiously.

"You see what I mean," Detective Sergeant Cully remarks.

Stride's mouth forms a straight line.

"I hardly think your theory fits this scenario," he says stiffly.

"Really? So how do you account for it?"

Stride goes on calmly writing.

"There will be a logical explanation."

Cully gives him a sceptical look.

Stride closes the book.

"I find myself very uneasy, Miss King," he says. "Ve-ry uneasy indeed. Can you think of any reason why this might have occurred?"

"Really, I do not know. Mr Moggs, do you know?"

Moggs shakes his head.

Stride mutters something under his breath. He gives the door a hard accusatory stare as if it has done the marks all by itself.

"The papers are full of the presence of a gigantic hound," Moggs remarks. "I have heard it has been rampaging everywhere and running wild across the city. Maybe it found its way here."

"Now, now young man," Stride says dismissively. "I shouldn't believe everything you read in the papers."

"Indeed so," Moggs agrees. "As the late Mr King frequently used to remark: a journalist is just another name for a vulture with a notebook."

"And how right he was," Stride mutters. "So, neither of you have anything further you can tell me? No reason you can think of why this ... event should have occurred?"

Josephine shakes her head. There is a short silence.

"Then I will leave you, for now," Stride says.

He pauses.

"If you have anything further that you wish to discuss – anything you think might be relevant – do not hesitate to call upon me at Scotland Yard."

"Indeed I will not," she assures him.

The two detectives take their leave.

"What do you think has happened, Mr Moggs?" she asks, when the sound of their footsteps has faded.

"I do not know, Miss King. It is a mystery, indeed."

They stand side by side contemplating the wrecked office door.

"With your permission," Moggs says, "I shall now go and find a carpenter to plane the door."

"I think that would be a very good idea, Mr Moggs."

Moggs glances at her.

"But first, may I bring you a cup of strong coffee? You look a little shaken, if I may say so."

And, truth to tell, she does feel a little shaken. So many tumultuous events are piling in upon her one after another that she is in danger of being overwhelmed.

"Thank you. That would also be very acceptable."

Moggs nods briefly. He straightens his muffler and buttons up his overcoat.

"A gigantic hound?" she queries.

'Just something I read in the newspapers," he says. "Do not give it a second's thought, Miss King. As the Inspector said, there is bound to be a logical explanation. I shall return shortly with the coffee."

***

Meanwhile, Stride and Cully have reached street level.

"There's more to this than meets the eye, Jack," Stride murmurs. "First we have the brutal murder of Mr King. Then the mysterious removal of his body. Now this. Three events that I'm beginning to suspect could all be linked in some way. Though I'm not sure how or why."

While they have been engaged inside the building, the group outside has increased incrementally, the laws of causality stating that wherever two or three are gathered together a crowd will eventually form. Also, that among the crowd there will inevitably be a member of the press.

Stride's mouth sets in a grim line as he spots the jaunty cloth-capped figure of Richard Dandy, chief reporter on *The Inquirer*. *The Inquirer* is the sort of paper that claims it speaks for "The Ordinary Man In The Street."

"Good day, gents both," Dandy greets them breezily, elbowing his way to the front of the crowd, pencil poised, notebook at the ready. "Busy morning?"

"No busier than usual," Stride snaps.

"The Ordinary Man In The Street might be tempted to ask what two of London's finest detectives are doing in this neck of the woods."

"Might he?"

Dandy Dick, as he is known in the trade, gives Stride the sort of smile that lies on sandbanks waiting for unwary swimmers.

"He might indeed. Specially since we have this very dangerous gigantic hound on the loose. I'd've thought the mighty detective police had more important things to be getting on with."

He scribbles a couple of lines, angling the notebook towards him so that they cannot see what he is writing.

Stride sucks in his breath.

"So, give us a clue – what's going in there?" Dandy Dick asks.

"There is nothing going on, and I do not have any clues to give you."

The journalist nods sagely, then writes something else down.

"Thank you very much, Detective Inspector. You've been very helpful." He grins, tips his cap, and disappears into the crowd, leaving Stride staring after him in bafflement.

"What did I say?"

Cully shrugs.

"Who knows? Whatever it was, at least he's leaving us alone now."

He frowns.

"That door. I still think it might—"

Stride clicks his teeth impatiently.

"Well, don't think. I'm the one paid to think, not you. Right, I'm going to return to Scotland Yard. You stay here. Somebody must have seen something, heard something. Ask questions, and get some answers for God's sake! We can't let that bastard Dandy steal a march on us."

He hurries off in the direction of the Strand. Cully turns back to the crowd. Having noted the departure of the police, combined with the failure of any blood-soaked, blanket-covered bodies to emerge from the building, they are now reverting from suspiciously innocent bystanders to suspiciously innocent bystanders melting away into the surrounding streets and alleyways. His chances of finding out anything do not look good.

***

Mrs Thorpe's private sitting-room is cosy and warm. A bright fire crackles in the grate and the little rosewood tea-table is well furnished with silver teapot, cream jug, sugar basin and plates of delicious little cakes. This is where the angel in the house entertains her intimate friends.

The current intimate friend is Mrs Carlyle. The two ladies have known each other since they were day pupils at Miss Jemima Prudholme's Academy for Girls from Genteel Families.

Mrs Carlyle has recently managed to secure husbands for both her daughters, who, in Mrs Thorpe's opinion, are not particularly attractive girls. They are not nearly as talented as Isabella, who can sing, play piano, dance, and has studied geography, history, sketching, globes and mathematics.

Now the two ladies sit side by side on a sofa, balancing cups and saucers, little fingers crooked daintily, while they discuss the details of the lavish dinner party Mrs Thorpe is planning to hold shortly.

"You have secured the services of Monsieur Bouillon?" Mrs Carlyle inquires.

"Of course. Everything will be *à la Française*, as we prefer it," Mrs Thorpe replies. "We do not go in for dinners *à la Russe* here. Mr Thorpe likes to oversee the carving of the joints. Taylors will provide the fresh flowers and fruit."

Mrs Carlyle nods.

"I am sure it will be a perfect evening. And who have you invited for..." She lets the words hang invisibly in the air.

Mrs Thorpe leans forward and murmurs a couple of names. Her companion's eyes widen.

"I congratulate you, my dear. You have secured two of the most eligible young bachelors in London. Let us hope for a satisfactory outcome."

And Mrs Thorpe is indeed hoping for a satisfactory outcome. Hoping fervently with all her heart and soul. Because only a few hours earlier, she had another **difficult** conversation with Bella, stemming from a perfectly reasonable observation that if the girl had nothing better to do with her time, she might like to join one of Mrs Thorpe's church ladies' charity groups.

Mrs Thorpe bites her lip. She is sure she never spoke to her own beloved Mama in such a way. Indeed, she remembers herself as a most loving young creature, who would never stare at her Mama with hard eyes, and raise her eyebrow is such a supercilious fashion.

Mrs Carlyle straightens her gloves, and prepares to depart. Mrs Thorpe accompanies her friend to the hallway, where a maid waits to show her out.

"We shall meet again soon, my dear," Mrs Carlyle says, proffering the fingers of a gloved hand. "I am sure the dinner party is going to be a great success. Isabella will be the cynosure of every eye. You will be announcing her engagement in *The Times* before you know it."

Mrs Thorpe smiles thinly and prays that she is right.

***

While Mrs Thorpe and her dear friend have been tea-drinking and plotting, a cab has just pulled away from outside the house in St John's Wood, where a doorbell has been rung, and an official-looking letter delivered.

The letter has been carried by Annie to the book-lined study, where Josephine is once again dealing with the pile of funeral correspondence that never seems to get any smaller. The letter, which is from the solicitor Mr Able, has been handed over with a dignified gesture, the disapproving sniff being an optional extra.

Dear Miss King [Mr Able writes],

It has come to my notice that the Will of your late uncle, Mr Herbert King, has been asked for at Doctors' Commons, and has been examined. You may not be aware that once a Will has been proved and lodged, the law allows it to be examined, for a small disbursement.

As there is nothing in the Will that could, to my knowledge, be contested, and I am not aware of any individual who might have an interest in examining it, nor has any subsequent claim been made in person or writing to this office, I have made enquiries to ascertain the source of the request. I have discovered that it was made by Mr John Skittles, of Smallbone, Skittles & Smallbone, a firm of solicitors.

As I am your legal guardian, I immediately applied on your behalf to the individual named above, asking why he found it necessary to examine the Will. I have now received a reply, stating that he was acting under instructions from a client, but that it would be a breach of professional confidence for him to reveal more.

Be assured that I am pursuing this matter vigorously, and will write more when I have further information.

Your very obedient servant,
Sept. Able

A curious communication. Josephine places the letter next to the letters of condolence, deciding to think about it later. Meanwhile Annie remains standing in the doorway, awaiting instructions.

"Thank you, Annie."

The maid eyes the letter with interest.

"You may go."

A pause, a toss of the head, followed by a flouncy departure.

Josephine sighs. She wishes that her education, inadequate as it was in every single respect, had at least touched upon how to handle sulky staff. Resignedly she reaches for another letter of condolence, dips her pen into the inkwell, and begins to write.

Meanwhile Detective Inspector Stride and Detective Sergeant Cully are staring down at the early evening edition of *The Inquirer*, whose front page headline declares in big bold letters:

DETECTIVE INSPECTOR STRIDE OF SCOTLAND YARD SAYS HE "DOESN'T HAVE A CLUE"!

Stride jabs a finger angrily at the incriminating headline.

"I did not say that!"

"I think you did," Cully says.

"Yes all right, maybe I said *something* to that effect. But not in the way *he* puts it. The bastard's twisting my words."

They read on.

"What a load of utter cock!" Stride splutters. "'*Local residents report hearing fearful howling... things going bump in the night... terrible screams ... churchyard haunted for weeks by a ghostly apparition in black robe...*' Who are all these 'local residents'? Why didn't they come forward and talk to us, instead of to the press?"

Cully shrugs.

"I did my best. But people prefer talking to the newspapers. It gives them what I believe is called in the newspaper trade 'the oxygen of publicity'."

Stride mutters words to the effect that if he had his way, he wouldn't give them the oxygen of oxygen.

"And look here!" he exclaims, stabbing the paper viciously with his finger. "Did you read this? '*The ordinary Man in the Street is beginning to wonder whether the new detective division is worth all the thousands of pounds of taxpayers' money spent upon it.*' Do you know what I feel like doing to our smug self-satisfied Mr Dandy? Do you? I'd like to pull his head off with my bare hands, and use it as a football."

"I don't think that's actually legal."

"Then it should be," Stride exclaims. "Spreading lies. Misquoting people in public office – it's not on. I tell you what Jack, if this state of affairs is allowed to continue much longer, the press'll become an even bigger menace to law and order than the bloody criminals are. Mark my words!"

Detective Inspector Stride crumples up the newspaper and throws it angrily on to the floor. It will be later found by a cleaner, whose family is always desperately short of paper for the outside privy. Sadly, because it would give Stride great satisfaction to know that this will be its final use, he will never find out.

***

Dusk falls, and the lamplighters begin their rounds. The little flames flare and burn. The lamps are like eyes: they observe the dark, spectral side of the great city. They bear witness to the strange and terrible life of London at night.

In the flickering golden glow, they spy something moving erratically along the street. Something that makes progress, then stops and rests against a wall. The approaching Something develops a wretched threadbare topcoat, a battered shako still bearing the faint outline of a skull and crossbones, and boots that seem to be on the wrong feet.

As the Something draws closer, the prow of a red-veined nose, a pair of blood-raddled eyes and an unkempt beard also become apparent. The figure shuffles into a dark doorway, and pulls a bottle from one pocket.

"Forward the Light Brigade. Charge for the guns," it mutters in a hoarse whispery voice, before sinking to the ground in an insensible heap. Private Jim Jarndyce, late of the Light Brigade, and subsequently late for everything else, has returned to his old haunts.

***

Dawn arrives, accompanied by a milky vapour that hangs in the streets like the damp shed skin of a cloud, coating faces with moisture droplets. It also brings a ragged street-urchin carrying a broom who picks his way along the grease-slimed pavement. He is followed a few paces in the rear by the shambling mumbling object of the night before.

"Only a few more miles," Oi announces jauntily. "Soon be there. Look lively!"

The object shuffles along, looking more deadly than lively.

"No food, no fuel," it mumbles.

"Yeah, right. Plenty of food where we're goin'," Oi says encouragingly.

A few more miles brings them to the Marylebone Road. The boy continues to half-support, half-drag his companion, who has a tendency to suddenly stop dead, regardless of any approaching traffic.

Oi takes the shambling figure by the arm.

"Come on old soldger. Best foot forward."

The old man rips off a shaky salute.

"Private Jim Jarndyce reporting for duty, my lord. Forward the Light Brigade! Death or Glory!"

Eventually the two travellers reach St John's Wood. They stand (or rather, one of them stands, the other sways) in front of a handsome new house, whitewashed, and shiny painted, but with the blinds drawn down halfway, and a black bow on the door-knocker.

Private Jarndyce, whose relationship with time and geography is fluid at best, points a shaky finger.

"Is this the 'orspital? Will the kind lady with the lamp be there?"

Oi shakes his head sadly.

"Right, old'un," he says. "It's down the area steps for the likes of you and me. And let's hope the skivvy ain't a tartar, or we'll be back on the street afore you've said your piece."

A short while later, Josephine is interrupted by a knock at her bedroom door. She has just time to squirrel the diamond away in a drawer, before Annie the parlour-maid enters, her expression even more hoity-toity than usual.

"If you please, miss," she says, "there are two ... **persons** to see you."

In the basement kitchen Josephine discovers Oi sitting on the step on a piece of newspaper. He has a slice of bread in one hand, clearly the result of some sort of charm offensive upon Mrs Hudson, the cook. A peculiar smell seems to be coming from somewhere just beyond the open kitchen door.

Oi pauses mid-bite.

"Said I'd let yer know when old Jim came back to Lunnon," he says, nodding towards the area.

Josephine crosses the kitchen, and discovers the wreck that was once Private Jim Jarndyce of the Light Cavalry Brigade, but which is now just a shaking, shivering, mad-eyed heap of rags and bones. They stand and stare at each other in wordless amazement.

Still chewing, Oi appears in the doorway.

"Has he told yer?"

She shakes her head.

"Come on, old'un," Oi coaxes. "You remember: it was a dark and misty night..."

The bundle of rags jerks into semi-animated life.

"It was a dark and misty night and I woz restin' my eyes when I heard blood-curdlin' screams," it recites. "An' I looked and looked an' I didn't see nuffink and then I heard footsteps."

He stops, swaying to and fro as if blown by some internal gale.

"Go on," Oi prods. "And then someone ran past you, right?"

The old man takes a couple of shuffling steps towards Josephine, who feels her eyes beginning to water from the smell.

"Whoever it woz," he whispers hoarsely, "they looked like a

person, and they wore clothes like a person, but they woz running on all fours, like an animal."

"What do you mean?"

But Private Jarndyce's brief visit to the real world is over. Staring distractedly about him, he starts mumbling about cannons and sabres.

Oi shakes his head.

"You won't get nuffink outer him now," he says.

Josephine instructs Mrs Hudson to supply them both with food. Then the dazed old man is hauled and manoeuvred back up the area steps, leaving her completely mystified and wondering what on earth it was that he thought he saw.

Sadly, she will never find out. Sometime during the night, Private Jim Jarndyce will be summoned by a greater commander to appear on a higher parade ground. In the morning he will be found cold and lifeless in a doorway, his pockets still full of bread and cheese.

***

But before this unfortunate discovery is made, a dinner party is taking place at the Hampstead mansion of Mr and Mrs Thorpe. It is a dinner party for which no expense has been spared, from the elaborate place-settings and the snowy linen to the great epergnes of hothouse flowers and greenery.

The menus (written in French of course) have been carefully planned by the gracious hostess of the feast. No bread and cheese here. The food has been cooked by a French chef, specially hired for the occasion.

Naturally there will be several courses, beginning with *potages*, passing through *poissons* and *relèves* and ending with *entremets* – these last being placed on stands on the sideboard, to be admired by the guests before being demolished.

Amber sherry awaits in cut-glass decanters. Hock and champagne sit in silver wine-coolers, and sweet dessert wines are lined up like infantrymen awaiting the signal to go.

The guests eat and drink and are exceedingly merry. Although not all of them. Isabella Thorpe, for one, does not seem to be participating in any aspect of the evening's entertainments.

Her plate of *Suprème de Saumon Richelieu* sits untouched in front of her. Her wine is untasted. The expression on her face indicates that given a choice – which of course she has not been given – she would rather be anywhere else on earth than here.

The two eligible bachelors sitting on either side of her have both been trying to engage her in sparkling witty conversation ever since the *Consomme à la Doria*. To no avail, and as her plate is discreetly removed by the specially-hired waiters, to be replaced by some *Côtelets Hasseur aux Pointes*, they give up, turning instead to the ladies sitting on the other side, who are only too happy to flirt and receive their attentions.

Isabella stares at her thin bony hands, which remind her of bird claws. She knows that Mrs Thorpe has deliberately arranged the guests so that she sits between young George Murray (two thousand pounds a year) and even younger Henry Soane (will inherit large family house and successful business one day). She presses her lips together and crumbles her slice of bread.

Isabella remembers passing a butcher's shop recently, and seeing a freshly killed pig's head in the window, an apple in its mouth. Blood caked its nostrils , and it was surrounded by flies. It made her feel sick and dizzy. All those flies buzzing around the poor dead animal, its eyes blindly open.

And now here she is. She has turned into the pig, artfully arranged in her mother's shop window, and the young men are the flies. Buzz, buzz.

A *tarte aux framboises* is placed in front of her. Reluctantly, she picks up her fork, breaks into the pastry crust. The raspberry juice gushes out, drips onto the plate, red like blood.

The fork clatters onto her plate. The room swims. She feels

all eyes swivel towards her, has the sensation of falling forwards. She hears a glass smash, smells freshly laundered linen. Then darkness descends.

***

It is a few days later and in the thin light of an early dawn, a boat is making its way along the river Thames, the liquid coin that runs through the heart of the city. Two people are in the boat: a man plying the oars, and an adolescent boy with his hand on the tiller.

They make steady progress, always keeping a wary eye open, for the tide has just turned and is running fast, and there are already barges and sailing colliers dropping down the river.

A slant of light touches something wrapped in a tarpaulin, lying on the wooden planks at the bottom of the boat. Something that bears the outline of a human form. The boat passes under Tower Bridge and continues downriver until it reaches the wharf known as Dead Man's Stairs.

The oarsman guides the boat towards the water-lapped wooden piles. His companion steps nimbly ashore and ties it by a rope to one of the iron rings attached to a post. The two then lift the gruesome contents out of the boat and carry it the short distance to the Wapping Headquarters of the River Police, where they dump it unceremoniously on the floor.

"'Nother one for you," the oarsman says gruffly.

The desk sergeant sighs, reaching for pen and ink. He opens the Occurrence Book.

"Male? Female?"

"Man. Been dead a while."

"Papers?"

"Nuffink."

"Pockets?"

A shake of the head.

"Where?"

"Putney."

"Anything else?"

In reply, the man stretches out his hand.

"'Arf a crown. Finder's fee."

The desk sergeant unlocks a cash box.

"Sign here."

The man makes a cross in the book, puts the money into his pocket, and signals to the boy that he is ready to go.

Out on the slipway, the boy turns to him.

"Why didn't you tell 'im abaht the marks?"

"None of our business," the man says quickly. "Let 'em work it out for themselves. We got our money. That's all wot matters."

The boy stares back at the police house.

"Poor sod. I ain't never seen nuffink like that afore. What you suppose happened?"

The man unties the boat without answering.

"You comin'?"

The boy pulls off his cap, scratches his head. For a moment he seems to hover between staying and going. Then he turns and joins his companion in the boat. The man picks up the oars, and rows the boat back out into midstream. He does not speak again.

***

Meanwhile Isabella Thorpe has been put to bed and the doctor has been summoned. He has diagnosed nothing fatal. (*"Green sickness, Mrs Thorpe. Yes indeed. Green sickness. Very common complaint amongst young gels."*) He recommends that she needs rest, and should be kept warm and comfortable. The main thing though, is to ensure that she eats enough to build up her strength.

Nothing flavourful, naturally, as bland food is supposed to be more easily digestible to somebody with a lowered constitution.

So out go soups, roast dinners, pies, tasty desserts, cakes and fruits – not that Isabella ever partook of them in the first place – and in comes toast-and-water and calves-foot jelly.

So concerned is Mrs Thorpe for her daughter's health that she has purchased Mrs Beeton's excellent book on cooking for an invalid, and is personally supervising the cook in the preparation of the bland tasteless meals which Isabella has to force down.

After three days of this excruciating torture, Isabella decides to stage a recovery. She declares that she feels much better. She staggers out of bed, and allows herself to be helped into her clothes, which now hang even more loosely on her wasted frame.

Mrs Thorpe is overjoyed. She tells Isabella that in the afternoon they will go for a little ride together in the brougham – the fresh air will bring the roses back to her pale cheeks.

But Isabella has other plans. She has had quite enough of her Mama's fussing, so she suggests that Gussy could jog along on his horse instead.

Gussy – how lovely, Mrs Thorpe declares. And possibly one of Gussy's Dragoon friends also? And while she thinks about it, wouldn't it be nice to invite poor little Josephine King along too, as she and Isabella are such good friends. Perhaps Isabella would like to write her a little note?

Isabella would not particularly like to do that, but her instincts of self-preservation whisper that any reluctance on her part could be interpreted as a relapse, and send her back to her bed and the grim regime of force-feeding. So the little note is duly written and dispatched. An acceptance is received, and nobody is any the wiser.

But the best laid plans of mice and men, and of Mrs Thorpe, "*gang aft aglay,*" as the Scottish poet says. For when the carriage bearing the two young ladies draws up at the barracks later that day, it is to discover that Gussy's horse has cast a shoe in the night, and cannot be ridden out today.

81

Thus Isabella and her companion make their unaccompanied way towards Regent's Park: Isabella disappointedly, Josephine secretly relieved. They progress in silence for a while. Then, as the carriage turns into Regent's Park Road, Isabella asks listlessly,

"Should you like to visit the Zoological Gardens? I believe it is quite amusing."

Josephine nods her agreement. There are giraffes and camels at the Zoo. She has never seen giraffes and camels before. At the very least, they have to be more entertaining than her withdrawn and uncommunicative companion.

"But are you quite well enough?" she asks politely.

Isabella waves a languid hand.

"Oh yes. A short walk, and something amusing, is just what the doctor ordered."

They alight from the brougham, pay their shillings, and pass through the turnstile. Once inside, however, it soon becomes clear that Isabella has wildly misjudged her ability to walk any distance at all, for after only a few yards, she collapses onto a bench.

"You go on," she says, gasping for breath in an alarming manner. "I shall be quite all right here."

Josephine stands by, staring down at her helplessly.

"Really. Go!" Isabella urges.

Josephine goes.

Isabella settles down with a contented, if weary sigh. The animal smell is almost overpowering, but she reminds herself that at least she is not in her bedroom, and that her Mama isn't here. Life has its little upsides.

Best of all, nobody is making her eat anything – though she cannot help notice that every animal in sight appears to be eating something revolting, and with great relish. She closes her eyes, trying not to breathe too deeply.

Meanwhile Josephine strolls round the Zoo, amazed at the grace of the giraffes, the comicality of the camels and the merry antics of the monkeys. There is so much to see. She wishes she had brought her sketchbook with her, but promises herself that this will be the first of many visits, and she will bring it next time.

The minutes slip away unnoticed, and it is only when she reaches the clock tower that she realises she has been away from Isabella for over an hour. She does not wish to be impolite, so she stops and retraces her steps.

Turning a corner, she spies a woman dressed in black and heavily-veiled. The woman is bending down in front of one of the cages. Her attitude is one of intense focused concentration, as if she is listening intently to something.

Josephine observes her from a distance. For a few minutes the woman remains utterly still, as if she was a wax statue of herself. Then suddenly she straightens up, and hurries away towards the East Tunnel.

And then something strange happens. All the animals rush to the front of the cage and begin to howl. Eerie and alien, the sound rises and falls. It is like a siren, silver and unearthly, seeming to come from everywhere at once, as if the sky itself is screaming.

Josephine puts her hands over her ears, feeling the hairs on the back of her neck stand on end. An oily slick of fear clings to her skin.

Eventually, the howling dies away.

She approaches the cage. Dark sinuous shapes prowl and pace. A notice informs her that the animals are *Mongolian Wolves (Canis Lupus Mongoliensis). Danger: Visitors are advised to take care. These animals may bite.*

She stares into the cage. Mad yellow eyes stare back.

For a moment the whole pack forms up behind one grey wolf, as though they are getting ready to attack. Then, as if realising they have made a mistake, possibly identified the wrong prey, they slink back into the shadows.

Puzzling over this strange event, she makes her way back to

the bench, where she discovers Isabella sitting exactly as she had left her.

"Did you hear those wolves howling?"

Isabella gives her a dreamy, half-vacant stare.

"No. What howling? What wolves?"

Josephine sighs. It is quite clear that Isabella is not well. Not well at all.

But returning home in the brougham, it seems that the outing has done Isabella some good after all. She is still barely communicating beyond what politeness demands, but her cheeks have a pale pink flush, and her whole demeanour seems more enervated.

There is a reason for this change, but it has nothing to do with the fresh air, nor the companionship, nor the carriage ride. Unbeknown to Josephine, Isabella has had a little adventure of her own.

While she was sitting on the bench, a young man had happened to pass by. Their eyes had met. He had smiled at her. She had smiled back – well, he was very handsome, with beautiful dark brown hair and wonderful deep blue eyes.

He had uttered a remark about the weather. She had said something – oh, she can't now recall what it was. Next minute, he was sitting next to her on the bench – not too close, they were in a public place, after all – and they were making polite conversation.

The brougham drops Josephine back in St John's Wood, then carries Isabella steadily towards Hampstead. She has been thinking about the young man ever since she got into the carriage. His name is Henry Papperdelli, and he is member of the Pre-Raphaelite Brotherhood – whatever that means.

Henry is studying art at the Working Men's College and lives with a whole lot of other artists in a rented house in Red Lion Square, Bloomsbury. This is an area of London which Isabella is quite sure her Mama would not regard as respectable at all.

Back at the house, Isabella scurries up to her bedroom. She takes off her warm shawl, sits down at her dressing table and studies her reflection in the looking-glass. Her skin is so pale. Her cheekbones stick out. Her eyes are violet-lidded with fatigue, and her thick coils of chestnut hair make her head look top-heavy, as if her neck is too fragile to support it.

She bears no resemblance whatsoever to the round, rosy-cheeked, rosebud-lipped girls that she sees in fashion plates or on the covers of song sheets. Not that the young man seemed to mind, though.

Isabella smiles a sly, secret smile at the wan, etiolated girl in the looking-glass. Henry wants to paint her portrait. He said so. It is a truly shocking suggestion.

She can't wait to see him again.

***

Midnight. The bewitching hour. Out in the street, gas-lamps flicker like corpse candles. Darkness creates a sense of the uncanny. It blurs and dissolves the uncertain boundaries between real and imagined.

In the pitch-black silence of the sleeping house, Josephine awakes. She hears a noise. It sounds like glass breaking. Hovering on the edge of consciousness, she lifts the bedcovers and slides out of bed. Wrapping a shawl around her shoulders, she stumbles to the door, stepping out into the dark space of the landing.

The air seems to vibrate with something she cannot define, but she knows instinctively, deep down at her core, that it is not good. If she were a cat, every hair on her back would be standing upright. She looks down into the hallway.

Moonlight streams through the stained-glass panels of the front door, throwing rainbow patterns on the walls, silvering the fur of the animal-skin rug that lies on the hallway floor. It takes her a moment to realise: *There is no animal-skin rug on the hallway floor.*

Her breath catches in her throat, as the rug suddenly raises its head and gets to its feet. Evil yellow eyes stare intently up at her. Next second, a massive grey wolf bounds towards the stairs, teeth bared in a snarl of rage.

For a split second she freezes, her heart hammering in her chest. Then she runs into her uncle's room, slamming the door shut. Just in the nick of time. Loud snarling and heavy thuds come from the other side of the door, followed by the rasping sound of claws being drawn down the wood from top to bottom.

Josephine reaches under the bed and pulls out her uncle's Afghan pistol and a small box of bullets. When she'd first arrived in London, he had taught her how to load and fire it. They'd subsequently spent many happy hours shooting starlings off the summerhouse roof. Her uncle had said that the ability to fire a gun was more useful than all the rubbish they filled her head with at school.

How right he was.

Now she loads the gun, trying to keep her hands from shaking. Then, taking a deep, calming breath, she opens the door a crack and peers out.

There is no sign of the wolf.

She is just setting off to find it when she hears a low, wicked growl behind her back. Spinning round, she sees the wolf crouched in the gloomy darkness of the top landing. Its pupils glow fiery red.

A bright comet tail of fear runs down her spine, but she raises the gun, and holds it out in front of her, gripping it with both hands. She hears her uncle's voice:

"*Sight straight along the barrel, Josie. Steady hands. Squeeze the trigger gently ... gently ... remember, it kicks back when it fires.*"

The wolf springs. She fires. The wolf howls in pain, and leaps over the banister, spattering her with blood. It somersaults through empty air until it lands heavily in the hallway below, where it bounds towards the baize door leading to the basement kitchen.

A moment later Annie appears on the top floor landing, her hair in curling-rags, her eyes starting out of her head. The maid takes one startled look at Josephine, clad in a blood-bespattered night-gown, clutching a smoking gun in both hands, and starts to scream at the top of her voice.

A couple of hours later Josephine is back in her bed once more. She is wearing a fresh nightgown and there is a glass of hot milk on her bedside table. All traces of the grim night visitor have been cleared away. The broken scullery window has been temporarily boarded up. Everything is safe and sound. But she does not feel safe and sound. Not at all.

Something is niggling away at the back of her mind like an aching tooth. It resolves itself into a series of thoughts: The wolf had seemed quite at home in the house. It had not tried to run away when it saw her. It was not afraid.

She pushes the thoughts a little further along a path she does not want to go down. The wolf had seemed to deliberately wait for her to come out of her uncle's room. Almost as if it had known who she was, and what it had to do. As if somebody had given it careful instructions.

She recalls her visit to the Zoological Gardens earlier that day. The way the wolves had stared at her, then slunk away. She tries not to think about the implications of all of this. But they are the sort of thoughts that have glue on them.

***

The following morning finds Detective Sergeant Jack Cully staring gloomily down at a dead body lying in the gutter, and searching for the right words of comfort to say to the man standing next to him, who stifles a sob, wiping his streaming eyes on his sleeve.

"I can't believe she's gone," the man hiccups. "She was only there yesterday, so alive and well."

Cully takes out his notebook, flicks it open and licks his pencil.

"So, when was the last time you saw her?"

The man heaves a great sigh.

"Last night, must've been about six. I always say goodnight to her before I leave."

"And you didn't notice that... um... that..."

"Alice – her name's Alice."

Cully nods.

"You didn't notice Alice was missing?"

The man shakes his head.

"I can't stand the thought that she suffered. Do you think she suffered, officer?"

Jack Cully is damn sure that Alice suffered. She must have suffered to hell as she tried to make her way back, bleeding from the bullet wound in her side. The carriage that ran her over was probably doing her a favour.

"No," he lies. "I'm sure she went peacefully."

The man sniffs noisily.

"She was my favourite wolf," he says. "The others, well they're just wolves. Nothing special about them. But Alice – she was different. She used to look at me, you know, almost as if she could read my thoughts."

Jack Cully doubts this. He recalls an aunt who used to make the same claim for her pet goldfinch. Until the day it flew out of her parlour window and disappeared. Probably straight into next-door's cat.

"So she's never got out before?" he asks.

The zookeeper shakes his head.

"Never. And I don't understand how it happened this time. She's never tried to escape before. Never. It's a complete mystery."

He bends down to stroke the damp, bedraggled fur.

"I'm so sorry, Alice," he whispers.

Jack Cully turns his head away. And glares at the little knot of journalists scribbling and sketching frantically in the background. He can just visualise the midday headlines: **MONSTER WOLF SLAIN! FEAR DEPARTS FROM CITY STREETS!** Caustic comments would be written about the incompetence of the detective police.

He closes his notebook with an air of finality. But a few concerns linger on, like wisps of smoke after a bonfire has been extinguished. His main concern is that the paw-prints he'd seen in the cemetery were very much bigger than the paws of this dead wolf. And he doubts that Alice would be capable of committing all the offences named in the newspapers, let alone digging up and dragging off a dead body. Still, as his boss always says: *"Give me solutions, Jack, not problems."* So that is exactly what he is going to do.

***

And Detective Sergeant Jack Cully will get away with it, because even now, in one of those strange serendipitous events, Detective Inspector Stride is about to arrive at the Wapping Headquarters of the River Police.

Stride has been summoned by his opposite number, who has apprehended a small wherry containing stolen goods, traceable directly back to a violent robbery carried out by an East End gang that Stride's men have been watching for the past few weeks.

In the course of the visit Stride will, naturally, cast a professional eye over the gruesome *Body Found* posters pasted to the front of the police building. Despite the best efforts of the police artist (who could render a picture of his own mother unrecognisable), Stride will recognise a face that he has seen before. Upon enquiry, he will be shown the remains of the body, will identify and name it, and will arrange to transport it back to its last-but-one resting place. He will also observe certain marks that he does not recall seeing on the body when he last viewed it. But he won't understand what they mean, and so he will ignore them.

***

Meanwhile Josephine is travelling across London in an omnibus. She has managed to secure one of the coveted separate compartments. It is about the size of an upright coffin, but at least she does not have to travel squashed up against some man reeking of cigar smoke.

She is grateful for this short period of solitude, having lain awake most of the previous night, the inside of her mind shiny with the clarity of sleeplessness. Every creak and groan had startled her upright, ears straining for the sound of imaginary paws padding upstairs. She had not realised that the scariest place in the whole universe could be her own bedroom.

Now, nerves pulled tight by too little sleep, she is on her way to talk things over with the only person she feels she can confide in. Alighting at Holborn, she pays the conductor her sixpence before making her way to the offices of King & Co.

Trafalgar Moggs is seated in his usual place behind the desk, filling in ledgers. He gives her a long searching look, then quietly sets down his quill.

"Good morning Miss King. This is an unexpected visit. Something is troubling you?"

She fumbles awkwardly with her bonnet strings.

"Yes, something is troubling me greatly, Mr Moggs."

The clerk rises.

"Let us repair to the inner office," he suggests. "Then you can tell me what it is."

A short while later Josephine is seated behind her uncle's desk, relating the terrifying events of the previous night.

"This is a very great mystery, Miss King," Moggs murmurs when she has finished. "I confess I am puzzled what to suggest.

Other than perhaps the animal was being kept as a pet in some menagerie, then escaped, and perhaps that was why it did not seem afraid of you." He frowns. "The newspapers are still full of reports of a 'gigantic hound'. It has been seen all over London."

She picks up her uncle's brass letter-opener and turns it to and fro.

"The marks upon the office door here were remarkably similar to the marks left by the animal last night. Should I talk to Detective Inspector Stride?"

"Do you think the two events are linked to Mr King's murder?"

She shakes her head.

"I cannot see how."

"My advice," says Moggs, "would be to let well alone. I have read in a magazine that, given the millions of human beings all jostling each other for space within a few square miles, every possible combination of events – both striking and bizarre, may be expected to take place."

She sets down the letter-opener.

"Then I shall follow your advice, Mr Moggs."

They sit in silence for a few seconds.

"On a different topic altogether," the clerk says, "what have you decided to do with the jewels?"

"I have not yet reached a decision," she confesses. "I know that both you and Mr Able think that I should put them in a bank. But is that what my uncle would say?"

Unexpectedly, a smile crosses Moggs's face.

"Your uncle would probably say that a banker is just another word for a thief in a suit," he remarks drily. "But I think you should at least get the diamond valued, Miss King. Maybe that would help you to make up your mind one way or the other."

"Where could I go to do that?"

"If I were you, I'd take it to Garrards the jewellers – just off the Haymarket. They make jewellery for the Queen herself, so they should know what they are talking about."

***

Robert Garrard of R & S Garrard & Co, Royal and Crown Jewellers, stands in his Panton Street shop staring out through the curved glass shop window. He hears the sounds of horseshoes slipping on damp cobbles, the cry of newsvendors shouting the early evening headlines.

Beneath his feet, the hiss of grinding-wheels comes up from the basement workroom, where his apprentices melt gold in crucibles, and cut and shape stones into wondrous things, such as the diamond necklace and drop earrings that he has recently delivered to Her Majesty, Queen Victoria.

The diamond, known as the Lahore Diamond, was presented to the Queen by the Directors of the East India Company, along with the Timur Ruby (which itself weighed an unbelievable 322.5 carats). It had been an even more remarkable jewel than the famous Koh-i-Noor Diamond (105.6 carats), which his firm also reset as a pendant in a necklace of Oriental inspiration. Since inheriting the business from his father, also called Robert, he has measured out his days in stones and carats.

Robert Garrard is a man in the prime of life. Sleek, handsome, his hair dyed brown, and oiled back from his face, he exudes the thrust and energy of someone much younger. Even the whores on the Haymarket say it is a pleasure doing business with him. Now, hands clasped behind his back, he rocks gently to and fro upon his feet, and thinks about diamonds.

There is no other stone like the diamond. No other jewel that can take upon itself so many hues. He has seen diamonds yellow as sulphur, orange, pink and black. He remembers the Pigot Diamond (48.63 carats), which Rundell & Bridge sold, cut, for thirty thousand pounds. A white oval, with only the tiniest red foul.

The finest stones are always white, clear and transparent.

Simpler than water, untouched and elemental. Like the magnificent stone he has just handled.

A short while earlier, Robert Garrard had been standing behind the counter discussing various commissioned pieces with his shopman, when the door had opened to admit a redheaded young woman dressed in full mourning.

Stepping over the threshold, she had glanced cautiously about her at the tables displaying gold and silverware, copper and jewellery. Light reflected off cut surfaces, glowed gently from gilded items. Garrard had already decided what this visit was about: the young woman had some pieces left to her by the deceased. Probably trinkets of very little worth that she now wished to sell, in order to prevent herself from slipping into poverty and destitution.

He had stepped forward, assuming a benign, fatherly expression.

"Good morning, young lady. I am Robert Garrard, the owner of this establishment. How may I be of assistance to you?"

A pair of shrewd green eyes had regarded him levelly from under a rather damp bonnet. A gloved hand had delved into an inner skirt pocket and pulled out something wrapped in a clean cloth, which was placed it upon the shiny wooden counter.

"I should like you, please, to tell me the value of this."

"Of course, young lady. It would be my pleasure."

He had nodded, smiling condescendingly, and folded back the cloth to reveal a very large cut diamond. It had winked and glittered, as if it had just woken up.

Garrard had licked his lips and stared, knowing it for what it was. Automatically, he had taken a loupe from his pocket, and picked up the stone delicately, sensing its oily hardness drawing heat from his fingers.

Even without weighing it on the scales, he had estimated its weight at over two hundred carats. More than any other diamond he had ever seen or handled. More, even than the

93

Koh-i-Noor.

Suddenly, he had found that he could not breathe. He had felt as if he was going to scream. He had concentrated hard on the stone, pushing his emotions aside.

"Where did you get this?"

"My uncle left it to me in his Will," the young woman had replied coolly. "He brought it back with him from his travels abroad."

Garrard had tried to re-gather his thoughts.

"It is a very old diamond," he had said at length, "probably originating in the Konar region of Afghanistan. Many fine white diamonds came from there. How did your uncle come by it?"

"He was given it as a gift. My uncle's lawyer referred to it as 'The Eye of the Khan'."

Garrard had breathed in sharply.

"I have heard the name before. There are tales and rumours about a diamond of that name. It was mined in the Kollur mines centuries ago. Over time it was supposed to have passed through the hands of many famous Mughal and Persian rulers. The last known record of it was a very long time ago. It was always assumed that it had disappeared."

"How can a diamond disappear?"

He had smiled wryly.

"It is all too easily done. War and death are the most usual methods. With some stones, every facet may stand for a bloody deed. And then there is also the curse. Many famous diamonds are cursed."

She had looked at him inquiringly.

"The famous Koh-i-Noor Diamond, for instance, carries a curse," he had told her. "All the men who have ever owned it have lost their thrones, or had some other terrible misfortune befall them. Fortunately, it is now owned by our beloved Queen. Diamonds and curses. They follow each other like day and night."

Carefully, as if swaddling a new-born baby, he had wrapped the diamond up and pushed it gently towards her.

"Take very good care of your diamond, young lady. You are extremely lucky to own it."

"So how much is it worth?"

Garrard had shaken his head.

"You can't put a price upon something like that. It is worth whatever the one who desires it will pay. In whatever currency they choose. You are keeping it locked up somewhere safe, I presume?"

"Oh, I am. Thank you very much for your help."

She had stuffed the diamond back in her pocket. He had winced.

"Please don't worry, Mr Garrard," the young woman had reassured him as she headed for the shop door. "I shall be taking a cab home."

***

While Robert Garrard continues to stare out of his shop window, cursing himself for not getting the young woman's name and address, the subject of his thoughts is actually standing just a few streets away in front of a newsvendor's stand.

She is staring at a headline, which proclaims:

RARE MONGOLIAN WOLF SHOT IN FRENZIED ATTACK!

After purchasing a copy of the paper she picks up a cab on the corner, and directs the driver to take her straight home. Inside the cab, she reads the story with growing dismay.

The wolf was called Alice. Oh dear. And according to its keeper, Mr Alfred Garnett (35): *"Alice was the sweetest wolf you could ever imagine and would never hurt a fly."* Josephine finds this difficult to reconcile with the snarling red-eyed creature that she had encountered the night before, but the accompanying drawing of a large beast, eyes closed, tongue lolling, lying in a pool of its own blood, does indeed bear some resemblance. Though it is hard to think of it as "Alice" – a name which she does not associate with a wild animal.

More worrying, however, is the revelation that the police believe the shot that killed Alice was fired in the St John's Wood area.

"Residents of this peaceful suburb were awoken in the middle of the night by the sounds of gunfire."

This is followed by the declaration that

"We will make every effort to search out, track down and apprehend the villains who have perpetrated this mindless act of cruelty upon a dumb and helpless animal. They will meet the sternest punishment,' promises Detective Sergeant Jack Cully of the detective police."

It appears that while acting in what she innocently believed to be self-defence, she has committed a crime, for which she will be sternly punished if she is caught. So she must take steps to ensure that she isn't caught.

The cab stops outside the house. She pays the cabman and hurries up the front steps. But even as she is fumbling in her pocket for the key, a voice addresses her.

"Miss King?"

She turns, the colour draining from her face as Detective Inspector Stride, accompanied by the other detective whose name she has just read, hurry across the street towards her. Josephine takes one look at the expression on their faces and feels a hollow sinking sensation in the pit of her stomach. They are here to question her about the wolf.

Suddenly she finds it difficult to swallow. The gun, she thinks frantically. She should never have left the gun in plain sight on the floor of her bedroom. If there is to be a search of the house they will certainly find it.

And then her goose will be well and truly cooked. (Not that she will ever get to eat it. From now on it will be bread and water, and a hard bed to lie on.)

"We were just on our way to see you, Miss King," Stride says. "May we step inside for a moment?"

Squaring her shoulders, and mentally assembling the basics she will need to take with her to prison, she opens the front door with trembling hands. She has never been arrested before. She wonders whether she will have to wear handcuffs.

"You recall my colleague, Detective Sergeant Cully," Stride says as they follow her into the drawing room.

Her heart sinks a little further.

"We wish to talk to you about something that has recently occurred."

She braces herself.

"Your uncle's body has been found."

She stares at him, feeling her jaw drop open in sheer disbelief. This is not what she is expecting to hear. For a moment, she is so astonished that she wonders whether she has understood him aright.

"His body? But I thought you said it had been taken by people for purposes which were unsuitable for an impressionable young female mind to know?"

Stride has the grace to look embarrassed.

"That appears now not to be the case."

"Where was it found?"

"Err ... it was taken from the river and brought to the River Police headquarters at Wapping."

Josephine's stare goes on a couple of seconds beyond the comfort barrier.

"How on earth did it get into the river?"

"We are not at this stage in our enquiries able to answer that, I'm afraid, Miss King. Possibly it was placed there by a person, or persons, unknown."

"The same person or persons unknown who robbed and

brutally murdered him in the first place?"

"That too, is part of the ongoing investigation."

"Are you any nearer to finding out who they are, and arresting them?"

"The detective police are making every effort to apprehend the person or persons unknown who are responsible for the crime," Stride says.

She gives him the look that used to get her supper taken away from her at the Bertha Helstone Institute.

A difficult silence ensues. Rashly, Stride rushes to fill it.

"I am most sincerely sorry indeed that you have been troubled with this matter, Miss King. Naturally, I and my fellow-officers appreciate that you must be shocked and distressed by the news.

"We have arranged for the body to be quietly and discreetly returned to Kensal Green Cemetery, and interred in its former resting place. I hope this is in line with your wishes."

She inclines her head.

"As soon as I have any further news, I shall inform you immediately," Stride says. "In the meantime, if you have no further questions, I will bid you good day, Miss King."

Stride puts on his hat and signals to his companion that he is ready to depart. At the door he turns, as if he has suddenly remembered something.

"Just one more thing, Miss King. Last night, I don't suppose you heard any gunfire?"

Her eyes widen.

"Gunfire? No, Detective Inspector. I did not."

Stride prides himself upon his ability to read most people, but once again Josephine King is proving to be a closed book in a locked bookcase.

"Ah. Well. Thank you, Miss King. Then I shall trouble you no further."

She is still puzzling over this unexpected turn of events when Annie scuttles into the room.

"The police detectives have left, miss," she announces. "Was it about the burglar that broke in last night?'

"Yes, that's quite right, Annie," she agrees, the lie coming out with alarming fluency. "Sadly, I was unable to give them a description, and as nothing was stolen, I fear they are not going to pursue the matter any further."

The maid nods.

"Just as well you had Mr King's gun, wasn't it?"

"Yes it was," she agrees again. "And now I think I would like a cup of tea. And a slice of Mrs Hudson's delicious seed cake – a big slice. Can you bring them both up to my room, please."

Later, after hiding the gun somewhere safe, and mentally strapping her Inner Liar into a backboard, Josephine unwraps the Eye of the Khan. She gazes at it, loving it with her eyes as it glitters in the pale sunshine of the late afternoon.

She knows with a sudden certainty that she cannot part with it, will never be able to consign it to the darkness of a bank vault, to be buried away like everybody else she has ever loved. For most of her life she has lived with the constant sensation of loss. It is as if there has always been a love inside her waiting to happen, and now the diamond is what it has happened to.

A jewel without price, Mr Garrard had said. She holds it the palm of her hand, the weight of it catching her by surprise all over again as it radiates light, like the face of an angel.

**

Much to her surprise, Isabella Thorpe has also come into possession of something of great value. Not a diamond, although to her it is almost as priceless; it is her freedom. Here she is, on her own, with no Mama in attendance, seated at a table in one of those delightful little tea-rooms that have suddenly sprung up like mushrooms all over the West End.

On the table is a pot of tea for one, and a plate of delicately-sliced bread-and-butter. There is a spot of hectic colour in each cheek, and she has an air of suppressed excitement. Her gaze keeps straying towards the street door.

Eventually the door opens, and oh – be still her beating heart – it is him! Isabella cannot breathe. She wonders whether she is about to faint. He is surprised to see her. She is surprised to see him. It is a game they play. You never know who might be watching from behind a newspaper, or from under a fashionably ribbon-trimmed hat. Her Mama knows many people in town, and the last thing Isabella wants is for some nosy acquaintance to go hurrying round to Hampstead tattling tales.

Thus, they arrange to meet "accidentally" in public. Yesterday it was outside a shop in Oxford Street, and today it is in this innocent little tea-room. Always at the same time of day, when Isabella is supposed to be taking a carriage ride for her health.

A smiling waitress hurries over, and pulls out the chair opposite. He sits down, wafting the most delicious smell of cologne and tobacco. Lips parted, she breathes him in like incense.

The temptation to reach across the table and stroke his beautiful silky hair is almost overwhelming. A strange, but not unpleasant, sensation starts spreading through her lower body. She presses her gloved hands together, and clasps them in her lap.

"Isabella." He murmurs her name as if it was something delicious to eat.

She swallows, then picks up her teacup with an unsteady hand, and sips from the side.

"Are you well today, Isabella?"

"Quite well, thank you Henry."

His blue, blue eyes look straight into hers. Isabella feels as if she could dive into the depths of them and be forever lost. The waitress hovers nearby waiting for his order. He requests China tea, and a selection of fancy cakes. They chat idly about the weather while he waits to be served.

When tea arrives, he picks up a fork and plunges it straight into the heart of a sponge cake. She watches the soft yellow pieces disappearing into his red mouth, and feels her chest tightening. There are cake crumbs on his moustache. She wants to lick them off. Heat gathers between her thighs. She tries to ignore it.

"So, Isabella," he says, "have you thought any more of what we talked about last time we met?"

"Oh. You mean paying a visit to your studio?"

Of course she has thought about it. Lying in her bed, she has tried to picture what an artist's studio would look like. She remembers a school visit to Paris, the walk through Montmartre, with its small painted houses and green shutters, the hushed instructions to ignore the brightly-clad ladies with bare feet, lounging in doorways and smoking cigarettes. She recalls hearing violin music floating out of a shuttered window, and there had been the sound of excited laughter, the smell of heat, and coffee, and forbidden things.

"I am not sure it would be considered quite proper for me to visit you alone," she murmurs.

"I quite understand. Of course I should always make sure that one or more of my friends' wives were there to chaperone you. Or perhaps you could bring one of your own woman friends?"

What woman friends? Isabella thinks bitterly. Oh yes, she knows lots of young people her own age. Since returning to London, her Mama has introduced her to the cream of young female society. But under the veneer of affection, they watch her like vicious young birds of prey, ready to tear her apart with their talons should she attempt to flirt with any of "their" young men.

Not that she would. Not for a single second. "Their" young men are boring, vacuous and self-important. Their affected drawling voices get on her nerves. The way they look her up and down as if she were a piece of horseflesh disgusts her.

The thought of marriage to one of these, of being alone with him, having to let him touch her, and do all those things whispered about in midnight dormitory conversations, makes her feel physically sick.

She watches Henry lift the delicate china cup, and place his full red lips gently around the rim. She imagines his lips pressed against hers, and a sudden pulse inside her throbs: *yes ... yes ... yes.*

"Then perhaps ... I will come and visit you," she whispers.

"That is excellent news, Isabella. You cannot imagine how eager I am to begin painting your picture."

Henry smiles, and helps himself to another slice of cake.

***

A starry, starry night. Both above and below, for at their huge brightly-lit Park Lane town house, Sir William Snellgrove and his elegant wife Lady Harriet are holding a party for their friends and acquaintances.

The Snellgroves move amongst the upper echelons of London society. Lady Harriet Snellgrove is one of the great society hostesses of the day. She is also the owner of a priceless collection of jewellery, and a wardrobe full of exquisite clothes, all tailor-made for her at an exclusive salon in the heart of Paris.

This lavish event is taking place just a stone's throw away from some of the worst slum dwellings in London, where families live ten to a room in damp crumbling buildings, sleeping on soiled straw, burning floorboards for heat, and using the gap underneath as a toilet.

But here in the Snellgrove mansion, everything is light and gay and brilliant. No expense has been spared, from the footmen in matching wigs and uniforms, to the decorated ballroom hung with artificial flowers, and looking like something out of the Arabian nights.

The street outside is crowded with carriages, while knots of curious bystanders pack the pavement to watch the glittering guests descend from their glossy equipages. The guests enter the house via a strip of crimson carpet, under a striped awning, where they are graciously received before the ladies in their silk ball gowns are conducted upstairs to the ladies' dressing room, where a couple of maids await to rearrange head-dresses, or repair a ripped seam.

Amongst the guests are white-gloved bank directors and members of the select aristocracy in evening dress, guardsmen in glittering uniforms, duchesses blazing in diamonds, and, of course, all the young beauties of the season. It is a brilliant and distinguished circle.

The supper-room is ready, the fare provided by a confectioner and caterer. The table groans under the liberal weight of hams, tongues, and fowls cut up and held together by ribbons. There are jellies, blancmanges, trifles and tipsy-cake – a veritable cornucopia of delicious things to eat.

Music drifts out of open windows as the final few guests make their entrance into the ballroom. Amongst them is Lord Frederick Hartington and his wife Lady Caroline, members of that very select group of aristocratic families who have entrée to Buckingham Palace itself.

Also arriving with them is the beautiful Romanian Countess, a friend of Lady Caroline. They met when the latter was taking the waters at Baden-Baden. Now the Countess is here in London, at Lady Caroline's invitation, enjoying the pleasures of the great city.

How exquisite she is, in her gossamer-fine silk gown and her white evening gloves. Her rich glossy hair is adorned with a diamond and black ostrich-plume headdress. Her face is covered with a modest lace veil, which only seems to enhance her smooth creamy white skin and dark sparkling eyes.

The Countess drops a low graceful curtsey to the host and hostess before she is led to the row of gold and crimson chairs that fringe the ballroom. Of course she will not dance tonight –

she is not part of the London social scene – but her animated expression, and the way she surveys the giddy young ones who valse and polka, shows how much she envies them their *joie de vivre*.

At 10pm precisely, supper is served. Everyone moves towards the supper-room. The Countess and Lady Caroline sit together. It is noted by all the company how much the stiff, aloof Lady Caroline seems to enjoy the foreigner's presence. Why, on two occasions, she is actually observed to smile.

Towards the end of the feasting, however, the Countess's manner appears to alter. The bright smile is replaces by a look of disquiet. Every now and then she raises her hands to her face, as if something there is hurting her. She keeps glancing round, passes a gloved hand across her brow. Finally she murmurs a few words to her companion, who nods in agreement. The Countess rises, slipping unobtrusively out of the supper-room.

Unseen by any of the guests (who are far too busy enjoying themselves) and unobserved by the house-staff (who are far too busy waiting on them), the Countess glides upstairs towards the upper regions of the house.

A short while later, a hooded and black-cloaked figure emerges from the house and hurries away.

***

It is the morning after the party, and it doesn't take long for the report to arrive on Detective Inspector Stride's desk. By 7.30, when a whistling, breakfasted and newly-shaved Stride strolls into police headquarters and heads for his office, the atmosphere is so thick with anticipation that you could almost slice it and hand it round on plates.

A little knot of day constables gather behind Detective Sergeant Jack Cully, as he moves circumspectly towards the closed office door. They stand outside, waiting for the stormclouds to break. They listen as the whistling slowly fades away into silence. Cully checks his watch and holds up one finger.

Exactly one minute later, there is a roar:

"Cully! Get in here! On the double!"

Cully opens the door and enters. Behind him, the men exchange meaningful glances. One man grins, drawing an index finger slowly across his throat. They edge closer to the door. A slow morning is just about to speed up.

Stride waves a piece of paper in the air. His expression is bordering upon apoplectic.

"What the hell is this?"

"It's one of the night constables' reports."

Stride reads aloud:

"Last night, a party took place at the Park Lane abode of Sir William Snellgrove. During the course of the party, a maid in the employment of the family was brutally attacked and killed while carrying out her duties."

"Yes," says Cully. "I thought you should see it first thing. It seemed rather important."

Stride seizes the word, and gives it a quick verbal battering.

"Seemed important? **Seemed?** Of course it's bloody important! How did it happen?"

Cully spreads his hands.

"There was a big crowd outside the Snellgrove mansion – people like to watch the rich having fun. Maybe there were some felons amongst the crowd who took advantage of the situation to try to rob the house—"

"And were the police in attendance?"

"There were some constables watching the proceedings."

"Clearly not watching enough," Stride says, rising from his chair. "Right, we need to get round there at once. Aristocracy doesn't like to be kept waiting. How many detectives can we put on this?"

"We have five officers currently free. The rest are either trying to find the gang who robbed and murdered the businessman

Mr King, or the person who shot that wolf."

Stride pauses, then shakes his head.

"Take all them off those inquiries for now, Jack. We've got no leads on the King murder, and at the end of the day, a dead wolf's a dead wolf. This takes priority over everything else."

Cully opens the door. There is the sudden clomp of many pairs of boots, followed swiftly by the noise of people trying to fill a small space they previously did not occupy.

***

A short while later Stride and Cully arrive at the Snellgroves' town house in Park Lane. They are shown into the drawing-room by a snooty parlour-maid, who instructs them tartly to wait.

"Keep your eyes in, Jack," Stride murmurs to his colleague, who is making a mental inventory of the vast array of expensive and delicate objects that furnish the room.

But Jack Cully is not thinking what his boss thinks he is thinking. He is thinking instead about the book he has just finished reading. It is called *The Communist Manifesto* by Mr Karl Marx.

Right now Cully is asking himself why these people have so much wealth, while every day he encounters rickety children paddling in filth, and young women forced to sell their bodies to keep themselves from starving.

Eventually the door opens, and Sir William Snellgrove stalks in. He gives Stride and Cully a look so stiff they could have ironed sheets on it.

"At last!" he exclaims. "A heinous crime has taken place in my house. I expected the police to attend far sooner than this."

"We came as soon as we could, sir," Stride replies evenly. "And now that we are here, I should like to view the unfortunate victim."

Sir William Snellgrove favours them with another long

disapproving stare. Then he leads the way up the richly-carpeted stairs, along the richly-carpeted landing, to a small dressing-room on the first floor. Brushing aside the group of servants gathered outside the door, he ushers the two detectives across the threshold.

"There, officer," he says, gesturing towards an open window, in front of which lies something covered with a green woollen cloak.

"The discovery was made early this morning," Sir William continues. "The gel failed to appear for her normal duties, and was subsequently found here. The room, as you can see, is not much used. Last night, it was employed as a repository for the outdoor garments of some late-arriving guests."

Stride crosses the room, bends down and folds back the cloak. From the angle of the head, it is quite clear that the unfortunate victim's neck has been broken. Her throat has also been torn open. But that is not what causes the expression on his face to change. He beckons to Cully.

"Take a look at this."

The young woman's face is frozen into a look of sheer terror. Even in death, her eyes seem to be starting out of her head, her mouth gapes in a rictus of fear.

Sir William Snellgrove peers over Stride's shoulder.

"Good gracious," he exclaims, "the gel must have had some sort of fit."

"That's not a fit, sir," Stride counters grimly. "The poor young woman was clearly frightened out of her wits."

He steps carefully over the body, and peers out of the window.

"It's a sheer drop down to the pavement. Whoever did this can't have entered that way. So it must have been a person, or persons, already in the house."

Sir William bridles indignantly.

"What are you suggesting, officer? That one of my own people may have killed this poor unfortunate gel? That is outrageous – all the staff in this house are hand-picked by myself or my wife, and have worked in my employment for years. You could say they are practically part of the family."

Stride pulls out his notebook.

"What was the name of the deceased, sir?"

"Mary Smith."

"Jenny Brown," comes a voice from the landing.

His face expressionless, Stride writes both names down.

"I shall arrange for the body to be transported to the police morgue."

During this exchange Cully is still staring thoughtfully down at the poor dead terrified face.

"Throat torn open. Frightened to death. Remind you of anybody else, sir?" he murmurs.

Stride breathes in sharply, but does not reply. He makes a final careful inspection of the room, writing further notes as he goes. Then he thrusts the notebook briskly into his topcoat pocket.

"Has anything of value been taken?"

Sir William shakes his head.

Stride nods.

"I should like to talk to her ladyship now, if I may."

Sir William gives him an indignant look.

"My wife has retired to her room. She is far too indisposed to talk to anybody right now."

Stride fixes his gaze upon the far wall.

"I do not think the murderer entered through the walls," Sir William says sarcastically. "Nor down the chimney."

"I am sure you are right, sir." Stride's voice conveys nothing.

Sir William fidgets with his waistcoat buttons.

"Now look here, officer, I understand you will have to ask questions, carry out a full investigation, that sort of thing. All I ask is that everything must be done with the *utmost* discretion, d'you see? Not a word of this must get out. My name *must not* appear in the gutter press. People would gossip. My reputation as a host would be in tatters."

Stride's face is a study.

"Oh, we would certainly not want that to happen, sir."

Sir William subjects him to a long stare.

"Very well then. Is there anything else I can assist you with?"

"The names of your house staff. Oh – and a list of all the guests who attended the party last night."

Sir William's lips twitch, but he gives a curt nod and leaves the room.

"It is identical to the Herbert King murder, isn't it?" Cully remarks when the room is empty.

Stride's mouth tightens.

"Similar, Jack, I grant you. Similar."

He stares into the middle distance, his expression inscrutable. Then he turns to face Cully.

"'Right Jack, onwards and upwards," he says firmly. "Onwards and upwards. We're not going to learn any more standing around here. Let's start asking questions. And remember, these people are not like you and me, so mind your manners."

Cully nods. By the time he has finished spending the day questioning rich people and snooty house-staff, all of whom seem unfamiliar with words like *please* and *thank you*, he will have become more and more convinced that Mr Karl Marx's opinions about the unfairness of society, and the need for a redistribution of wealth, are quite correct.

***

As Cully is preparing himself for this ordeal, in another part of London Josephine King is once again climbing the steps to the offices of King & Co.

She is wearing a brand-new black bonnet and a grimly-determined expression, and she carries a large notebook under one arm. In the outer office she is greeted cautiously by

Trafalgar Moggs, who half-rises from his stool.

"Good morning Miss King," he says. "I shall be with you in half a jiffy."

Josephine crosses the floor and enters her uncle's office, where she positions herself behind the desk, setting the notebook down in front of her. As Moggs comes in, she sits a little more upright and tries to look brisk and efficient.

The clerk is carrying a set of ledgers, which he places on the desk.

"You are certain this is what you wish to do, Miss King?" he asks.

She nods.

"Quite certain, Mr Moggs. My uncle left me his business in his Will. It is my duty to make sure that it is run properly. And I cannot do that unless I understand what exactly the business is."

It is either that, or staying at home, answering endless letters of condolence and fending off Mrs Thorpe and her not-very-subtle hints about the attractions of her son.

"I see," Moggs says slowly, picking his words with care. "It is quite unusual ... for a young woman ... like yourself ... to be concerned with business affairs."

Josephine gives him a cool stare.

"The Queen was the same age as me when she came to the throne."

"But she had ministers to advise her."

"And I," she says crisply, "have you. So, Mr Moggs, where shall we begin?"

***

Meanwhile, Gussy Thorpe has been summoned to the family abode for a scolding. He is hovering in the over-furnished drawing room, his big body bumping into little side tables and upsetting their contents. Delicate porcelain statuettes teeter and fall like china in a bull shop.

Gussy knows what this is all about. Demmit. Rolling noisily out of the notorious Cave of Harmony in Covent Garden a couple of nights ago, where he and his friends had been enjoying themselves with rum, cigars and bawdy songs, he'd run slap-bang into one of his parents' toffee-nosed friends leaving the Italian Opera House.

At the time, he thought he'd got away with it. But now he strongly suspects that the spoffy old cove has peached to the guv'nor, which means he's in for a wigging. He sucks his thumb, a habit retained from his childhood that still returns whenever he is feeling anxious.

Eventually the door opens and Mrs Thorpe comes in. Gussy feels his sagging spirits lift. Mater never blows up like the governor, in fact, she's a regular brick, and has even been known to slip him some tin when funds have got low. He grunts an awkward greeting.

Mrs Thorpe gives him the more-in-sorrow-than-in-anger look. Gussy looks at the floor. Suddenly he is nine years old again, and standing outside the headmaster's study.

Mrs Thorpe shakes her head.

"I am very disappointed in you, Augustus."

The Disappointment shuffles his feet. He knows he is in trouble when the mater calls him by his full name.

"Well, what do you have to say?"

The Disappointment clears his throat a couple of times.

"I believe I have mentioned to you, on several occasions, that I hoped you would try to find some nice military friends to introduce to your poor sister Isabella. And what have you done? Nothing."

Ah. Gussy brightens. This is not what he thought.

His mother continues her tirade.

"You have not brought a single young man round to meet her. In fact, you haven't been near the house for days. Why is that, pray?"

Gussy mutters something about being "fwightfully busy on pawade."

"No Augustus, this is not good enough." Mrs Thorpe shakes her head again. "You know poor dear Isabella has been so unwell – her only pleasure in life is her little outings in the barouche. The least you could have done is invite some of your friends along to amuse her."

"What fwends?" Gussy queries dubiously.

"Oh, really! All those young men you seem to spend all your time with. What about that friend you're always mentioning: George Osborne? Isn't he the son of Mr Frederick Osborne, the owner of the Osborne Private Bank? I'm sure he and poor Isabella would get on splendidly."

Gussy winces. Of all the reprobate crowd he hangs out with, George Osborne is undoubtedly the worst. It was George who sold him those pictures of ladies with no clothes on, lacing their boots. It was George who introduced him to Madame Beauty. (*All clean girls, sir. Do anything you like. Money on the night-table, after you've done.*) The thought of his sister becoming acquainted with George Osborne in any way sends a shiver down his spine. Gussy is very fond of his sister, though he rarely shows it.

"Yes, Augustus? What do you have to say?'

Gussy opens and closes his mouth a couple of times in a codfish sort of way.

Mrs Thorpe ignores him. She repeats her instructions to invite George to accompany Isabella on her next carriage-drive.

"And I'm sure I don't have to remind you," she adds for good measure, "that your father is still debating whether or not to purchase that commission you want."

Gussy makes his way out. He doesn't want to think about what he has been asked to do. To take his mind off it, he decides to think instead about last night's visit to the Alhambra Music Hall, where he'd seen the daring Monsieur Léotard on his Flying Trapeze, and some very naughty French dancers.

The girls had kicked their legs right up into the air, so you could see they were not wearing anything underneath their skirts. He'd enjoyed that very much. Maybe he'll call in tonight, and see it all over again.

***

It is two days later. A bitterly-cold morning. Cold to the bone. Warehouse-cold. Murder-cold. Detective Sergeant Jack Cully is making his way towards Scotland Yard to begin his shift. He is just about to cross the road and enter the building when he sees something that makes him stop dead in his tracks and breathe in hard.

A small group of reporters is gathered outside. Even from a distance, Cully senses the anticipation. They look like cats waiting in front of a mouse hole. He swears under his breath, then swears again as he realises his presence has been noted by two of the Fifth Estate's most persistent: Dionysius Clout and Richard Dandy.

Cully darts between a couple of carriages and gains the opposite pavement.

"Morning Sergeant Cully," Dandy Dick greets him genially.

"***Detective*** Sergeant Cully."

"If you say so. Is it true then?"

"I doubt it," Cully snaps.

"You're sure about that, are you? Because the Man In The Street, and in this case, we're talking a very nice street, and a very nice nobby man, has every right to sleep peacefully in his bed without his servants being strangled to death under his very nose. And this ain't the first time it's happened recently, is it?"

Cully stiffens.

"I don't know what you mean."

Dandy Dick produces the ever-ready notebook, and flips it open.

"Does the name 'Herbert King' ring any bells? Nice gent.

113

Own business, hobnobbed with the h'aristocracy. Strangled upon Westminster Bridge only a short while ago. And now, this. Does the word 'pattern' ring any bells?"

Cully cuts across him.

"Two murders is hardly a pattern. And I don't think it is any of your concern."

Dacre rounds on him.

"Two murders amongst the h'aristocratic classes most certainly *is* our concern. Found out who killed Mr King yet? Thought not. Arrested any of the criminals yet? Thought not. Arrested anyone for anything? Thought not."

The small group of reporters begins derisively chanting: "Thought not ... Thought not ..."

Cully bridles.

"If you'll excuse me, **gentlemen**, I have work to do."

"How is the gov'nor? Taking it all in his **stride**?" Clout sneers, to hoots of derisive laughter.

His mouth set in a rigid line, Cully elbows him roughly out of the way, and gains the front entrance.

"Oi, Cully!" Clout shouts after him. "You want to watch yourself – I could 'ave you for assault!"

And I could have you arrested for loitering, and polluting a public thoroughfare by your presence, you useless fat arsehole, Cully doesn't say. But he is certainly thinking it as he hurries inside.

He is also thinking that once his boss finds out that information about the Snellgrove murder has escaped the hallowed Park Lane confines and filtered down to the gutter press, he, Jack Cully, is going to get it in the neck. Even though it was not his fault.

"Where's old eagle-eyes?" he inquires, as he signs the duty roster.

The duty sergeant grins.

"Summoned to Marylebone first thing," he says. "Very important business. Left you a note."

He hands Cully a piece of paper.

114

Cully reads, his eyes widening.

"Oh Hell! Hell and back again!" He stuffs the note into his greatcoat. "If anyone wants me, tell them I'll be back when I'm back," he says, as he heads for the rear exit. "And whatever else you do, ***do not*** talk to that lot out there!"

***

Jewels and weapons have coexisted together for over fifty thousand years. Jewels are made out of love of something beautiful, weapons out of a need to kill. Love and death. It is how we define ourselves, what we are.

The sequence of events that has sent Detective Inspector Stride and now Detective Sergeant Cully hurrying to Marylebone police station actually began in the middle of the previous night. Josephine had been startled awake from a terrifying dream in which she had been running down endless corridors, carrying a pile of heavy ledgers and pursued by numbers that refused to add up.

She'd sat up. Moonlight was ghosting through the blinds, silvering the familiar outlines of the furniture. On her chest of drawers, the diamond was glimmering to itself in the dark. It drew her eyes to it, so that eventually they'd seen nothing else. She'd risen from her bed, and picked it up, gazing mesmerised into its cool white depths.

The room had been close and stuffy. She'd parted the curtains and lifted the sash window slightly, letting the night breeze fan her face. Down below all was still. The pale golden glow of the streetlamp was creating a chiaroscuro of light and dark. The unsteady gas flames flared and waned, giving everything an aura of perceptibility. As if objects were both present and absent at the same time.

She was still not sure whether she was fully awake or wholly asleep, so when a dark hooded shape had emerged from a pocket of shadow, and moved into the pool of light, it was as if what she was seeing was not a dream, but not quite a reality. Like being trapped in between two states.

The formless shape had stopped directly opposite the house and turned, lifting its head until it seemed to be staring directly at her and at what she held in her hand. There was something disquieting about the way the light both disguised and revealed, so that the figure appeared to be both human and unknown at the same time.

For a moment she had hesitated. Then, putting the jewel down and wrapping a warm shawl around her shoulders, she had slipped her feet into her boots and stumbled downstairs. Unlocking the front door, she'd hurried out into the silent street.

"Hello," she'd called out. "Who are you?"

The shape had turned. For a moment, she had caught sight of its face, but it was a face that did not make sense, because it did not resemble anything she had ever seen before. Then, opening its mouth in a snarl of rage, it had dropped onto all fours and bounded off, melting into the shadows at the end of the street.

Josephine had felt a comet's tail of fear run down her spine. She had not understood the old soldier's words. She had not believed him. But now she had seen it for herself. Now she did believe him, even though she still did not understand.

Suddenly footsteps had approached from behind. She'd whirled round, her heart beating wildly. A police constable had materialised.

"Are you alright, miss? I thought I heard shouting."

Josephine had realised the impression she might be conveying. She'd drawn herself up with as much dignity as she could muster, given that she was standing in the street in the small hours of the morning clad only in her night attire, a shawl, and a pair of unlaced boots.

"Thank you officer, I am perfectly fine."

The police constable had surveyed her thoughtfully. Then

he'd extracted a notebook and pencil from his pocket.

"So miss, perhaps you could explain to me why you are out here at two in the morning?"

He'd paused, then added, "…and why you are carrying a pistol?"

She had stared at him, aghast. She did not remember grabbing the gun from the chest of drawers where she'd hidden it last time, but she must have done, because here it was, in her hand. And then, just to add to her problems, a gust of wind had bowled down the street, slamming the front door shut.

Josephine had explained that she'd been accidentally locked out of her own house. Then she had attempted to rouse Annie the parlour-maid by ringing the bell, by banging upon the door and finally by shouting through the letterbox.

In the time it had taken to realise that the noise was not penetrating the attic bedroom, the constable had blown upon his whistle and been joined by a fellow-constable. The latter had expressed the opinion that, given her compromising attire, the lateness of the hour, and her inability to explain satisfactorily why she was in possession of a loaded gun (albeit only partially loaded), the young lady had probably escaped from some private asylum.

Josephine had been duly escorted to Marylebone police station, where she'd been given a rough blanket and a mug of lukewarm cocoa, then placed in an overnight cell to await collection by the asylum owner in the morning.

Wrapping the thin blanket around her, she had settled down on the wooden plank bed. The bare whitewashed walls and the pervading smell of disinfectant were an unpleasant reminder of her school days – an impression further reinforced by the sound of muffled sobbing coming from the cell next door. She had spent the rest of the night working on an escape plan, based upon a novel she'd recently read.

In the morning, over a bowl of thin porridge (another unpleasant resonance with her past), she'd requested paper and pen and composed a letter to Detective Inspector Stride. The letter had been dispatched to Scotland Yard, where it was handed to the duty constable, who placed it on Stride's desk, where it was picked up and read at 7.00 am.

***

By the time Cully reaches Marylebone Police Station, Stride has arranged for Josephine's release and she has been sent home in a carriage. And after finishing their mugs of tea and enjoying a nice chat with their colleagues, Stride and Cully also depart.

"Somnambulism," Stride murmurs thoughtfully, as they stroll towards the cab rank. "I have come across it before. There was a similar case a couple of years ago – a young woman climbed onto a roof in the middle of the night, wearing only her night-gown, fell to her death. Fast asleep the whole time. Doctor put it down to having recently given birth to twins."

"But Miss King has not given birth," Cully says. "And as she did not attempt to throw herself off a roof, I don't see the similarity."

Stride rolls his eyes.

"She has been under a great deal of strain recently, has she not? The murder of her uncle, and the ... ensuing events. And you must remember that the female mind is not the same as ours. It works in peculiar and unpredictable ways."

"Is that why you kept hold of the gun?"

"One of the reasons. Can't have sleepwalking young women with firearms wandering the streets at night, can we? God knows what might happen. But I'm also following a little theory of my own, Jack. I'm going to ask Carson in firearms to examine it. If the bullet matches the one that killed that wolf – well, then we have an explanation for our little mystery. It may not be the first time she has done this."

Cully still has doubts about the identity of that poor beast. And he distinctly recalls Miss King saying she heard nothing on the night in question. However he sees no reason to stir the pot. Sufficient unto the day. He recalls his earlier encounter with Fleet Street's finest. Best once again to keep his head down and say nothing.

Stride and Cully approach Scotland Yard, where to Cully's relief the unwelcome denizens of the press have disbursed in search of other prey. They alight from the cab and enter the building.

***

The elderly couple running the coffee stall at Westminster Bridge have been doing a brisk trade in hot drinks and bread-and-butter since crack of dawn. They've erected a little awning to shelter themselves from the raw winter cold. Whenever there is a lull, they gather round the small brazier to warm their hands.

"I see another one has gone," the old woman remarks, blowing on her fingers.

"Mrs whatever her name was … over the way from us. Meant ter tell you. Brought her out this morning. Stiff as a board. Thought I hadn't seen her around for a while. Not a scrap of food in the house they say, nor a stick of furniture. Burned the lot trying to keep warm."

"It's an 'ard world right enough," the old man agrees.

"Harder for some," his wife says, nodding towards the small shivering figure of the crossing-sweeper, who has been battling against the filthy streets and the biting wind since early dawn. "I see the hoity-toity gel come by earlier."

She spoons coffee dregs into a mug and adds some lukewarm water.

"'Ere, take him this as we're quiet. And there's that slice o' bread that fell on the ground earlier. Give it a quick wipe; it'll do nicely. He ain't going to fuss over a bit of dirt. And find out what that gel wanted."

The old man takes the delicate viands over to the boy, who falls upon them like a starving animal. His benefactor stands by waiting for the mug to be returned, and trying to ignore the chewing and slurping noises.

Eventually the boy finishes eating and drinking. He wipes his mouth with a ragged sleeve, then absentmindedly sucks it. They exchange a few words. Then the boy is summoned by a tall top-hatted City man waiting to cross the road. He darts off, leaving the coffee stall owner to return to his wife.

"What did yer find out?"

"Gel wanted to talk to Old Jim Jarndyce."

"Going to find it a bit of a job then," the old woman says tartly.

"When he told her Jim'd gone, she was proper cut up abaht it."

"Why? What's it to her?"

"Nuffink. He says she gave 'im some money for a fish supper."

The woman laughs harshly.

"Take more than one fish supper to save the likes of him. Ain't going to make old bones. I see it in his eyes. Death eyes. Be dead and buried by Christmas, I reckon."

She greets the next customer with a leering smile.

"Yes sir? Nice cuppa coffee for you? Slice of bread-and-butter to go with it? There you go. Have a good day, sir."

***

A wan afternoon sunshine is doing its best to break through the smoggy clouds that envelop the city. An omnibus clops slowly along the road. Inside the fuggy carriage, a tired mother, with a sleeping child on her lap, sits between a red-haired young woman dressed in shabby black and a man reading a newspaper.

The mother is thinking about the pile of washing awaiting her return, and the meal she will prepare for her husband, when she suddenly becomes aware that the young woman is leaning across her in a rather intrusive manner and staring at the centre pages of the man's newspaper. Intrigued, she follows the young woman's gaze and reads:

MURDER IN PARK LANE ABODE!! SERVANT GIRL STRANGLED TO DEATH!! SECOND SIMILAR MURDER TO OCCUR IN CITY!! DETECTIVE POLICE BAFFLED ONCE MORE!!

The young woman utters a little gasp, then rises swiftly to her feet and pushes her way to the back of the omnibus. A moment later she alights and disappears into the swirling crowd.

The mother adjusts the heavy child. There are far more important things in life than sensational stories in the newspapers, she thinks. None of them are ever true, anyway. Her head begins to nod, her eyes close. A few minutes later she too, is fast asleep.

***

Meanwhile, just off the genteel elegance that is Hampstead High Street, a new tea-room has recently opened. The Lily Lounge is a warm and welcoming place where, for a reasonable outlay, the patrons can partake of an afternoon tea consisting of a variety of hot beverages, a selection of freshly-made sandwiches, scones, luscious iced and cream cakes, and fruit tarts.

The two proprietresses and their staff, all neat and discreet in dark skirts, blouses, starched white aprons and caps, glide unobtrusively between the tables, carrying silver trays laden with tasty goodies. Occasionally they might pause to recommend a type of tea here, a variety of cake there.

Other than that, their presence barely registers with the

customers, who gossip and chat and show off their purchases. After all, these waitresses are only glorified servants by another name, and the customers are well-used to having servants in the background of their lives. So they eat and drink and pay them no mind.

Lilith Marks is serving tea to a couple sitting at a corner table. The woman is wearing a fashionably-styled tartan silk dress. Her face is heavily veiled, her leather gloves impeccably tailored. Something foreign about her appearance, Lilith thinks to herself, as she crosses the teashop floor, tray balanced on her arm.

Her companion is a thickset middle-aged man in a dark gabardine, his hair shiny with macassar oil, gold rings on his fleshy fingers. He has a hooked nose and small eager eyes.

The man has a small velvet bag, from which he now brings out a magnificent emerald bracelet. He shows it to the woman, who leans forward and picks it up, laying it across her gloved palm and then holding it up to the light. Lilith serves the tea. Neither of them notices her.

Lilith recognises the bracelet at once. It belongs to a Mrs Diana Meadows. Lilith remembers Mrs Meadows's husband, Mr Lionel Meadows, a rich City financier, showing it to her in her drawing room shortly after he had bought it. A present from a guilty husband.

Lilith had studied the bracelet and pretended to admire it, secretly marvelling at how men always thought they could buy their way back into their wives' affections with presents of expensive jewellery.

Eventually he had put it back in his pocket and they had gone upstairs. Because at the end of the day she had a living to make, and standing around admiring another woman's emerald bracelet was not the way to make it.

The woman at the table turns the bracelet so that the light catches the stones, making them sparkle. She nods approvingly, then points out a couple of small things to the man. An earnest discussion takes place. The man makes a few notes. Then the woman returns the bracelet to the man, who replaces it in the velvet bag.

The transaction completed, the couple turn their attention to the tea and cakes. They make a hearty meal. When they have finished, the man clicks his fingers in Lilith's direction, the universal male gesture to bring him the bill, which she does, handing it to him with a polite smile.

The man throws some coins on the tablecloth. He barely acknowledges her. The couple leave the table, and Lilith begins to clear the tea things. She does not know the name of the foreign woman. But she does know the identity of her companion. She knew him the moment he walked into her restaurant.

He is Isaac "Ikey" Solomon. She and Ikey go back a long way, to the bad old days of poverty and deprivation, when she was little Lil Malkovitch living in Bethnal Green, working in her parents' sweatshop and dreaming of better days.

Ikey Solomon lived three doors down. He used to walk out with her older sister Essie, till he threw her over for someone else. Someone better. Ikey's dad ran a nice business buying and selling antique and modern gems – a business which, by the looks of it, Ikey has now inherited. It shouldn't be too hard to track him down.

***

The following afternoon finds Isabella Thorpe sitting in the shiny cherry-coloured barouche. She is wearing a stylish pink dress chosen especially for the occasion by her Mama, who fails to recognise that pink does not suit her colouring. Her is hair newly curled and pinned, her bonnet fashionably trimmed with pink feathers and ribbons. But this time Isabella does not ride alone. Sitting next to her is young Dragoon Guardsman George Osborne, buck about town, lady-charmer, his black moustaches shiny with wax, his hair smelling of macassar oil. Sitting opposite her is Gussy, bumbling, a bit of a buffoon, but harmless. Mostly.

Isabella grips the side of the carriage with a gloved hand. She wishes, oh so fervently she wishes, that she were somewhere else, and with someone else. The pain of longing is almost overwhelming. The other source of her misery is the close and unwelcome proximity of George Osborne's leg, which is pressing against hers. She is sure he is doing it on purpose.

Isabella feels small and oppressed. George Osborne is so big, so loud, so boastful. So full of his own importance. Ever since his first "Ah Miss Thorpe, howdy-do?" as he mounted the carriage-step and extended two fingers, he has done nothing but brag about himself and his exploits.

Meanwhile, unaware of his fair companion's aversion, George Osborne, of celebrated blood and (he thinks) irresistible to the fair sex, twirls his moustaches and lights up a cigar – because everybody knows that ladies love the smell of a good cigar, don'tchyer know. Isabella is forced to shrink even further into the corner of the barouche, for fear that her dress might catch fire.

"Your brother's got a devilish fine horse," the Irresistible One observes. "But still not as fine as Black Beauty, my nag. Now there's a real charger, eh, Miss Thorpe." And he gives her one of the famous killing glances that usually has the effect of making young ladies blush, and do things with their fans.

"I say, Guster old chap, why don't you sell me your horse?" Osborne continues. "He'd make a nice pair with mine."

"By Jove – hang it, George," Gussy exclaims. "I mean, demmit!"

Osborne grins maliciously at him.

"I could always tell your governor about the cash I won off you at billiards. What d'you say?"

"Gad, George – why won't you let a fellow be!" Gussy expostulates.

A free-and-easy exchange begins between the two young bucks, from which Isabella, being neither a member of the Dragoon Guards nor a patron of the Cocoa-Tree, is of necessity excluded. She clenches her hands in her lap, and prays for this torture to come to a speedy end.

The barouche glides smoothly along the Mall towards the Knightsbridge barracks, where the two bucks will alight. Isabella thinks of Henry Papperdelli, and his deep blue eyes and curly brown moustache. He will be waiting for her at the pre-arranged rendezvous, but waiting in vain. She has not had time to send him a note alerting him to her absence. What conclusions will he draw? Will she ever see him again?

Tears of self-pity fill her eyes. She presses her lips together tightly. For a well-bred young lady to show any emotions whatsoever in a public arena is totally unacceptable. Her Mama and her education have drilled this into her.

At long last, and not a moment too soon for Isabella, the barouche halts outside the barracks. George Osborne jumps straight down and strides towards the gate. Gussy lingers by the barouche for a moment. Like everybody else in the Guards, he knows the dark stories about Osborne: the gambling, the opium-swigging, the drunken bouts, the whoring. Indeed, he has witnessed (and participated in) many of these activities himself.

But Gussy has his instructions. And like a dutiful son short of cash and in need of a commission, he intends to carry them out to the letter.

"He's a good fellah," he says.

"Is he?" Isabella replies wanly.

"Demmit, Iz, you could do worse."

"Could I?"

She turns her face away, unwilling for him to see the despair in her eyes. For a moment they silently contemplate the awful truth that cannot be spoken. Next minute there is a shout of "Gustus – presence needed!" from inside the barrack walls.

Gussy bites his lower lip, then sighs resignedly.

"Take Miss Isabella home, James," he commands the coachman.

And James, who has equally never disobeyed an order in his life, and never will, slaps the reins and urges the shiny well-fed horses to "trot on."

***

A couple of hours later, Josephine has returned from a day spent learning the mysteries of ledgers under the tutelage of Trafalgar Moggs. Now she sits at her writing-desk, studying the contents of a further letter from her solicitor, Mr Septimus Able.

Dear Miss King [he writes],

Further to my previous correspondence upon the subject of the Will of your late uncle, Mr Herbert King, I am now able to shed more light upon the matter.

I informed you in my previous letter on the subject that I had discovered that the request to see the Will was made by Mr John Skittles, of Smallbone, Skittles & Smallbone, a firm of solicitors, on behalf of a client of the firm.

If it were any other firm involved in this unaccountable examination of your late uncle's Will, I should have had difficulties in proceeding with the matter.

Fortunately, Willing & Able were involved in a recent legal matter concerning one of the firm's senior partners, and I was able to use this to good effect.

The name of the client is Countess Elenore von Schwarzenberg, a Romanian lady who is visiting London.

I have also ascertained that she is currently residing at number 55, Russell Square. If you so wish it, I am happy to proceed further in this matter, and await your instructions.

Yours sincerely

It is a puzzling letter, and Josephine has spent some time reading and rereading it in an attempt to work out why this Romanian Countess would be interested in her uncle's Will. She has come to the conclusion that there is only one way to find out, and so, having carefully considered Mr Able's kind offer, she has decided that she will save him the trouble, and proceed in the matter herself.

After a light snack, Josephine takes a cab and arrives at the north end of Russell Square. Ahead lie the grand terraced houses where the bankers, the merchants, the Sirs and my noble Lords live. Green-painted wrought-iron railings surround the plane-tree'd gardens, the statue of Lord Bedford at the centre and the pump on the east side.

There are Watch Boxes along the perimeter. Some of these are occupied by policemen, but they barely register her presence. She has already noticed how useful it is to be a young woman wearing mourning dress. As far as the world is concerned, she might just as well be clothed in invisibility. She crosses to the west side, surreptitiously checking the numbers upon the doors, until she arrives at Number 55.

At first glance the house seems unoccupied. There are no lights in the hallway, no servants visible in the basement kitchen. Leaves are piled upon the front step and in the area. The Venetian blinds are drawn down at every window. The house gives off an unfriendly air, as if it repels visitors.

Undeterred, Josephine extracts a calling card from her reticule. She mounts the steps and knocks on the door. She hears the sound echo through the house, but no footsteps are heard in response. She waits for a while, then knocks again. Again, nothing happens. Disappointed, she turns from the door.

However just as she is preparing to leave, she senses movement behind one of the ground-floor blinds. A slat is carefully raised. Something gleams behind it. The liquorice shimmer of a human eye.

A second later, the slat is lowered. The house goes on giving an impression of non-occupancy to the passing world. But as she walks away, Josephine cannot help the sensation that somebody inside the house is watching her. And not in a good way.

***

Night falls, and with it comes rain, drumming off roof tiles, waterfalling in torrents from leaky gutters. Rain whips the surface of the muck-encrusted streets into thick brown soup. Rain coats ancient brick buildings in a slimy sheen of wet. Rain glugs and gurgles into drains and culverts.

There is a peculiar quality to London rain. It is grey-green in colour and viscous, as if the sooty fat from a million chimneys and stoves has risen up, formed into layers in the sky, and is now being dumped back on earth in liquid form.

Safe and warm in their high-pillowed Hampstead bed, Mr and Mrs Thorpe lie side by side like effigies upon two ancient tombs. Mr Thorpe is not listening to the falling torrents, instead he is listening to his beloved consort, whose conversation somewhat resembles the rain in that it gushes on and on without much apparent cessation.

"Isabella looked very well today," Mrs Thorpe says. "That pink dress suits her admirably. She always looks pretty in pink and it is such a suitable colour for a young girl, I always think. I am sure young George Osborne was impressed. How could he not be? And Mrs Carlyle has secured Isabella an invitation to the Osbornes' next At Home. George has two sisters, you know. It is important that our dear daughter makes a favourable impression upon them, after all, if everything goes to plan, she will be, in time ... family."

"Will she?"

Mr Thorpe frowns. It seems like only the other day they were having a conversation about his daughter's future. Now, that future appears to have arrived in the present.

"And what does Izzy say? Does she like this George fellow?"

"We call her Isabella now, remember? Izzy was for when she was a child."

Mr Thorpe has a sudden memory of a pretty ringletted girl in a white frock, climbing on his knee, and demanding imperiously to listen to his pocket watch ticking. His little Izzy. Where did the time go?

"Isabella knows that George Osborne is quite a catch. He is handsome, and his father owns a private bank. Why, half the women in London have their eye on him for their daughters. And he looks so fine in his uniform." Mrs Thorpe gives a tinkly half-laugh. "It takes me back to my youth. We had a garrison of the Ninth Hussars stationed nearby – all the girls were in love with a redcoat."

"But Izzy isn't you," Mr Thorpe says. "I shouldn't like to think of her marrying someone she didn't like, and being unhappy."'

"Isabella will do as she is told," Mrs Thorpe says tartly. "Mrs Carlyle tells me there are already things being whispered about her – that silly fainting business, the quizzical way she looks at people, and does not encourage friendship amongst other girls. We cannot let the impression get about that she is odd or different in any way, or she will never find a husband. It is not a question of like or dislike. Isabella must be guided by her Mama and Papa. As was I."

And with this emphatic pronouncement, Mrs Thorpe rolls over onto her side. An indication that the conversation is at an end. This is usually greeted by Mr Thorpe as a welcome sign that he can finally fall asleep. But tonight he remains wide awake, listening to the endless rain, and thinking about what his wife has just unwittingly revealed.

***

Meanwhile, in another bedroom in St John's Wood, another wakeful soul is also finding it hard to fall asleep. Josephine lies upon her back, staring up at the ceiling. She is aware of her breathing, surrounding her like an envelope. She listens to the rain falling, the clop of hooves and grind of wheels as a late carriage passes beneath her window. A bell in a distant church chimes the hour.

She also hears the noises of the house. Water moving in pipes, the creak of floorboards. A door suddenly swings open. She screams, sitting bolt upright, nerves pulled tight. But it is only her wardrobe door, which she had not closed firmly enough. She sees her ghost hanging in its mirror.

Josephine slips out of bed and goes to the dressing table. Opening the top drawer, she takes out the diamond. Her diamond. It glows softly, catching photons of stray light. Nothing human could be so beautiful, she thinks. She feels a need to keep it close, to protect it. She returns to her bed. The diamond sleeps in the cagework of her hand.

***

The next morning finds Isabella Thorpe seated in the dining room. She is surrounded by silver-domed dishes containing bacon, scrambled eggs, chops and kedgeree.

In front of her is a rack of toast, and there is butter and marmalade in small cut-glass dishes. The table is positively groaning with all the ingredients that go to make a good middle-class Victorian breakfast.

Isabella is also groaning with the effort of trying to force down a very small slice of plain unbuttered toast and a cup of black tea. She is under strict instructions from her Mama to eat breakfast, a meal she usually avoids at all costs.

After breakfast, she and her Mama are going shopping for a

new winter dress. Something becoming, her Mama says. Something that will transfer her daughter's feet from under the Thorpe table to under somebody else's table, Isabella thinks. Oh yes, she isn't fooled for a moment.

In the afternoon, she is to call upon the Misses Eliza and Harriet Osborne, sisters of George Osborne, who have let it be known that they will be "At Home" to visitors from three o'clock. Isabella sips her tea, and rearranges the crusts on her plate. Her Mama might try to get her feet under someone else's table, she thinks grimly, but she can't make her eat.

She forces down another miniscule mouthful, then rises from her chair.

"I've finished and I am going to my room," she tells the housemaid, who bobs a curtsey.

Ignoring the usual head-spinning, stars-in-front-of-her-eyes sensation that always accompanies climbing any stairs, Isabella enters her room, and sits down at her dressing table to await the arrival of Withers, the lady's-maid. While she waits, she plans her itinerary for the forthcoming visit.

She will stay at the Osbornes' "At Home" just long enough not to cause offence. She will pretend to partake of the light refreshments on offer. She will make vapid conversation about nothing in particular. Fifteen minutes later, she will take her leave.

For Isabella has discovered that the Osbornes reside just a stone's throw from Red Lion Square, which is where Henry Papperdelli lives. The discovery fills her with light and joy. She has already sent him a note suggesting that they might meet at the corner of the Square at a quarter past three.

She can actually sense her heart beating faster at the prospect, as if it is marking the time until the desired event takes place. She has not seen him for days and days, and she thinks about him constantly. It feels as if something is eating away inside her. The irony is not lost. Hearing Withers' light step outside her bedroom, Isabella carefully wipes all joy from her face, leaving it bland and expressionless.

***

A couple of hours later, Detective Sergeant Jack Cully is returning to Scotland Yard having enjoyed a hearty luncheon. Easily recognisable as a member of the police force in his buttoned-up navy topcoat with its distinctive silver buttons, he has adopted the "walk-fast-and-look–worried" pose that he hopes will prevent members of the public from stopping him in the street, and bothering him with their problems.

Jack Cully knows nothing about troublesome drains, cats up trees and the annoying behaviour of lodgers. He does know that his feet and hands are cold, and he is gasping for a mug of hot, well-stewed black tea. So it is with some exasperation that he feels a hand laid gently on his sleeve, and hears a voice saying,

"Excuse me, officer? Could I trouble you for a word?"

Cully turns, and sees a woman standing on the pavement. She has a neat, well-cut dark street-dress and a check wool shawl, and her luxuriant dark hair is pinned up under a smart bonnet.

Her clothes say she is a respectable member of the working community. Her sumptuous bosom, bold black eyes and full red lips suggest something rather different. Cully recognises her type instantly. Oh yes.

"Well, **madam**, what do you want?" he says coldly, laying emphasis upon the second word to indicate that he, Jack Cully, is a man of the world, and he knows exactly whom he is dealing with here.

The woman laughs. She takes a small pasteboard rectangle out of her reticule, and hands it to him.

"My business card," she says briskly.

Cully reads:

The Lily Lounge (*select tea-room*)

12 Flask Walk
off **Hampstead High Street**
London NW3
(Mrs L. Marks, proprietress)

"Oh ... err," he stutters. "How may I help you, Mrs Marks?"

Lilith regards his discomfited expression with infinite satisfaction.

"I believe I have some important information to impart," she says.

She beckons him closer, whispers into his ear. And then watches as his eyes widen in amazement.

Detective Inspector Stride has just lit his third pipe of the day, when the door to his office opens and Jack Cully enters. Wearily, Stride glances up from the piles of reports, which he is now rearranging into different piles of reports, in the hope that something he may have missed first time around might suddenly and magically present itself to him now.

"There is a lady in the interview room," Cully says. "She wants to talk to you."

***

Meanwhile, Isabella Thorpe, having successfully evaded the malign clutches of luncheon, arrives at the Osbornes' town house precisely upon the stroke of three. Here she is shown into the dusk-rose-coloured drawing-room, where she perches on a hard rosewood chair and tries not to wilt under the watchful-eyed scrutiny of Eliza and Harriet Osborne.

George's two sisters are wearing identical dresses in bright mauve, currently a very fashionable colour but one that is hard to pull off, especially in the case of Harriet the older one, whose face at twenty-nine is starting to lose its youthful bloom, and to take on a pinched, tight-lipped expression.

Both women have dark corkscrew curls, small dark

suspicious eyes and horsey acquisitive teeth. They sit side by side on the sofa, regarding Isabella as if she was some strange species that they had never encountered before.

Isabella has the distinct impression that they are mentally putting little red crosses against the bits of her that they don't like. And they clearly don't like very many bits. Conversation is difficult and stilted. They have absolutely nothing in common, and the Osbornes do not do "small talk." Fortunately, there is a clock on the mantelpiece, so she can keep tally of the minutes, which are passing ... very ... very slowly.

"Georgie tells us you've recently returned from France, Miss Thorpe," Harriet remarks. "I went to *Paris* once." She says the word *Paris* in exactly the same tone of voice in which she might have said *sewer*.

"It is a delightful city, I think," Isabella replies.

"Do you? Food was disgustin'. They don't hunt much, the French."

"I believe they do not."

"We love huntin'. Do you hunt, Miss Thorpe?"

Isabella shakes her head.

"Georgie always hunts whenever he's in the country. Do you ride, Miss Thorpe?"

"I'm afraid not."

An awkward silence falls.

"I say, why do you keep looking at the mantelpiece?" Eliza asks.

"Oh, I ... was admiring the little china Cupid," Isabella lies.

"Really? Can't stand it myself."

Oh God, deliver me, please, Isabella prays.

And as if God has heard her, the door suddenly opens.

"Miss Violet Monk," the servant announces.

A second later a tall, rangy young woman with a weather-beaten expression and muddy boots bundles in, followed by two tumbling puppies. Eliza and Harriet immediately jump to their feet uttering squawks of delight, and fall upon the puppies as if they were sugar-plums.

Nobody notices Isabella as she creeps unobtrusively from the room. Out in the street it has started to rain. Luckily, she has had the foresight to bring an umbrella. She opens it, and walks as fast as she can in the direction of Red Lion Square.

And there, standing on the corner, is Henry. He sees her, and raises his hat in greeting. And suddenly Isabella feels bright and clear, like a piece of glass. Touch her, and she will shatter with happiness.

Love is blind, so they say. Or at least, it is not as observant as it should be in the circumstances. So enraptured is Isabella by the sight of Henry Papperdelli that she fails to notice a striking red-haired young woman in a black bonnet making her way towards Russell Square.

It is only as the young woman passes by, rain dripping from her bonnet, that Isabella recognises her. Their eyes meet. Both colour up. Isabella is the first to regain her composure. She turns her face to one side, cutting Josephine, who walks on, head held high.

"Who was that young lady we just passed?" Henry asks, as they turn into Red Lion Square. "She seemed to know you."

Isabella smiles sweetly up at him.

"I've never seen her before in my life," she says.

***

Still puzzling over her unexpected encounter, Josephine arrives at her destination, Number 55 Russell Square. She has decided to revisit the house where the mysterious Countess is residing, in the hope that today, the lady (or maybe one of her servants) will be at home.

For a moment she stands outside, screwing up her courage to sticking point. Then, squaring her shoulders, she marches up the steps to the front door and knocks smartly. This time she does not have to wait long before the sound of heavy footsteps approach the door, which opens to reveal a manservant.

He is big – the sort of big that makes the rest of the world look small. Tall and broad-shouldered and grey. Josephine has never seen such a grey man. Iron-grey hair, grey clipped moustache, cold grey eyes that stare down at her in a grey unfriendly manner. Grey trousers, topped by a grey coat with a lot of ornate gold braid. One of his hands is wrapped in a cloth bandage. Something stirs at the back of her mind. Unlikely though it is, she is sure she has seen him before, and recently so.

"Yerss?"

She takes a step back.

"Umm ... I was wondering whether I might leave a card."

The grey manservant frowns dubiously.

"Perhapss."

Josephine smiles brightly, taking the little pasteboard square from her reticule.

"The Countess is at home?" she inquires. "Because I was—"

"She iss about to go out," the manservant says.

He takes her card.

"Goot bye."

He closes the door. Heavy footsteps retreat into silence. Well, she thinks, at least she has made contact. Now etiquette dictates that the Countess will leave her card, and then they will actually meet, and she will finally find out how this mysterious Romanian Countess knew Uncle Herbert. And why she wanted to look at a copy of his Will.

***

At about the same time as Josephine is making her way back to St John's Wood, Lilith Marks emerges from Scotland Yard. She secures a hansom and gives the driver directions. She needs to be back at the tea-room as soon as possible. The afternoon rush will be at its height.

Lilith eases herself into the cracked leather seat, reflecting upon what she has just done. She knows she has made the right decision, though it went against the grain of a past when her relationship with the forces of law and order had been very different indeed.

As the cab trots its way through the congested city streets, she thinks about Herbert King, the lover with gentle hands and laughing eyes. She recalls the look on his face as they made love, the sweetness of his body on hers. The way he paced himself, holding back until she experienced her own pleasure at the moment of climax.

But even more, she thinks about Essie, the glorious big sister who used to swing her into the air, singing *"Here we go up, up, up ... Here we go down, down, down ..."* When Ikey Solomon had abandoned Essie for a girl from a better, richer family, he had not only broken her heart, he had also ruined her reputation. Everybody knew she had been discarded. No nice young Jewish man would look twice at Essie after that, let alone want to marry her. Essie Malkovitch was damaged goods.

Lilith will never forget the day Essie left her home and her family, declaring that she had to strike out on her own and make a new life for herself, somewhere where nobody knew her name, or her shameful story.

In the forever hours of any sleepless night, Lilith still sees her younger self standing alone in the middle of the street, tears streaming down her cheeks as she watches her big sister walk away, head held high, carrying her pathetically small bundle of clothes and possessions.

Nobody ever saw Essie again. She simply disappeared.

Some time later, the news filtered back to the small close-knit Jewish community that a young woman called Essie Malkovitch had died in childbirth in a workhouse in the north of England.

Revenge is a dish best served cold, so they say, and Lilith has waited a long time to serve up this particular one. Now, at last, she has placed it upon the table. Nicely chilled.

A couple of hours later, Stride and Cully arrive outside a building on Commercial Road. A sign above the door reads: *I. Solomon & Co. Goldsmith, Dealer in Fine Antiques and Second-hand Jewellery.*

Practically a racial profession, Stride thinks. Along with second-hand clothes dealer, moneylender, or (if you were fortunate enough to have a surname like Rothschild) rich banker. He pushes open the door, a small brass bell mounted on a spring tinkling as they enter.

The interior is dark, ill-lit by flickering gaslight. There are displays of jewellery in glass cases all around the walls. Tables with large Chinese vases and ornate silver candelabra. Paintings of long-dead people in old gold frames hang on the walls. Unknown ancestors regard Stride sourly.

A heavily-bearded middle-aged man in a long dark gabardine stands behind the counter. He has a jeweller's loupe in one hand, a pearl necklace in the other. He is examining the necklace closely, pearl by pearl.

There is something unpleasant about his body stance, a kind of eagerness. He glances up, recognises the two officers for what they are, and sets down the loupe. He smiles. Cautiously.

"Gentlemen? Good day to you both. How may I be of assistance?"

"Am I addressing Mr Isaac Solomon?" Stride enquires, his tone flat and expressionless.

"Indeed you are."

"I am Detective Inspector Stride. This is my colleague Detective Sergeant Cully."

"So, gentlemen, you are both welcome in my little emporium."

Stride gestures towards the pearls.

"Nice necklace."

"Baroque. The quality is good, but it needs some work before it is fit to be sold."

"Where did you get it from?"

Solomon shrugs.

"Ach, you pick up this, that and suchlike from families who no longer want them. You know how it is."

Stride doesn't know how it is. He has never possessed any this or that, let alone any suchlike, in the first place.

"How do people get to hear about your business?"

"Word of mouth. Sometimes they read one of my advertisements in the newspapers."

"Oh?" Stride's eyebrows raise.

"Oh yes, Inspector, you have to move with the times. The modern man of business has to advertise. It's the new way of doing things. All above board and legal, of course. Wouldn't want to fall foul of the law, would I?"

"No, indeed. You wouldn't want to do that," Stride nods slowly. He takes a long leisurely look around the shop. Nods again.

This time, Solomon's eager smile doesn't quite make it up to his eyes.

"So Inspector, maybe you could tell me the reason for your visit? I'm guessing you aren't here to buy a little trinket for the good lady."

Jack Cully stifles a snigger. Before he met Stride's "good lady" he used to wonder why his boss put in so many extra hours at work. Now he understands perfectly.

"You guess correctly, *sir*."

Stride digs out his notebook, makes a play of turning the pages, scanning the closely-written lines. Taking his time.

"Ah, here we are. The Lily Lounge tea-room, Hampstead. You were there with a lady, quite recently. A foreign lady dressed in black. You had in your possession a particular item of rather fine jewellery, I believe."

The Goldsmith and Dealer in Fine Antiques and Second-hand Jewellery gapes at him, the colour draining from his face.

"Perhaps I was. Maybe I did. I don't really recall. I see a lot of clients in many places. It's the nature of the business."

"The item in question, *sir*, was an emerald bracelet. Is that correct?"

"It might have been."

"Property of Mrs Diana Meadows," Stride says. "Removed by someone in the crowd while she was attending the Italian Opera. The story was in all the papers at the time; I'm surprised you did not read it. It was front-page news."

He pulls a wry face at the memory.

"Do you have any comment, *sir*?"

Solomon's face is a study.

"You mean, did I know it was stolen?"

"I don't know. Did you?"

"No. No. I swear on my mother's grave, no. I bought it in good faith."

Stride's face radiates pure scepticism. He has seen this kind of denial many times. The more they plead their innocence, the deeper their guilt. He flips to a clean page of the notebook.

"Who did you buy it from, if I might ask?"

Solomon shrugs.

"It was a man ... he came into the shop one day ... that is all I know, Inspector, believe me. He said it was a family heirloom."

Stride snorts.

"Did he now? Tell me about the lady who bought the bracelet."

Solomon spreads his hands.

"What can I tell you? I never set eyes on her before that day."

"Describe her to me."

"Ach. She was maybe thirty years old. Fashionably dressed. She spoke very well, but with a foreign accent. I got the feeling she was an aristocratic lady."

"What sort of a foreign accent?"

He shrugs.

"Foreign. French, German, I don't know."

"What did she look like?"

"I don't know that either." Solomon meets Stride's disbelieving stare. "She was wearing a thick black veil, Inspector. It would have been rude to stare. She had very dark eyes – that's all I can recall."

"And how was the meeting arranged?"

"The whole transaction was arranged through a manservant of hers. He approached me saying the lady wished to purchase some jewellery, particularly emeralds. I specialise in emeralds. He instructed me where to meet her with the bracelet, which I did. When she saw it, she said she wanted a new clasp put on – an easy quick little job. I told her when it would be ready to collect. The manservant came, paid me and took it away."

Stride notes this down carefully before he returns to his quarry.

"So, Mr Solomon, what else can you tell us? There must be something more."

"Ach, I'm telling you everything, Inspector," Solomon pleads. "You have to believe me."

"Actually Mr Solomon, I don't have to believe you. And I don't think that I do," Stride goes on, shaking his head. "I'm sure I don't have to remind you that dealing in stolen goods is a crime, *sir*. And that applies whether you knew they were stolen or not.

"Now, I hope you are not planning to take any journeys out of the city in the next few days. Because my officers will be back. With a warrant to search the premises. And they will also want to see a full inventory of everything you have bought or sold in the past few months. And then they will ask you to accompany them to Scotland Yard, where I shall be waiting to ask you some further questions. Do you understand, *sir*?"

Solomon nods unhappily.

"In the meantime, *sir*, if you should receive any more requests for specific items of jewellery, or any further visits from men wishing to sell you family heirlooms, you will come straight round to me. Is that clear?"

A further unhappy nod.

"Then we shall thank you for your co-operation, and bid you good-day. For now."

Stride gives the hapless jeweller his most unendearing smile. Then he turns on his heel and marches out of the shop. Cully follows him, leaving Solomon staring after them in dismay. To be visited by the police, in broad daylight and on a working day, spells disaster for his business. Once word gets round the tight little Jewish community of which he is a member, nobody will want to be seen entering his shop. Or meeting him in the street. Or sitting with him in the synagogue. He is finished. He slumps back into his seat and covers his face with his hands. Oy vay! What has he done that HaShem has brought such tsuris to his door?

***

The importance of the gentlemen's club cannot be overstated. It is a place where like-minded individuals of the male gender can meet together in convivial surroundings to share a drink, read the newspapers and discuss the burning issues of the day.

Mostly, however, the gentlemen's club is a refuge from the trials and tribulations of the matrimonial home. Thus, having finished work for the day, Mr Thorpe has called in at his club for a quiet drink and a bit of refuging before returning to Hampstead and to Mrs Thorpe, the angel in his house.

He sits half-buried in a deep comfortable leather armchair with high winged sides. A tray of whisky and water sits within easy reach on a rosewood wine-table.

"I see shipping stocks are up again," remarks a fellow-refugee sitting in a winged chair opposite. "Didn't your late friend Herbert King have stocks in shipping? Seem to remember I sold mine to him. Must be making a tidy amount for that niece."

Another refugee chuckles.

"I remember old Herbert. He was always a great one for the ladies, wasn't he? Had some little Jewess stashed away somewhere. Amongst others ... "

"Wonder what will happen to his business," the first refugee continues. "Nice set-up. I wouldn't mind buying it. Think I'll get in touch with his lawyer, get a feel for the lie of the land."

"He may have left it to his niece," Mr Thorpe says, remembering the thin redheaded young woman with downcast eyes and solemn demeanour who had sat opposite him in the funeral carriage.

"Well, she ain't going to want it, is she?" the refugee laughs. "Soon as she's out of mourning, she'll be gadding about town looking for a husband. That's what modern gals do nowadays."

Some more sipping.

"How's that boy of yours getting on, Thorpe?" another refugee asks. "Army life suiting him?"

Mr Thorpe grunts. As far as he can tell, Army life is suiting Gussy very well – in so far as it seems to consist of racketing about town spending money. His money.

"And your girl? Estella, isn't it?"

"Isabella."

"Got any plans for her future?"

Mr Thorpe shakes his head. If he *had* plans, Isabella would stay at home, where he could keep an eye on her. He glances at his pocket watch and eases himself out of the leather armchair.

"Better get off now," he sighs. "Don't want to be late for dinner."

The refugees watch him leave.

"Shame about old Thorpe," one of them remarks. "Used to have some go about him in the old days. None now. Blame that bitch of a wife. Got him completely under her thumb."

Mr Thorpe makes his way across the thickly-carpeted foyer and out into the noisy, smelly thoroughfare. He whistles up a cab, and tries to think positive thoughts about the evening ahead. There are many hours of domestic bliss around the fireside to get though before he can finally sink into the arms of Morpheus and fall asleep.

***

It is the following morning. While Josephine is away learning the rudiments of her late uncle's business, an important conversation is taking place in the St John's Wood house. The two participants are Annie, the parlour-maid, and Mrs Hudson, the cook.

The location is the basement kitchen. They sit opposite each other at the scrubbed wooden kitchen table. A plate of home-baked biscuits and a fat brown teapot fuel the discourse.

"***Delicious*** biscuits, Mrs Hudson," Annie remarks.

Mrs Hudson smiles in a satisfied manner.

"Thank you, Miss Price. Sadly I don't get many opportunities to do fine baking nowadays."

Annie sighs.

"Indeed you don't. Times have certainly changed. And not, in my opinion, for the better."

Mrs Hudson stares into her teacup.

"When was the last time we had a nice little dinner party? Or even a tea-party?" Annie persists. "Your talents are going to waste, Mrs Hudson. As are mine. When Mr King told me his niece was coming to live with us, I was really looking forward to arranging her hair, getting her ready for balls and evening-parties. Instead, she just scrambles into her clothes in the morning, and poof! she's off out."

"She likes her meals, though," Mrs Hudson remarks. "Empties her plate every time. And she's good with her pleases and thank-yous. I will say that for her."

Annie sniffs disapprovingly.

"When she's here, she is," she says. "But half the time, she's

144

gadding about who knows where with who knows who. And there's another thing – I don't feel safe sleeping here with no man on the premises."

"There is that, I'll grant you," Mrs Hudson concedes.

"And I don't like working in a house where there's been a death," Annie says. "It's unlucky."

"You'd be hard put to find a place where that hasn't happened," Mrs Hudson remarks. "And it's not as if he died here in the house, is it?"

Annie tosses her head.

"Maybe. But we still had the coffin here. With his dead body in it. And then there was that funny business with Mr King's gun." She purses her lips. "And the visit from the detective police the other week. Never got to the bottom of that little episode. And that time recently when she crept in bold as brass mid-morning and swore she'd been out for a morning walk after her breakfast. But I know she hadn't had any breakfast. And I'm sure she wasn't wearing her own clothes either. Every time I ask Miss Hoity-Toity she just shrugs me away. Says it's **personal**, if you please. Personal! And me having worked my fingers to the bone for her uncle for more years than I care to recall."

She helps herself to another biscuit.

"Well, I've made up my mind, Mrs Hudson. It's my half-day, and I'm going straight round to give my particulars to a couple of reputable agencies. I've already let a few friends in service at good houses know that I'm looking. I've got my references all sorted. And if you'll take my advice, you'll do the same."

Mrs Hudson does not reply. Instead, she places the now empty teapot into the sink and takes off her apron. She goes into the pantry, emerging with a large wicker shopping basket and her hat and mantle.

"I'll bid you good day, Miss Price," she says. "And best of luck – if that's what you want."

"It is what I want."

Mrs Hudson opens the back door, and clambers up the steps to street level.

The maid waits until the footsteps fade into the distance. Then she helps herself to the rest of the biscuits, which she puts in her pocket.

"Shame to let good food go to waste," she mutters.

Shortly afterwards, Annie emerges from the front of the house, dressed in her best outdoor coat and bonnet. She glances up and down the street, before locking the front door and slipping the key into her pocket. Then she walks briskly along the road and disappears round the corner.

***

Annie is not the only one disappearing round corners today. Isabella Thorpe is also about to perform a similar action as she steps out of the shiny cherry-coloured barouche, which has just pulled up in Montague Street, close to the imposing British Museum building.

Isabella has started visiting the British Museum. At least that is what she tells her Mama. She has informed her Mama that she is engaged upon a course of study. The Egyptians. Sometimes it is the Babylonians. Or maybe the Ancient Greeks. She has bought herself a nice little leather-bound notebook in which to make notes. No notes have appeared yet, but then, they are early civilisations, and it is early days.

Isabella gives James the coachman instructions when she is to be collected. Then, as the barouche drives off, she walks briskly towards the imposing edifice of the British Museum, walks straight past it, and turns left into Great Russell Street.

She crosses Bloomsbury Square, continuing her journey until – oh look, here she is approaching Number 17 Red Lion Square. Behold, she stands at the door and knocks.

Isabella has never been inside a real artist's studio before, but after a couple of visits, she is getting over the shock nicely. She no longer blenches when she sees the uncarpeted floorboards (*naked* would be a better description, but she is a well-brought up girl and cannot bring herself to contemplate such a word).

She is also getting used to the plain, unpapered walls, the dribbly wax candles in bottles, the lack of curtains, the shabby sofa, and the paint-spattered chairs and table.

"It's a bit of a tumble rumble jumble," Henry had apologised, when he first introduced her to the studio.

And indeed it was. And it still is. But now she rather likes it. Isabella also likes Sissy, the wife of one of the other artists lodging at Number 17. She had met her on the first visit. Sissy is an extremely tall, pale-faced young woman, with violet eyes and a mass of long red-gold hair. Impressively, she is even thinner than Isabella.

Sissy wears strange unstructured dresses, which she told Isabella were inspired by medieval book illustrations. She makes them herself. Sissy used to work in a haberdashery shop, until she was "discovered" by Henry's friend. Now she keeps house, and models for her husband's paintings.

Isabella is also modelling for a painting. It is to be called *The Princess's Dream*. She is the Princess, of course. The modelling involves sitting as still as she can, in an extremely uncomfortable position, for a long time.

She must not move, or she will destroy the "Muse." Sissy has explained the importance of the Muse to her. She must not speak either. Or breathe too loudly. The Muse is very exacting in its requirements.

But oh, the pre-painting stage makes it all worthwhile, because it involves Henry placing her in the window-seat and draping the flesh-coloured silk shawl about her shoulders. Then she takes the pins out of her hair, and he arranges it to fall in decorative waves upon her shoulders.

Isabella is prepared to endure any hardship for the shiver of sweetness that runs down her spine every time he touches her.

He is touching her now.

"You have such beautiful hair, Isabella," he murmurs, his fingers teasing out her curls.

His mouth is so close to her ear that she can feel his warm breath fan her cheek. Isabella wants to turn her face to his, to feel his lips upon hers, the soft brush of his moustache. She wants to be enfolded in his arms, and held close to him. It is all she can do not to cry out in ecstasy.

"Yes!" Henry exclaims as he steps back. "That is the look I want! Hold the pose!"

He disappears behind the easel, and begins painting furiously while Isabella stares out of the window, wishing she could hold the pose forever.

The Princess's Dream will involve peacocks and pomegranates and a crystal fountain. Her own dream seems so modest in comparison. Freedom to choose, to live the life she wants with the man she loves. Her head droops, her lips part in a sigh.

"Please hold still, Isabella," orders the man she loves.

And silently, dutifully, Isabella obeys.

***

While Isabella dreams and longs, and gets a crick in her neck, back in Hampstead her Mama is entertaining Mrs Osborne (mother of George, and wife of Mr Frederick Osborne, owner of the Osborne Private Bank). It is the first time the two ladies have met *tête-à-tête*.

They have progressed through the various stages from leaving cards at each other's houses, to acknowledging the cards. Now they face each other across the walnut tea-table.

Mrs Thorpe plies her guest with tea and small iced cakes. Mrs Osborne accepts gracefully. The rituals are followed rigidly and formally. They chat about the weather, the servant problem, the difficulty of getting chintz muslin at this time of year.

Eventually, when plates have been filled and emptied, Mrs

Thorpe sidles cautiously up to the matter in hand.

"Isabella has spoken so often of her visit to your *delightful* girls!" she gushes.

Mrs Osborne, who is aware that her daughters have many qualities, but that delightfulness is not one of them, accepts the compliment in the spirit in which it is offered.

"They also tell me they were charmed by your daughter Isabella," she lies.

This is all very positive, so Mrs Thorpe plucks up courage and takes another step along the primrose path towards prospective matrimony.

"We both – and I speak for Mr Thorpe as well as myself – value the *positive* influence that George has been upon our son Augustus since he entered the Regiment. I think Gussy would be quite lost without his good friend George at his side to guide him."

Mrs Osborne is no fool. She knows all about her son's heavy drinking, reckless betting and gambling. She should do – it is her money that pays his creditors, and stops him from disgracing the family name by appearing in the debtors' lists.

That is why she and her husband have decided upon this course of action. George must marry, and as soon as possible. Marriage should settle him down, sober him up, and put an end to his rackety life and roistering ways for good and all.

She has made judicious inquiries, from which she has learned that the Thorpes are wealthy. New money, of course, and the family has no social cachet or ton whatsoever, but one has to make do in these straitened times. Sadly, George's roistering reputation is too well-known amongst her own tight little social set for him to stand a chance with any of her friends' marriageable daughters.

At least it means that the girl will come with a good dowry. Let him run through that for a change, she thinks sourly.

"So where is *dear* Isabella this afternoon?" she asks. "I was so looking forward to making her acquaintance."

"Oh, she is probably shopping somewhere," Mrs Thorpe says, laughing lightly. "You know what these girlies are like."

She glances at her watch. She had given Isabella strict instructions to be back by three. It is now nearly a quarter to four. Though maybe, upon reflection, it is better this way. She doesn't want Mrs Osborne to encounter any of Isabella's strange behaviour. Once it gets out that her daughter faints, barely eats, and is currently turning herself into a bluestocking, her chances of making a good match are practically negligible.

That is why she has made up her mind that Isabella must marry as soon as possible. She hopes that Mrs Osborne, who moves in a totally different set, has not heard any of these damaging rumours.

"Not that she is an extravagant girl," she adds hastily. "Her time in the French convent school we sent her to has taught her the value of thrift and economy. Nuns, you know," she adds, leaving her visitor to draw her own conclusions about the parsimonious habits of nuns.

"Ah. Nuns. Quite."

Mrs Osborne accepts another small cup of tea, but no cake. Actually, she isn't bothered by Isabella's non-appearance. According to Hattie, the girl is a niminy-piminy little thing, with no figure, and absolutely nothing to say for herself.

All the better, as far as Mrs Osborne is concerned. The last thing she wants in a daughter-in-law is one of those spirited modern misses, constantly complaining and carping about her son's treatment of her.

"We shall be glad to welcome George into our house whenever he cares to call," Mrs Thorpe says carefully.

"And of course, the same is true for us with regards to dear Isabella," Mrs Osborne replies, equally carefully.

There is no more to be said. Both ladies understand each other perfectly. After a small diplomatic pause, Mrs Osborne rises, bids her charming hostess farewell, and is shown out by the parlour-maid.

***

It is just a short distance away from these proceedings to the bustle that is Hampstead High Street, and the Lily Lounge tea-rooms. At this time in the afternoon, it is heaving with customers, the air steamy and bright with light chatter.

The young waitresses barely have a second to catch their breath in between taking and serving orders. The richly-spiced fruit cake, white-iced and renamed Christmas cake in honour of the upcoming season, is proving a great hit. Lilith makes a mental note to make several more for next week, while she prepares and then serves another afternoon tea to a couple sitting at a discreet table at the rear of the tea-room.

A balding, high-foreheaded elderly gentleman, impeccably dressed in a dark three-piece suit and spotless white cravat, is entertaining a fine lady, enveloped in rich velvets and laces. Frederick Hartington, Lilith thinks. Old Harty-Tarty. Large as life and still as snooty.

He accepts a cup of Indian tea from her hand with the barest of nods, and not even a flicker of a smile. Clearly he doesn't recognise her with her clothes on. So much for their past relationship, she thinks. Though it was never her face that he was interested in. One of the "backdoor boys," as she remembers it.

So it's true what they say, Lilith muses. If you remain in one place long enough, everybody you know will pass by eventually. Though in the case of Harty-Tarty, now tucking into a scone laden with jam, the word "know" has rather more of a Biblical than a social meaning.

Lilith observes the couple from a distance. The lady is not his wife. They are having far too enjoyable a time for that to be the case. Judging by her clothes, she is clearly high-class. Her maroon velvet gown can be priced in guineas, and she has diamond earrings that look real, not paste. Through her discreetly-lowered veil, Lilith can see that her skin is very

151

smooth and porcelain-white.

Lilith frowns. Something about the lady's demeanour strikes a chord in her memory. She is sure she has seen her before. She racks her brains. Yes, she remembers now: it is the same woman who took tea with Ikey Solomon. The one who purchased the stolen emerald bracelet.

So what, Lilith wonders, is she doing here now? Buying more jewels? Intrigued, she watches from a distance. But this time it appears to be a totally the innocent tea date, if anything connected with Harty-Tarty can ever be designated innocent.

The couple chat animatedly. At one point, Harty-Tarty even leans across and pats the lady's hand in a consoling manner. Eventually, they finish their tea and he signals for the bill. Lilith directs one of the waitresses to attend to him, while she continues to watch from behind the counter.

She sees the lady wrap a warm woollen shawl around her shoulders, then fasten it with a beautiful and rather unusual brooch. The brooch is made of lapis lazuli and marcasite.

Lilith grips the side of the counter, feeling the breath suddenly leave her body. She recognises the brooch at once. It is hers. A present from her dead lover, Herbert King. *"L & M — your initials,"* he'd joked. *"As soon as I saw it in Garrard's window, I thought of you."*

She is quite sure that it is hers, because one of the tiny chips of blue stone is missing. It had fallen out shortly after he'd given it to her. She recalls that he called round unexpectedly one evening, and she had asked him to get the brooch repaired. He'd put it in his pocket, then walked out into the night.

A few hours later, he was dead. Attacked and left to perish in a gutter. And now here is her brooch, still apparently missing its stone, being pinned to the shawl of a stranger, who is even now getting up and heading for the door.

Lilith hastens into the back room, where two newly-hired waitresses are resting their weary feet.

"Sorry, ladies. Tea-break is over," she says. "I need you to serve. I must go out on important business."

She crams on her bonnet and mantle and follows the lady into the street, where she sees her bid a cordial farewell to Harty-Tarty then climb into a closed carriage.

Frantically, Lilith waves down a passing hansom.

"Follow that carriage!" she commands.

The cabman whips up the horse, and the cab sets off in hot pursuit. Down the High Street they bowl, the cab swaying and jolting over the rutted road, the horse slipping and sliding on the slimy surface.

Lilith clings on for dear life. She is not a religious person, but she finds herself praying: *Oh God please. Please God*, over and over again, as the cab lurches down Haverstock Hill at a terrifyingly fast pace.

As they rattle along the setted stone surface of Chalk Farm Road, Lilith levers open the sash window, and thrusts out her head. The carriage is still just in sight, though moving quickly away through the traffic.

She curses under her breath. The two sleek carriage-horses are much faster than the cabman's nag, which is already beginning to jerk its head and froth at the mouth with the exertions it is being made to perform.

"Please don't lose them now!" Lilith shouts.

"Matter of life and death is it, lady?" the cabby responds, never taking his eyes off the road ahead.

"Yes. Yes it is."

He pulls sharply upon the right-hand rein, and the cab turns crazily on two wheels. They speed towards King's Cross. Lilith clutches the sides, her eyes wide. Her bonnet has fallen to the floor, her hair is unpinned and streaming back in the wind, and she is attracting some unwelcome stares and comments from passers-by, but she barely notices. Her gaze is fixed upon the black outline of the carriage as it moves further and further away, until suddenly it disappears completely.

Lilith throws herself back into the seat with a groan of

despair.

The driver eases back on the reins, and the sweating, panting horse slows to a trot.

"I'm sorry, lady. They turned off up ahead. Did my best for you, but we've lost 'em."

Of course they have lost them. What was she thinking of? Lilith clenches her fingers into tight fists. This was a mad enterprise from the start. She gets down from the cab and pays off the driver, giving him a generous tip for his efforts on her behalf. Then she crosses the road, and picks up another ride back to the Lily Lounge.

The return journey gives her time to calm down and reflect. Perhaps all is not lost. She does not know the identity of the lady wearing *her* brooch, nor where she lives, but she does have the means at her disposal to find out.

She will employ sexual blackmail. Somewhere in the collection of letters she has recently had returned to her by Herbert's niece is a *very* interesting one from Harty-Tarty – one that she is sure he would not like his wife to read.

The cab drops her at the end of Flask Walk. She clambers out, surprised at how shaky her legs feel. Seeing the brooch again has brought so many memories flooding back. All of them good.

Lilith pushes open the door to her place, and surveys the busy scene. Cakes are being consumed, tea is being drunk. Money is being made. She has come a long, long way from those dark days in Bethnal Green.

And she owes it all to one lovely man who saw something in her that nobody else saw, and was prepared to give her a chance to fulfil her dream. For his sake, and his alone, she will endeavour to discover the name of the lady. She will find out how she got hold of the brooch. Then she will go to the police.

Lilith moves to the back kitchen, and picks up the steaming kettle. A cup of hot sweet tea to calm her down, that is what she needs right now. After which, she has to make an important call.

***

There are no cups of tea on offer at Number 17 Red Lion Square. No cake either. Art needs only itself for nourishment; it is not slave to food and drink. So Isabella goes on modelling, and Henry goes on painting, until suddenly she realises that she has stayed far longer than she should have done, and that James the coachman will be waiting for her in Montague Street.

Slipping the rosy, flesh-coloured silk shawl from her shoulders, Isabella scrambles to her feet and looks around frantically for her mantle and thick woollen shawl. She is late. Very late. Oh dear. What if James has not waited for her? She has no money. How will she get home? What will her Mama say?

It is one of those afternoons when the sun shines hot but the wind blows cold. Clutching her mantle to her, bonnet tied askew and hair falling around her face, Isabella hurries as fast as she can towards the British Museum.

Henry does not accompany her – she cannot risk being seen alone with him again. Though truth to tell, he has barely registered her departure, being still in thrall to the Muse.

At last she spies the familiar barouche, and hastens towards it. With the briefest of apologies to James and instruction to drive as fast as he can, she mounts the steps and sinks back against the butter-soft leather upholstery.

Stars dance in front of her eyes, and her breath comes in great heaving gasps. As the coach jerks into motion, she leans forward, trying to fight off the tidal waves of giddiness that threaten to overwhelm her.

Isabella has had nothing since a cup of weak tea at breakfast, and now it is nearly five o'clock. But she cannot succumb to the giddiness. She must not be ill again. She has to be well, or how will Henry finish the painting?

She is his Princess; he needs her. The thought is sustaining. She holds on to it, and to the side of the carriage, and prays that when they arrive home she will be able to sneak in without anybody noticing how late she is.

At last the barouche draws up in front of the Hampstead house, and Isabella is handed down. She enters the hallway as noiselessly as she can, and tiptoes towards the stairs.

If only she can rest for twenty minutes, with her eyes closed, she is sure she will feel so much better, and then she will go downstairs and try to eat her dinner, and nobody will be any the wiser about her little escapade.

She pushes herself to reach the first floor landing, pausing for a few seconds while her head spins and black shapes dance and pivot in front of her eyes. Then, with a sigh of relief, she opens the door to her room.

And freezes on the threshold with horror.

For there stands her Mama, arms folded, and an expression as black as a thundercloud upon her face.

"Isabella!" she exclaims angrily. "Where on earth have you been? And what has happened to your hair?"

***

While Isabella is being put to the torture of the maternal Inquisition, Josephine is sitting on edge of her bed, unlacing her boots. It is good to be out of the nipping December cold. She throws herself back with a sigh of contentment.

Who would ever have thought her life would turn out like this? Certainly not Miss Fox, who taught Divinity and Bible Reading at the Bertha Helstone School. She can still feel Miss Fox's sharp bony fingers biting into the flesh of her forearm, hear Miss Fox's shrill voice screaming *"Josephine King, you are a vile little heathen, and one day you will burn in the flames of Hell."*

This alarming statement would usually be followed by Miss

Fox locking her in the classroom cupboard. Sometimes she stayed in the cupboard all day.

And yet here she is, no longer reviled and apparently unflamed. She has money in the bank to spend, a priceless diamond, a house, and a business to run. She has prospects.

And now she also has a job to do. One that she has been putting off for far too long. It is the time to pack up and dispose of her uncle's clothes. Winter is here, and there are many poor and destitute people who'd be grateful for a warm coat, or a woollen muffler, to keep out the cold.

She has been given so much. It is wrong not to share some of it with the less fortunate. And there are so many less fortunate. She thinks of Oi, the crossing-sweeper, who seems to be getting thinner and more wizened every time she sees him. She worries about him. About his cough.

The blinds are drawn down in her uncle's room, as they have been since the day he died. The fire has not been lit. The room smells of emptiness and dust, backgrounded by the lingering scent of his cologne.

She decides to start with the chest of drawers. She opens each drawer in turn, lifting out shirts, socks, cravats, ties and underclothing, and placing them neatly upon the bed. Then to the wardrobe, from which she extracts suits and waistcoats.

Next she arranges the fine leather shoes and overshoes in pairs on the floor. Finally, she takes her uncle's two topcoats: the one he had on when he was found murdered in the gutter, and the ulster that he wore on milder days.

She checks the pockets of both coats and finds a small envelope. Her uncle's name is written on the front in a flowing italic hand. Intrigued, she opens the envelope and pulls out a folded piece of paper. As she reads what is written, the room begins to revolve around her. The air sings in her ears. She feels ice-cold.

The front doorbell rings.

***

Annie is downstairs laying the dining room table when she is interrupted by the loud and urgent ringing of the bell. She goes to see who on earth is calling so unexpectedly. She opens the door and there standing on the doorstep is a woman, dressed in good-quality work clothes.

She looks like a respectable shop assistant. Except that no shop assistant ever had such bold black brows and full carmined lips. And no shop assistant would stand in such a provocative way, with her hand on her thrust-out hip.

Annie gives a little gasp of horror, and attempts to shut the door in the woman's face, but Lilith is far too quick for her.

"Annie, I need to see your mistress," she says, placing a foot squarely in the doorway. "Now," she adds for good measure.

Annie tries to dislodge the unwelcome intruder, but Lilith has fought off the amorous advances of far too many drunken men in her time, and she is much stronger. She puts her shoulder to the door and shoves it open.

"You can't come in," Annie protests.

But Lilith is already in, and is taking off her bonnet.

"Kindly tell her that I am here," she says coolly. "You know who I am, presumably."

Annie's mouth opens and closes like a codfish.

"Or would you prefer me to go and find her myself?" Lilith asks, and she starts towards the drawing-room.

"I believe Miss King is upstairs," Annie says stiffly. "Stay here, I shall go and see."

The refusal to allow Lilith to wait in the drawing-room is a snub of the highest order.

Lilith shrugs, then pulls a face behind the maid's back. A few minutes later Annie returns, her expression even sourer than before.

"You are to go up," she says. "It is the first room on the left."

The words *and don't touch anything on your way, whore*, linger unsaid in the air between them.

Light-footed, Lilith runs upstairs and enters Herbert King's room. Josephine is standing by the bed. Lilith takes one look at the piles of clothes, then at her paper-white face, the eyes huge pools of unhappiness.

"You poor dear girl. You shouldn't have to do this all on your own!" she exclaims, reaching out and hugging her.

It catches Josephine off guard. She has not been hugged since she was a small child. The breath goes out of her, but she holds on to the older woman's shoulders briefly, before letting go.

Lilith steers her to the bed, clears an area and they sit down next to each other. She reaches out and briefly touches one of the piles of clothes.

"What are you going to do with these?"

"I thought of giving them to a charity for the poor and needy."

Lilith nods approvingly.

"Yes," she says. "That is exactly what he would want you to do. You must think it strange that I have called round at this time of day, but something has happened and I wanted to tell you as soon as possible."

She relates the incident of the stolen brooch.

"I shall make it my business to find out who this woman is, and where she lives, I promise you."

Josephine regards her thoughtfully.

"I may know who she is," she says. "And if it is the same lady, I also know where she lives. I found this letter in my uncle's coat pocket."

She hands Lilith the piece of notepaper.

Lilith reads: *Remember our rendezvous tonight. Make sure you bring the diamond with you, as we agreed. EVS* .

"Who is 'EVS'?" she queries.

"I think she is a Romanian lady called Countess Elenore Von Schwarzenberg," Josephine says. She relates what Mr Able, the solicitor has told her, then tells of her two visits to the house in

Russell Square.

Lilith listens intently.

"Where is the diamond?" she asks abruptly, when Josephine has finished speaking.

Josephine leaves the room, returning a short while later.

"Here," she says, placing it into Lilith's hands.

"Ah," Lilith breathes. She holds the stone gingerly, as if its brilliance might burn her palm. The house is very still. They sit together with the diamond. Human and inhuman.

Eventually Josephine breaks the silence.

"The letter is dated the day of my uncle's death. Mr Moggs, the clerk, told me he remembers the post arriving, so it must have been delivered to the office. But for some reason, he didn't take the diamond with him to the meeting."

"Clearly he did not. We do not know the reason why. But whatever the reason, sometime after the meeting he was set upon and murdered." Lilith frowns. "I think that we need to find out more about this Countess Elenore von Schwarzenberg. Her behaviour is very strange – one might say very suspicious. For I know that Herbert would never have parted with my brooch voluntarily."

"The detective police believe my uncle was murdered by a gang of thieves who stole his personal belongings," Josephine says. "Surely she cannot be a member of such a gang, for how could a woman perform such a terrible crime as murder?"

Lilith smiles grimly. She knows women who routinely carry knives under their skirts, and wouldn't hesitate to use them. She has seen drunken female fights where eyes were lost and ears bitten off.

She once witnessed a woman strangle a violent client with her bare hands, when she caught him trying to rape her eight-year-old daughter. In Lilith's experience, anything a man is capable of, a woman can do, just as well and probably lot better. Certainly with far less pity. And this woman is a foreigner to boot.

160

Lilith is about to impart this wisdom when there is a knock at the door, and Annie enters.

"Your supper is ready, miss," she says sourly to Josephine. She glares at Lilith and flounces out.

Lilith rises from the bed.

"Then I will leave you to eat it, for I have work to do."

"Oh." Josephine feels her cheeks going red.

"Not that sort of work," Lilith regards her with a faint glint of amusement in her dark eyes. "I have changed my ... occupation since we last met. Now I run a tea-room in Hampstead with a friend of mine. I have the day-book to write up, and stock-cupboards to check, before I retire for the night."

She smoothes down her dress.

"I only hope we have enough of my Christmas cake left, for it seems the customers cannot get enough of it. I shall write to you as soon I have found out more about the Countess. Meanwhile, I think we should keep this to ourselves. We need more proof before we go to the detective police with our suspicions."

Her gaze moves to the Eye of the Khan.

"If I were you," she says, "I'd take that diamond straight round to your bank tomorrow, and ask them to look after it. It is clearly not safe in this house. And while it is in this house, neither, I think, are you."

***

Morning arrives, and finds Isabella Thorpe in the shrubbery where she has gone to hide from her Mama. There is nothing to compare with a leafless shrubbery in a cold wind for the promotion of gloom and despondency. Isabella Thorpe should know, for she has been wandering in it for over an hour. Now she feels so gloomy and despondent that she wants to die. Or at least, if that option is not open to her, then she'd like to run away.

She has even mulled over a stratagem, whereby she will secretly sell off some of her fine silk dresses and jewellery, and then decamp to Number 17 Red Lion Square, where she will live in poverty with Henry, and suffer and starve. Because it would just serve her Mama right if she did.

Except that deep down, Isabella knows that she won't do anything of the kind. The starving probably wouldn't be a problem, but she is used to being surrounded by nice things. The unpapered walls, and the bare floorboards, and the absence of lady's-maids and carriages and expensive dresses, would be more than she could bear. Suffering in poverty is all very well and good, but suffering in comfort is far more enjoyable.

But Isabella is a firm believer in destiny. She has read numerous works of fiction, wherein she has learned of the role destiny plays in the happy outcome. Destiny brought her and Henry together, so destiny will find a way to keep them together.

The other destiny, who is (via her Mama) trying to effect a similar togetherness between herself and George Osborne, is not a force she recognises.

And now here is her Mama, striding purposefully towards her, and at her back is the dreaded doctor. Isabella feels an icy coldness steal over her. She wraps her shawl around her bony frame, and tries to look healthy.

"Isabella, my love," her Mama coos. "There you are. I have been looking for you."

"I told you I was going for a walk," Isabella replies dully. "Walking is good for me."

"So it is," Mrs Thorpe agrees, her false ringletted front bobbing in agreement. "But maybe now it is time to stop walking. Have you had any breakfast?"

Isabella carefully considers the implications of this seemingly innocent question. If she responds truthfully (in the negative), she suspects a swift return to the former regime of enforced rest and supervised meals. Then it suddenly dawns on her that her

Mama has not stipulated an actual time when the breakfast was had. An escape route opens up.

"Of course I have breakfasted," she says.

And it is true, she has. Several days ago, and very reluctantly.

"That is very good," the doctor says. "And how are we feeling?"

Isabella's smile is as wide as Africa.

"Oh, I am quite well, thank you, Doctor."

"Uh-huh, uh-huh. And may I please examine your pulse?"

Isabella extends a pitifully stick-thin arm. The doctor extracts a watch from his waistcoat pocket and places a thumb upon her wrist.

"Perhaps a little hectic, Mrs Thorpe," he murmurs.

"But I have been exercising, Mama. Don't forget that," Isabella interjects.

Mrs Thorpe glances from daughter to doctor. It is clear that she wants to believe one of them. But which one? Isabella decides to press home her advantage. After all, what has she to lose?

"I'm sure my Mama will tell you that the regular meals, and the regular exercise in the carriage, have greatly improved my health. Would you not agree, Mama?"

Mrs Thorpe frowns gently. It is true that the fainting fits and strange behaviour have all but disappeared lately. She is unsure whether this can be put down entirely to carriage rides, and the small amount of food Isabella consumes. The trouble is, she knows no other reason for it.

"She is certainly ... better in herself," she says cautiously.

"There!" Isabella exclaims brightly. "You see, Doctor – all is well."

However, the effect of all this forced wellness is starting to take its toll. She is beginning to sway on her feet and see stars in front of her eyes. She thinks fast.

"Oh Mama, this walking has given me such an appetite. I should like nothing better than a cup of tea, and maybe some nice fresh bread-and-butter? Could you ask one of the maids to bring it to my room?"

"Certainly, my love," her Mama agrees. "Let us return at once. We don't want you to catch a chill, do we? Not when *you-know-who* is expected to call later."

She gives Isabella an arch smile, and takes her arm in a firm but motherly gesture that causes her to flinch.

"We must look our very best today," Mrs Thorpe says, hauling the reluctant Isabella towards the house. "Oh, and I have told James you won't be needing the carriage this afternoon after all."

***

While Isabella is trying to force down some bread-and-butter, a momentous event is taking place at the St John's Wood house, involving the packing of a certain box. Annie's box.

The snooty parlour-maid has finally made up her mind to leave, a decision reinforced last night in the white-hot fury of having to admit "that filthy Jewish whore" into the house. Enough is enough, and Annie has had quite enough, thank you very much. Oh yes, indeed she has.

As she packs her things, she runs over the little speech she intends to deliver to "that hoity-toity miss" (as she privately refers to Josephine) when she returns later that morning from wherever she has gone. The speech being delivered, she will pick up her box and flounce out. Probably slamming the front door behind her for good measure.

Annie has secured a new place in Kensington, with a good family, where she is sure that she will be treated as she feels she deserves, and she will never again have to show in street riffraff as if they were high society.

Meanwhile, unbeknown to Annie, a shiny midnight-black carriage pulled by a pair of matching black horses is making its way towards St John's Wood. It stops outside the house. The driver, clad in a thick grey coat, leaps down from the box, opens the carriage door with a flourish, and hands out the occupant. He is given some instructions. Then the horses are whipped up, and the carriage drives off.

Annie hears the bell as she is hauling her box down from the attic. She straightens up, wiping her sweaty hands on her apron, and hurries to answer the door. After all, until she steps outside the front door, she is technically still in the employ of the King family (minor branch), and so must perform her contractual duties. Though not, she reminds herself smugly, for much longer.

An unknown lady stands upon the top step. She is swathed from top to toe in furs, her face hidden behind a heavy black lace veil. Annie speedily readjusts her facial muscles from sneer to polite.

"Iss your misstress at home?" the stranger asks. Her voice is low and musical with just a trace of an accent. For some reason it reminds Annie of treacle.

"I am afraid she is currently absent, madam. Though she will be back very soon, I believe."

The caller proffers a visiting card. Annie glances at it and gasps.

"May I enter, and await her return?"

"Of course, my Lady," Annie says humbly. Dropping a curtsey, she opens the front door and the fur-clad caller sails across the threshold. Annie shows her into the drawing-room.

My Lady immediately strolls over to the fireplace, where a portrait of Herbert King hangs above the mantel.

"Ah, such a tragic loss to society!" she murmurs, applying a black edged handkerchief to her eyes.

Annie hovers in the background, maintaining a discreet but respectful presence.

"My dear, I am sure you have many menial duties to perform," my Lady says, still with her back to the maid. "I am perfectly happy to wait here. I will look upon this portrait, and remember."

"Yes, my Lady,"

Annie bobs another curtsey.

"Ah, how a cup of refreshing tea would comfort one on such a sad occasion," my Lady suggests, to nobody in particular.

"Of course, my Lady," Annie says. "I will see to it at once."

She hurries off to organise the tea, and gossip to Mrs Hudson about the unexpected and aristocratic caller.

A few seconds pass. Then the drawing room door opens. My Lady stands motionless upon the threshold. She appears to be listening intently for something. It cannot be the sound of returning carriage wheels, for she moves swiftly along the hallway in the opposite direction to the street.

Reaching the door leading to the basement, she softly closes it, before returning to the bottom of the stairs. Her questing nostrils flare, as if she is trying to scent out something. Then she slips out of her glossy pelts and runs nimbly up the stairs.

Some time later, Annie clambers the basement steps with a tray. Grumbling, she sets it down and opens the door, which she could have sworn she'd not closed. She picks up the tray and carries it to the drawing-room.

"Your tea, my Lady," she announces.

But the drawing-room, like the hallway through which she has just passed, is completely empty.

***

While Annie is standing in the drawing-room, puzzling over the mysterious disappearance of the aristocratic caller, Gussy Thorpe, big, bumbling scion of the Thorpe family, is in the barrack stables grooming his horse Charger. Of course there are orderlies and inferiors who would do the job for him, but Gussy is "demned fond" of his horse. Well, it don't answer a fellah back, so he prefers to do the job himself.

Gussy is having a bad heir day. He has just received another stiffish letter from the guv'nor informing him that unless he buckles down and mends his ways, the money for his commission will not be forthcoming. And his allowance will be cut to the bone. This is a terrible blow. When the only way to advance up the ranks is by purchasing a commission, to be denied the necessary tin is a bitter pill to swallow.

Gussy doesn't know what's currently eating the guv'nor. He (Gussy) has been as good as gold. He has hardly left the barracks – well, apart from trips to the Club, and to that new show in Town, and a few late ones at the Cocoa Tree… Other than that, he has been a positive hermit. And he ain't been really rip-roaringly drunk for over a week.

He sighs – a dangerous manoeuvre, given the tightness of his waistband. On the one hand, there's the guv'nor fossicking on about his spends, on the other, there's the mater trying to get him to court that sour-faced redhead. Between the two of them, Gussy doesn't know whether he's coming or going. No wonder he prefers the company of his horse.

And now the stable door opens, and the other current source of his misery comes swaggering in.

"Ah, there y'are Guster," George Osborne exclaims. "Been lookin' for you everywhere. Might have guessed I'd find you in here."

He peers at Charger's flank.

"Gad, that's a shine! Are you trying to wear the poor beast away?"

Gussy fidgets with the brush. George is supposed to be his best friend, having filled that role ever since public school days, but recently he's never felt totally at ease in his company.

Maybe it is the elegant cut of George's uniform – the result of being able to afford the best army tailor in London. Maybe it is George's nonchalant devil-may-care attitude. Or maybe it is George's finely-chiselled, handsome face, which is already beginning to show the early signs of a life of drink and debauchery.

Whatever the reason, Gussy only knows that he has been sedulously avoiding George Osborne. He wishes he could to do so now. Sadly, he can't.

"And how's my future brother-in-law gettin' along?"

George's black eyes sparkle wickedly, and he smacks Gussy on the back.

"Um ... I thought it wasn't settled yet," Gussy stammers.

"It will be, Guster. Only a matter of time. Just got to get round to poppin' the old question. Tie the knot next Summer, what d'ya think? I love a Summer wedding, don't you? All those fine looking gals in their light dresses."

Gussy swallows.

"But demmit, George, you hardly know Izz. How can you marry her?" (He pronounces it "mawwy".)

George Osborne grins at him.

"What is there to know? They're all the same, women, underneath. Eh, Guster?"

"But ... but ..." Gussy splutters, "you don't love her. And she don't love you."

George Osborne throws back his head and laughs. An ugly sound that makes Gussy's horse snort and stamp its feet.

"'Fore Gad, Guster, you are a fool sometimes! Love? What's love got to do with it? Marriage is a business deal. I get what I want, and so does she. Love? Listen, as soon as she's dropped a couple of sons, she can pretty much do as she pleases. I won't care."

Gussy grits his teeth, and resumes grooming Charger. He hates this conversation. He hates George Osborne. He turns his back, hoping that George will take the hint and depart.

"Meanwhile, I'm still a free man," George continues, evidently not taking the hint, and showing no sign of departing. "So I still have a right to my pleasures. How about it, old friend?"

"How about what?" Gussy asks sulkily.

"Tonight. You and me and a couple of the fellahs. Dinner at my Club, maybe take in a show after, then on to Mrs Frost's. I've had it on good authority that she's got some new girls in. Fresh from the country and young. Very, very young." George Osborne licks his lips. "How do you fancy some sweet virgin flesh?"

Gussy breathes in sharply.

"Oh don't fuss, Guster. Once I'm properly engaged, I'll forsake the 'ladies' and reform. You'll see. But in the meantime ... what about it?"

"I'm not sure," Gussy says unhappily. "The guv'nor wrote that he don't want me gettin' into any more scrapes."

George swats this ludicrous excuse aside, as if it were a troublesome gnat.

"Scrapes? Nonsense, Guster. What's life about if it ain't about havin' fun? Damn it, we're entitled to enjoy ourselves while we're young. Anyway, what do you think your pa got up to when he was your age? Much the same, I wager. As did mine."

The thought of his stern-faced, repressive businessman father ever frequenting the likes of Mrs Frost's establishment almost reduces Gussy to verbal incoherence.

"I'll think about it," he says at last.

"You'll do it, or I'm a Dutchman," George counters, with another hefty slap on his back. "Now hurry up groomin' that nag. I've got a little card game startin' in my room, and there's a seat for you at the table."

***

A little while later, Josephine returns to St John's Wood. She has visited several charitable institutions with parcels of her uncle's clothes, and the satisfaction of doing good is sitting inside her like a small warmth. She enters the hallway and is just hanging up her bonnet when Annie bustles out of the parlour, a duster in one hand, and an important expression on her face.

"There you are, miss. **Lady Hartington** called while you were out.

"Did she leave her card?"

Annie shakes her head.

"**My Lady** did not stay long. The aristocracy don't like to be kept waiting, miss. Perhaps you didn't know that?" she says pertly.

"I'm sorry, Annie, but as I was not expecting her, I cannot be held responsible for my absence. In any case, I had important business to attend to."

Annie's mouth closes in a firm line, but her face belies the opinion that no business could possibly be more important than entertaining a member of the aristocracy.

"Could you ask Mrs Hudson to make me a something to eat?" Josephine continues. "Then I shall have to go out again. I have an appointment at the bank."

Annie starts towards the kitchen, before remembering her primary purpose of the day.

"Before you go out again, I should like to talk to you, miss. If it is convenient."

Josephine sighs. Now what social *faux-pas* has she committed?

"Perhaps later, when I get back," she says, finally managing to hang up her bonnet. "Now please, can you go down to the kitchen."

Josephine climbs the stairs slowly. All the way back she has been steeling herself for this moment. Already she feels a sense of desolating emptiness, knowing that she will no longer see the diamond bubbling light, no longer cradle it in the palm of her hand, or feel its familiar outline under her pillow when she wakes in the middle of the night.

In her life so far, she has lost everybody that she has ever loved. It is a painful wrench to part with this, even though she knows it is for the best. She enters her room, and goes straight to the writing-desk, where she has taken to keeping the Eye of the Khan during the day while she is out.

She opens the top drawer. The diamond is not there.

She feels all round inside, her fingers expecting at any second to close on the stone's cold familiar hardness, but her hand comes back empty. She pulls the drawer out, and upends it. The diary, and a few keepsakes, fall to the floor.

The clock ticks like a whip.

Her heart lurches, falling away inside her, as if someone has stolen her soul. Suddenly she feels ice-cold. The air sings in her ears. Time runs backwards. She has been here before. She has never been here before.

While she is still reeling from the shock, Annie enters, carrying a plate of ham sandwiches.

"Your luncheon, miss."

Josephine stares at her.

"Have you been in my chamber since I went out?"

"No, miss."

Her brain is whirling with possibilities and impossibilities.

"Has anybody else been up here? Maybe Mrs Hudson? Think, Annie."

Annie frowns.

"No. Nobody has been here. Why do you ask?"

A germ of a suspicion begins to bud inside her.

"The visitor. Lady Hartington. Can you describe her?"

Annie purses her lips.

"She wore a beautiful long fur coat – mink, I think it was. Very expensive, I'd say. And one of those cunning new fur hats. Cossack style. I've seen one just like it in a magazine. All the rage amongst the upper classes, they say—"

"But her *face*, Annie," Josephine interrupts impatiently. "Describe her face."

Annie looks resentful.

"I didn't see her face, miss. It was covered with a black lace veil."

Of course it was.

"How long was she in the house?"

*"**As I said**,"* Annie replies pointedly, "it was only a short visit. I'd gone down to the kitchen to get her a cup of tea, and when I returned, she had left."

And taken the Eye of the Khan with her.

Suddenly feeling sick inside, Josephine sinks onto the bed.

"Well, I'm sorry, miss." Annie tosses her head. "It's not my fault if you weren't here. Perhaps she'll call again."

Oh no she won't. She has got what she came for.

She forces herself to stand upright.

"I must go straight out now, Annie. I do not know when I will be back. Please don't let anyone into the house. Anyone at all. Do you understand?"

Annie's face is one big resentful sulk.

"What about your luncheon?"

Josephine ignores the question. She pushes past the maid and heads down the stairs. She has suddenly remembered when, and from whose lips, she heard the name "Lady Hartington."

Annie hastens after her. She has a speech to deliver, and if she doesn't deliver it now, it will be too late. Her box is waiting by the kitchen door; a boy is coming round to collect it at 2.30. And Miss High-and-Mighty is well overdue for a few home truths.

"Miss, I have something to say to you. It's important."

Josephine whirls round.

"Oh for goodness sake, Annie! Can't you see I am in a hurry? What's the matter now?"

Annie bridles indignantly. She is not used to being spoken to like this.

Nevertheless, she draws herself up, clears her throat and launches into her prepared speech.

"It is my intention to leave your employment ***forthwith***," she begins, pausing on the "forthwith", a word which she thinks makes her sound grand and important. "I have recently managed to secure a new and better position with a very **respectable** family. However, before I depart, I would like to take the opportunity to offer a few remarks. Ever since your arrival, I have observed that—"

Josephine raises a hand.

"Fine. But I really don't have time for this now."

She crams on her bonnet.

"Good-bye Annie, and good luck."

She stumbles out of the house. Fortunately a cab has just drawn up at the corner of the street. She hails it, and gives the driver instructions where to take her.

***

A cold, sleety rain is falling, sharp as nails, as Josephine alights at Hampstead High Street. She left the house in such haste that she has not brought an umbrella. She hurries along Flask Walk, head down against the stinging drops trying to tie the strings of her bonnet a little tighter with freezing fingers, until finally she reaches the Lily Lounge.

It is not yet the hour for afternoon tea, so the Lily Lounge is unlit and the door is locked. She hammers upon it until a neatly-clad waitress appears. She gives Josephine a curious stare, then points to the Closed sign.

Josephine shakes her head, and indicates that she wants to enter. Now. After some mutual gesticulating, the waitress disappears, to be replaced by Lilith herself, who takes one look at her stricken face, and immediately unlocks the door.

"What on earth has happened?" she exclaims, drawing Josephine inside.

"The diamond has been stolen."

Lilith breathes in. Then she says calmly,

"May, cut our visitor a slice of the veal pie. A big slice please. Then butter some bread, and make us a pot of tea."

While May hurries to do as she is bid, Lilith leads Josephine to a table and pulls out a chair for her before she sits down opposite, taking Josephine's hand in hers.

"Tell me everything at once," she says quietly. "Leave nothing out."

She listens intently while Josephine relates the events of earlier on. Only when Lilith hears the name of the visitor does her expression change.

"It was not Lady Hartington," she states.

"I thought not. But how can you be sure?"

Lilith smiles wryly.

"Lady Caroline Hartington fell off a horse when she was in her early thirties. She injured her spine very badly, and she still walks with a stick. It would've taken two footmen to carry her up the few steps to your front door, let alone up the stairs to your chamber. She spends much of her time either in the country, or visiting foreign spas in the hope of finding a cure. Whoever called round was clearly an impostor."

"The Countess?"

Lilith nods.

"I think it very likely. I have made a few inquiries since we last met. It appears that Lady Hartington met this Countess at a Hungarian spa last summer. She was very taken with her, and a close friendship quickly developed between them. This led to an invitation to visit London for the Winter season, and stay in one of their houses. They own several houses, one of them in Russell Square.

"It is clear that the Countess has helped herself to Lady Caroline's calling card, then used it to gain entry to your house while you were out. Your servants would hardly have queried her identity, would they?"

Lilith pauses.

"But it also suggests to me that somebody has been watching the house, for she clearly knew that the diamond was there, and also which room it was being kept in. And, crucially, she also knew that you would be out when she called. Have you noticed anything unusual recently?"

A shiver runs down Josephine's spine as she recalls the strange unearthly figure standing in the midnight street in the moonlight, staring up at her window.

"I ... might have seen something, yes," she falters, and tells Lilith about the strange nocturnal prowler.

"Then that is how it was done."

"As easily as that?"

"Believe me, it is how most crimes are carried out," Lilith remarks drily. "And it is why so many criminals are never apprehended."

She sees Josephine's face fall.

"But that is not the case here," she adds quickly. "Now eat your pie, and drink your tea while it is hot, and then let us put our heads together and see if we can devise a plan to catch this evil Countess, and bring her to the justice she deserves."

While Josephine eats, Lilith walks quickly up and down, her lips tight, her brow furrowed in a frown of concentration. Eventually her expression clears, and she nods to herself in a satisfied manner. She approaches the table.

"I have it," she says. "Or at least, I think I see a way forward."

She pulls out a chair and sits down.

"In four days' time there is to be a Christmas Ball at the Hartingtons' house. It happens every year and is a huge society event. Everybody, including the Countess, will be there. The Ball goes on all night. If we could find some way to get into the house in Russell Square where the Countess is staying, we can search for the diamond. Once we discover it, we have the proof we require to report her to the detective police."

"But what if we don't discover it?" Josephine asks.

"Oh, we will," Lilith nods sagely. "It will have been hidden in a jewel case, or in a drawer somewhere. Rich aristocratic ladies keep their jewellery and precious items close by, in my experience. Besides, Lady Caroline always leaves London for the Continent straight after the Ball is over, and I'm sure the Countess will accompany her. She will be very anxious to get out of London quickly, so there'd be very little point placing the diamond in a bank or with a jeweller."

Lilith pauses.

"The only problem we have is finding a person who will help us break into the house. I do not suppose that you know any housebreakers or cracksmen, do you?"

For the first time since she arrived, a ghost of a smile flits across Josephine's face,

"No I don't," she agrees. "But I think I know someone who might."

Lilith's eyes widen.

"Then I suggest you make haste to contact them," she says tartly. "In five days, your diamond will be out of the country, possibly along with your uncle's murderer. We must move fast, for we have very little time."

***

In a city of nearly 2,800,000 people, you might think that the chances of casually meeting someone you knew would be statistically remote. In reality, you would be surprised how often it happens.

Isabella Thorpe and her Mama are shopping in Regent Street. They are just coming out of a haberdasher's store where they have been looking at a display of laces and ribbons.

Before that, they were looking at pins and fans in another store. They are having a nice little shopping trip. Mrs Thorpe arranged it. A bit of mother-daughter bonding.

To Isabella, it feels more like mother-daughter bondage. She is desperate to escape to Number 17 Red Lion Square, where she is sure Henry is waiting impatiently for her. She has had to put him off for several days now, and she aches inside with longing. She wants to feel his fingers caressing her neck again as he arranges her hair. Sometimes she can barely breathe for thinking about him.

Meanwhile Josephine King is hurrying along Regent Street, unaware of who is walking towards her. She has come from Westminster Bridge, where she has just given the crossing-sweeper some more warm clothes to tide him over the cold winter. And in return, he has given her some useful information.

There is nothing like running across an old friend in town. Sadly, this is nothing like running across an old friend in town. Josephine spots the Thorpes a split second before Mrs Thorpe's beady eyes light upon her, but it is a second too late to pretend otherwise than that she has been recognised. She pastes a polite smile onto her face, and mentally starts working on an escape route.

"Josephine! Josephine King!"

Mrs Thorpe hurries forward, holding out two fingers of her gloved hand.

"How are you, dear child?"

The Dear Child extends the requisite number of fingers.

"I am well, thank you, Mrs Thorpe. And how are you, and Isabella?"

Isabella Thorpe pinches her pale lips together, and gives Josephine a hostile stare.

"We were just looking around the delightful emporia," Mrs Thorpe continues. She always calls a shop an emporium; it elevates it – and therefore herself – to a higher status.

"Have you told dear Josephine your exciting news, Bella?"

Isabella gives her Mama a venomous look.

"Isabella has a beau," Mrs Thorpe trills. "George Osborne – such a nice young man. A military friend of Gussy's." She pats Isabella's shoulder fondly. "We are all so delighted, as you can imagine."

Josephine makes congratulatory noises, noting as she does

that the "we" of the statement does not appear to include Isabella, whose face is currently frozen into a rictus of disgust.

"And what about you?" Mrs Thorpe continues. "Have you made any decisions about your future? I inquire because Gussy was asking about you only the other day. The dear boy is very taken with you."

"Oh ... I ... am in the process of making many decisions."

"Not too many, I hope. And not without proper advice. Remember, Mr Thorpe and I are always available, should you require the guiding hand of long experience. You are still very young, my dear, and you should be spending your time enjoying yourself. Which is why we are here, of course. Come, Isabella, I spy bonnets!"

Mrs Thorpe sails off.

Isabella does not move. Instead she turns to face Josephine.

"You did not see me!" she hisses, icicles hanging from her words.

"Oh?" Josephine stares at her incomprehensibly. She does not have a clue what Isabella is talking about. "Did I not? When?"

"Near the British Museum."

Light dawns upon the confusion.

"Oh – you mean when you were with that—"

Isabella shakes her head.

"You. Saw. Nothing."

"Oh, I see."

"No, you did NOT see. Just remember," Isabella snaps, acid edging every syllable.

Then in a spectacular "cut", she spins upon her heel and stalks off.

Josephine shakes her head in bewilderment. For goodness sake. What does it matter what she saw? Why does it matter? It is not as if she and Isabella are friends. Far from it.

She makes her way down Regent Street to the omnibus stop in Piccadilly Circus. But her troubles are not yet over for the day, for barely has she stationed herself on the corner, when she finds herself accosted by a middle-aged man in a smart woollen topcoat with a velvet collar.

"My poor dear child, what are you doing standing here upon this gloomy afternoon?" he inquires.

Under his shiny top hat, the man has a thin, unhealthy angular face culminating in a grizzled moustache and a straggly beard. His eyes are sunk deep in baggy folds of skin. Josephine is tempted to say that it is none of his business, but for some unknown reason, he is regarding her with intense sympathy.

"I'm waiting for a bus," she says stiffly.

The stranger goes on staring at her in a rather disconcerting fashion. Finally he sighs deeply, and reaches into his topcoat.

"I have in my pocket a small pamphlet that may change your unfortunate life forever," he says. "May I beg you to accept it. I hope you can find someone to read it to you."

"What?"

"And here, my wretched girl, is some money to buy yourself some decent lodgings for the night." He hands her the pamphlet, together with some coins, before melting into the crowd.

She glances at the cover of the pamphlet.

"Urania Cottage: A Home for Fallen Women."

Cheek! Who does he think he is?

She turns over the pamphlet. There is a scrawled list on the back:

Washing bill
Buy fruit
Flowers for Nelly
New Title: No Expectations? Few Expectations?

While she is puzzling over this, her bus appears in the distance. She stuffs the offending pamphlet into her pocket and prepares to board.

***

London possesses a moral geography. The hours of day and night can almost be charted according to the shifting locations of prostitution. If Regent Street is its midday haunt, the Haymarket is its night-time locus.

Just off the Haymarket, there is a sign hanging above a bar. It depicts a gaudily-painted wagon piled vertiginously high with hay of a bilious hue. The sign tells you that the bar is called The Waggoner's Arms, but everyone locally calls it Candy's, that being the name of the owner.

If you push open the door of Candy's bar and step across the threshold, you will be greeted by the fragrant smell of beer and tobacco, and the lively hubbub of genial conversation. Here are gleaming brass fixings, big mirrors, and a roaring fire. Here the beer is served in glasses, not pewter tankards, and it arrives clear, with a good head on it.

Pennyworth Candy is a broken-nosed, meat-fisted mountain of a man. Ex-prize fighter, ex-various other occupations (about which it is probably better not to inquire), he towers over most of the customers. He is helped behind the bar by a bevy of attractive barmaids in frilly aprons, who smile, and serve, and listen sympathetically to your life-story. Of course, they will forget every word of it as soon as you leave, but you won't know that. It is that sort of bar.

On Saturday nights, a small stage is erected in one corner, a battered piano is wheeled out from the back, and patrons of a musical bent are encouraged to strike up a tune and bawl out a merry song for the mutual entertainment of their fellow-drinkers. There is never any trouble. Pennyworth Candy's reputation goes before him. It is said that when he enters a room, even the space gets out of his way. He is that sort of landlord.

At Candy's you are welcome to enjoy a quiet drink on your own. But you could also sit with one of the pretty young women who frequent the bar of an evening. Nice girls. Some used to be maidservants, until a "change of circumstances" had forced them to quit.

These girls are several notches below the likes of Lilith Marks, of course, but they are still a lot better than the bedraggled harlots, with their garish painted faces, who hang around outside and try to wheedle and drag you into the nearest doorway. As an added incentive, every girl is known personally to the proprietor, and is well-dressed and *clean*. They are all "that sort of girl."

If you like, after buying one of these beauties a few bevvies, you might be invited, for a modest fee, to visit her in her private apartment that is only a short step away, if you'd like to follow me, sir. Your choice. Or maybe not. No problem, sir. The night is still young, and there are plenty more where you came from.

And right now, one of these pretty young women, known to her friends as Fanny, is entering the bar. She brushes the damp from her cheap coat, and approaches the shiny counter, where Pennyworth Candy is pulling a pint for a customer.

"Wotcha Fan," mine host greets her. "Glass o' the usual?"

Fanny's usual is gin. She drinks it a lot. She holds out her hand for the glass, sips, then remarks casually,

"Young lady outside as wants to see you, Penny'orth."

Several drinkers set their beer glasses quietly down upon their tables. Several sets of eyes swivel round to fix upon the landlord. Something of interest may be about to happen, possibly involving a tragic tale of betrayal and abandonment. They sit back in their seats, and await developments.

Pennyworth Candy walks to the door of the bar and half-opens it. A brief conversation ensues. Then he ushers in a slender young woman dressed in black. She wears a plain black satin-trimmed bonnet, under which a riot of unruly red curls are struggling to escape. She is followed by a scruffy boy carrying a battered broom. He stares about him with wide greedy eyes.

Pennyworth Candy calls to one of the bar-girls.

181

"Poll, take the young 'un into the back and give him a good feed," He sniffs the air. "And a dip in some 'ot water wouldn't come amiss."

He shows Josephine King to a vacant booth.

"Something to drink, miss? What about a small glass o' sherry-wine? Doll, sherry-wine for the young lady."

Josephine slides into the padded seat, clasping her hands together tightly in her lap. She has never been in a bar before. The mirrors are confusing her sense of perspective, making the room seem bigger and more crowded than it actually is, and the noise is so deafening she can barely hear herself think. Also she is aware that she is under the scrutiny of many pairs of curious eyes.

Doll places a glass of sherry on the table. Pennyworth Candy folds his arms, and waits patiently for Josephine to explain herself.

"Believe me," she begins cautiously, "I have never done anything like this before."

"No, I kind of guessed that," the barman says drily. "You don't look like the sort. And you don't talk like it neither. But you've come ter the best place, my girl; I'll see you right. Now, the first thing I has to ask is: do you 'ave your own gaff, or do you want ter rent one of the upstairs rooms?"

"I'm sorry?"

"And I'll be quite 'onest with you: there are some gentl'men who'll go for ladies in black – particular if there's whips and suchlike involved, and you've certainly got the right hair for it. But you don't strike me as that type, so you might like to think about getting some new clothes before you starts. Unless you want to attract that sort o' customer, of course."

Josephine stares at him in horror.

"Why do you think I am here?"

Pennyworth Candy gives a sigh, followed closely by a world-weary shrug.

"Well, at a guess – you caught the eye of the young master of the house. Am I right? His ma found out. You was turned off. No wages, no character, no place to go. Yeah - it's not fair, and it's not right, but you ain't the first, my lovely, and you certainly won't be the last. Most of the girls here has a similar tale to tell."

Josephine turns bright pink. She is speechless with embarrassment. When her composure returns, and her colour goes back to normal, she explains the actual purpose of her visit.

The barman hears her out in silence. Then he shakes his head slowly from side to side.

"Sorry, miss. You've had a wasted journey. I can't help you. Look around you. This is my place now. This is what I do. I don't know how you got my name, or who gave it you or wot they said, but I ain't in that line o' work anymore."

"But you used to be," she persists.

He shrugs.

"Yeah I *used* ter be, for a while. Like I *used* ter go toe-to-toe bare-knuckle twenty rounds in the boxing ring. There's a lot I *used* ter do that I don't do any more. Learned the error of my ways, you might say. And I ain't about ter put myself on the wrong side of the law for some young woman I've never met who just walks in off the street and asks me."

He rises, and signals to one of the barmaids.

"Fetch the lad out of the back. We're done 'ere."

Josephine stares at him.

"Please Mr Candy, won't you reconsider?"

But Pennyworth Candy is already making his way back to the bar, taking with him her best and last and only hope.

"Well, thank you very much," she calls after his departing back, folding her arms and glaring at him defiantly. "My beloved late father always used to say that we were put on this earth to help one another. It's a shame that doesn't seem to apply to you."

Chin in the air, and back-ramrod straight, she marches towards the bar door, making absolutely no eye contact with anybody. She has just reached the door when a huge heavy hand is laid upon her shoulder and she is spun round.

Pennyworth Candy is standing right behind her. He is breathing heavily, and there is a strange wild look in his eye.

"You say that again," he says hoarsely. "And this time say it ter my face, so as I can hear you loud and clear."

Absolute silence falls. Quickly followed by an epidemic of foot-shuffling and throat-clearing, as the occupants of the bar suddenly discover a communal interest in the contents of their glass, or the unusual whorl and striation patterns upon the surface of the tables. Meanwhile the street-sweeper, now cleaner and replete, secretes himself behind one of the barmaids.

Pennyworth Candy's eyes are still fixed upon Josephine's face.

"Go on," he commands. "Say it."

She does.

"Now tell me your name."

She does.

"And your Pa – tell me his name."

She does.

The big man staggers back, as if he has been struck a mighty blow.

"I knew it had ter be him. You said it exactly like he used ter say it. And I must've heard him saying it a 'undred times or more when I was growing up." He shakes his head slowly from side to side. "So your Pa was Reverend Amos King, was he? God bless 'is memory. I was one of his Bermondsey Bible boys. Two nights every week I'd be dahn that church hall with the other lads, studying the Good Book. Then when we was done, we'd pack everything away, and your Pa'd teach us how ter box.

"He used ter say boxing was a discipline and it'd keep us out of trouble when we grew up. And he was right. That's how I got going in the boxing game. Started winning fights locally, then decided ter go Up West, see if I could make a living in the ring. And I did too, a nice living. Bought this pub from the

184

winnings. All thanks to your Pa. If it wasn't for him, who can say where I'd have ended up?"

The big man looks her up and down, an expression of wonder on his face.

"I knows who you are now. You're Little Jo, ain't you? Exactly the same red hair as your Pa. 'Course you was only a tiny child back in them days. And here you are, large as life, all growed up."

Pennyworth Candy snaps his fingers.

"Moll, bring us some of the best French brandy. Two glasses. And see we ain't disturbed. I got business to take care of."

***

Sometime later, Josephine and Oi leave the bar and enter the flickering fairyland of the Haymarket at night. It is several hours since they first passed through its streets, and now glitter and gaiety hold sway.

Amusement and pleasure is the business of the crowd. It is carried out in supper-rooms, music-halls and theatres, as well as down dark alleyways and in secret drug-dens and doorways.

They burrow through the crowd, occasionally having to advance sideways to avoid the promenading women, all stylishly decked out in bright colours, who might be mistaken for respectable females but for the calculating eyes that stare boldly out of painted faces, scanning every passing male with practised expertise.

"Keep your 'ead dahn, and walk fast," Oi advises.

They have almost reached Shaftesbury Avenue when a noisy gang of young men in military dress force their way through the crowd. Leading the gang, his eyes wild, his face flushed with drink, is George Osborne.

He carries a wine-bottle in his hand, which he is using as a kind of battering-ram to clear a path through. Josephine is forced to press herself flat against the nearest wall to prevent

185

being hit on the back, or knocked headlong into the gutter.

"Tally-ho boys!" George Osborne shouts as he rushes by, brandishing the bottle. "Onwards to Mrs Frost's! Keep up at the back!"

A familiar fat figure lumbers past her, breathing heavily. For a fleeting second their eyes meet, and a flicker of recognition passes between them. Then Augustus Thorpe, gay blade about town, disappears into the noisy crowd.

"Never trust a soldier, that's my advice."

Josephine turns. A young woman has just emerged from a doorway. It is Fanny, the girl from Candy's bar.

"I never goes with anything in a red coat. Not if I can 'elp it," she remarks. "They likes it rough, and they doesn't like paying for it after."

"Oh!" Josephine feels the colour rising to her cheeks.

"And that one out in front, George Osborne – Master Georgie-Porgy, we all call 'im – he's the worst of the bloody lot," Fanny continues. "He glassed up one of my friends so bad she had to go to 'orspital. Scars still not healed properly. And the girls say he ain't clean – if you know what I mean."

"No... really ... I—"

Fanny stretches herself.

"I'm just off for a tipple – done some good business tonight, so I reckon I deserves a night cap afore I turns in." She jingles some coins in her hand, gives Josephine a friendly nod, and saunters off back towards Candy's bar.

***

Lord and Lady Hartington's Christmas Costume Ball.

Just the thought of it sends frissons of delightful anticipation down the well-bred female spine. It is *the* event of the Winter social calendar. Anybody who is anybody in the upper echelons of London society expects to be there. So if you are not there, well, you know exactly who and what you are. And so does everyone else.

In houses all over London, mantelpieces have already been cleared to give the gold-leaf invitation cards pride of place. Each year a different theme is chosen. Prizes are given for the best, the most original or the most amusing costume. The supper table, courtesy of the Hartington chef, is to die for, and my Lord and Lady manage to secure the services of the best musicians in town to play for the dancing and evening entertainments. (This year it is rumoured that the great Mandolini has been persuaded into performing her Tosca.)

After the ball is over, my Lady, who unfailingly carries out her duties as hostess despite her physical disabilities, will quit the palatial Hyde Park mansion for warmer and healthier climes, not to reappear until Spring peeps over the windowsill.

The theme of this year's ball is Venice in Carnival, and dressmakers and mask-makers have been summoned from every corner of the city to discuss costume designs. Bribery is taking place on a vast scale. Mendacity stalks every boudoir. The trouncing and outdoing of one's friends and contemporaries is an integral part of the whole affair.

The prospect of the ball is also sending frissons down other spines, though in this case not necessarily of delight. At Scotland Yard, police officers are gearing themselves up for a night of mayhem and amok-running, as the general public enact their own form of carnival in the streets and alleyways surrounding Belgravia.

In the detective department of the Metropolitan Police, Detective Inspector Stride and his deputy, Detective Sergeant Jack Cully, are also viewing the evening with a sense of impending doom.

"It's going to be a repetition of the Snellgrove business. I can feel it in my water," Stride observes gloomily.

He waves a copy of *The Morning Star* at Cully.

"And have you seen this? I thought the *Star* was one of the better newspapers. Appears I was wrong. The infernal cheek of these hacks!"

Embarrassingly, many London papers are now running mock adverts on their front pages, ridiculing the seeming inability of the police to get a grip on events. *The Morning Star*'s contribution reads:

<u>Wanted Immediately at Scotland Yard:</u>
Bright, intelligent Men to train as Detectives
due to Current Occupants' failure to catch Criminals.
Ability to find own backside without map an advantage.
Remuneration offered. Apply in Person.

Cully stifles a grin.

"It's not funny!" Stride growls.

"No."

Stride taps his teeth with a pencil.

"Not even a mention that we discovered who shot the unfortunate wolf that escaped from the Zoo." He sighs exasperatedly. "Next time Colonel Moran, late of Her Majesty's Indian Army, thinks he hears howling in the middle of the night, hopefully he will remember he's in St John's Wood now, not the North-West Frontier, so he won't go out firing pot-shots at all and sundry."

"At least he came forward to confess in the end."

Stride rolls his eyes.

"There are too many people in this city who think they can take the law into their own hands." He gestures angrily at the newspaper. "And I know exactly who's giving them the idea. Bloody journalists."

"Maybe."

"So Jack, any ideas about how to stop the riotous populace from making hay while the gentry enjoy their little musical swoiray? It's too good an opportunity, isn't it? Half of London high-society will be heading to Belgravia for the night, leaving their homes and their valuables unguarded. What are we going to do?"

Cully recognises the question as rhetorical rather than actual, so waits to be told.

"I'll tell you. We are going to be a visible presence, Jack. Wherever crime takes place, we shall be lying in wait for it."

Cully mulls this over.

"So how will we know exactly where it is going to take place, so that we can arrange to be lying in wait?" he asks innocently.

Stride clicks his tongue exasperatedly.

"We will adopt the tried and tested methods. Identify the areas most likely to be targeted, and arrange for at least two men to be on duty in each area at all times. Watch Boxes manned. Boots on the ground. Eyes and ears at the ready. Good old-fashioned policing. I've told you time and time again: it's the only way to get the job done. And this time, there will be no gigantic hounds or wolves to distract us. Real or imaginary."

***

Different frissons are also being experienced in the Thorpe household. Here, Isabella Thorpe, in her new position as the possible future consort of George Osborne, son of Mr Frederick Osborne of Osborne's Private Bank, has been favoured with an invitation to the ball. So has her Mama, who will attend as chaperone.

Such despair. Such joy. It is a wonder that either lady can contain her emotions. But contain them Isabella must. Especially if she is to find a reason to escape the frenzied preparations for a brief few moments of honeyed happiness in the company of her beloved artist.

Relief arrives one morning in the unexpected guise of a business card from Harrison & Co, Theatrical and Masquerade Costumier, of 31 Bow Street. The card is brought in by one of the maids, and placed next to Isabella's plate of untasted breakfast. On the back of the card is written: *10 am.* She recognises the handwriting. Her heart pounds.

"What have you got there, my love?" Mrs Thorpe inquires, holding out her hand for the card.

Isabella moves to hand it over, but somehow the little pasteboard square ends up falling into her coffee cup.

"Oh dear! I am so sorry, Mama," she cries, making a feeble attempt to fish it out with a teaspoon. "Never mind. It was just a card from one of my friends. She has discovered a wonderful little shop in Covent Garden, and has arranged to meet me there, so that we can try on costumes for the ball."

Mrs Thorpe beams.

"How lovely. I am so glad you are finally making friends. I'm sure Papa will lend you the brougham – won't you, dear?"

The newspaper at the end of the table issues a grunt.

"Shall I come with you, Bella?" Mrs Thorpe says. "I haven't decided on my costume yet. I'd like to see what this emporium has available."

Isabella feels the colour drain from her face. This is quite an accomplishment, given that she has no colour to speak of in the first place.

"Umm ... But the invitation is for me alone, Mama."

Mrs Thorpe tosses her false-ringletted head.

"I see. Well, in that case, maybe we could meet later in town for a light luncheon?" she suggests.

Isabella pretends she has not heard. She rises from the table.

"Please excuse me, Mama, Papa, I must go. Withers is waiting to get me ready." And she scurries from the room before any more questions can be asked.

***

Satisfactory is a word much on the lips of Alf Harrison, proprietor of Harrison & Co, Theatrical and Masquerade Costumier, of 31 Bow Street. Every year at about this time he sits at the head of his kitchen table, raises a glass of beer, and toasts the aristocracy – Gawd bless 'em!

This year is no exception. Thanks to their balls and "swoirays" and parties, business is so brisk, so satisfactory, that he has had to take on his wife's brother's lad to help out in the shop.

The morning finds them engaged in a little staff training before the shutters are raised upon another day's hectic trading.

"Repeat after me," Alf commands, "Oh sir, that is a perfect fit! Ma'am – or Miss – I wouldn't have recognised you!"

The lad repeats it obediently.

"Good," Alf nods. "And watch the paste sparklers at all times. They may be high-class, but the gentry is as light-fingered as anyone else."

Alf busies himself straightening the stock. The lad is sent to raise the shutters and unlock the shop door to the first customers of the day, who are already gathered outside on the pavement.

Let 'em in, Alf thinks, stepping back behind the counter, and plastering a polite smile onto his face. Let 'em all in, with their posh voices and expensive clothes and unreasonable demands. He is ready. The lad is as ready as he'll ever be. Most of all, the till is ready. Let battle commence!

By mid-morning the rush has died down. Alf sends the lad out for coffee and ham sandwiches, leaving him alone in the shop with one gentleman customer. Arty type, Alf thinks. Hair a bit too long, cravat tied in too floppy a bow. Paint on fingers a dead giveaway.

The arty type strolls round, taking out this and that, stopping every now and then to check his pocket-watch. Eventually he pulls on a black Cavalier-style felt hat embellished with feathers, and starts striking poses in the full-length mirror.

Then the doorbell goes, and a young lady enters the shop unaccompanied. She glances round, her eyes taking in the velvet capes and bright feathers and masks.

Alf hurries forward to serve her.

"Mornin' miss. Looking for anything in particular?"

The young lady's eyes swivel to the arty type, still admiring himself. Alf sees them exchange a quick meaningful glance in the mirror. Then the young lady speaks, rather grandly.

"I think I shall just see what you have, thank you. Please attend to your other duties."

Oho, so that's how it is, Alf thinks. Tragedy, comedy, he's seen it all played out on the floor of this shop. And here we have – what? A little romance, away from the prying eyes of Ma and Pa? Not the first time his shop has been used for such clandestine meetings. He pretends to dust the counter.

The young lady (much too thin and pale for his liking, but there's no accounting for tastes) edges towards the arty type. Casually, she picks up a mask, and holds it in front of her face. The arty type picks up another mask. They move together towards the back of the shop.

Oh well. None of his business, Alf thinks. The door opens again, and two young ladies bounce in, laughing and chattering noisily. Their eyes light up as they spy all the wonderful clothes, and they launch themselves upon the rails with screeches of delight, like well-bred vultures. Alf is kept so busy attending to them that he takes his eyes off the secret lovers, and only remembers they are there when the pale thin young lady tries to slip discreetly past.

"Sorry, miss," he murmurs, stepping out of her way.

One of the screechers turns, then exclaims,

"Oh! Isabella Thorpe! It is you! Are you going to the Huntingdon Ball? So are we!! What fun!! Are you here to choose a costume? So are we!!"

Alf sees the young lady start and turn even paler, as if she has received a shock. Then she says, very coldly,

"Good morning, Charlotte and Editha. I hope you are both quite well."

The screechers stare at her.

"We hear George Osborne is paying you a lot of attention," one of them squawks. "Is it true?"

The pale young lady presses her lips together.

"George Osborne is so *manly*," the screecher sighs. "Those moustaches. Those black eyes. So *Byronic*!"

"We love a red coat," the other screecher adds. "Will he be at the ball? We have not seen him for ages. What costume is he going to wear?"

"I do not know," the pale young lady replies, stiffly. Then suddenly, she walks towards the door, and leaves. Just like that.

The screechers stare after her, open-mouthed.

"How rude!" one of the screechers remarks. "What an odd person she is!"

"Very, very odd, Edie. And of course, you've heard the rumour that..." The other screecher bends sideways, and whispers something into her companion's ear.

"Oh no! *Really?* Poor, poor Georgie!"

"He should have got engaged to my sister Violet. *Everybody* knows that," the first screecher declares indignantly. "After all, who is Isabella Thorpe? Her people are in *trade*. She don't ride. She don't hunt. She speaks *French*. Georgie's sisters are *devastated*. They absolutely loathe her. And they love Vi *so much*."

"It's too, too utterly awful."

"Quite."

They roll their eyes, before returning to the rails of costumes.

Alf watches them from behind the counter. So. Unrequited love. Tragedy rather than romance. He wonders whether the arty type knew of the presence of the other gent or whether it has come as an unwelcome revelation. He glances round the shop, but the arty type is nowhere to be seen. He has gone. And so has the Cavalier-style felt hat.

***

Managing expectations is always tricky, no matter how elevated your position in the social hierarchy. Such is the opinion of Lady Caroline Hartington. One would think organising a ball to be a mere bagatelle. But one would be quite wrong.

People expect so much nowadays, she muses. They want to be astounded, but they want to be reassured. They want novelty, but they also want tradition. They want the surprising, but they want the familiar. And they want it all at the same time. It is quite exhausting.

Lady Caroline rests upon a sofa in her elegant sitting-room. Her eyes are delicately closed. A lady's-maid is bathing her temples with *eau-de-cologne*, another wafts a tiny bottle of smelling-salts under her aristocratic nose. A third maid fans her gently.

Lady Caroline enjoys ill-health. Literally. She really does. It gives her a good excuse to opt out of doing anything, or going anywhere, or seeing anyone, unless she really wants to. Most of all, it keeps her old goat of a husband out of her personal domain, and out of her body and bed.

Like many young women of her class, Lady Caroline had married her parents' choice of suitor with only the vaguest idea of what married life entailed. The morning after the unspeakableness of her wedding-night, she had tried to run away. When that failed, she had gritted her teeth and resigned herself to her fate, until thankfully the fall from her horse had released her from "wifely duties" for ever.

Of course there has been a price to be paid. She knows all about her husband's little "adventures" in the more dubious quarters of the City. She knows about the high-priced whores he frequents. She also knows what he keeps locked away in a cabinet in his private study.

The only conditions she has always insisted upon are: no affairs with servants and no public scandal. And it is with the latter in mind that Lady Caroline half-opens her blue-lidded eyes and extends a limp-wristed hand.

"The list, if you please," she murmurs.

A maid gives her the list of guests invited to the ball. She reads down the names, and smiles to herself. He has, in the past, tried to sneak one of his fancy women onto the guest list, but she is no fool. She may not get about as much as she used to, but she still keeps abreast of society. She reads the court pages in the newspapers. She has intimate female friends. She is aware who is who, and who is not.

What she does not realise is that invitation cards can be copied, then written up and sent out without the hostess even knowing it has been done. And it has been done before. Many, many times. It has been done now, as a glance at the Maida Vale mantelpiece of Lilith Marks would immediately reveal. But Lady Caroline is as likely to pay a morning call to Maida Vale as to fly to the moon.

Lady Caroline lets the precious guest-list flutter down into her lap. The ball is tomorrow night, and still there is so much to do, so many things to think about. She sighs wearily, and lets her eyes close. Later, when she is sufficiently rested, she will send for the doers and thinkers, and see how they are getting on.

***

Finally, the morning of the ball arrives. In the kitchen of the Lily Lounge, Lilith Marks is icing fruitcakes for the week ahead while thinking about what she is going to wear. She has plenty of choice. Years as a well-paid prostitute have supplied her with a large and wide-ranging wardrobe. She has tight riding breeches (very popular with certain members of the upper class), low-cut dresses in every colour, style and fabric, maids' outfits, basques and bodices galore, whips, pistols, and drawers full of silk French knickers, garters and stockings (not always worn by her).

195

Lilith has mentally whittled it down to two outfits: a jolly Gypsy costume, or that of a noble Venetian lady. In the end she opts for the latter, as she guesses that plenty of other guests will have chosen something similar, and her role tonight is to call as little attention to herself as possible. She is not there to be seen, but to see. In particular, to see the Countess, and discover whether this is the same lady who visited the Lily Lounge on two separate occasions.

All she requires now is a suitable mask to hide her face, and a big feather fan to hide the mask, and she will be ready to go. Behind such a disguise, she could be anybody: a maid or a marquise. She could be a social beauty; she could be a spy.

***

It is Saturday night, and the stars are like fragments of a glass ball flung at the sky. The temperature is falling. In a few hours, frost flowers will bloom on pavements, in parks, gardens, and cemeteries. The gas lamps gutter and gleam with a cold light.

Detective Inspector Stride and Detective Sergeant Cully stand in a doorway opposite the palatial Hartington house, watching the people on the pavement watching the people in the carriages.

A team of uniformed constables thread their way through the excited crowd as conspicuously as they can. After all, with such flaunted wealth on show, there will be criminals galore out tonight: pickpockets, muggers, cut-purses, petty thieves. Probably even some journalists.

Cully stares up at the clear sky.

"Nice night for it," he remarks. "Full moon too."

Stride shivers and pulls his muffler more firmly around his ears. December possesses the streets, dark and bitter.

"Another ten minutes of this Jack, then I'm off to get a cup of something hot," he says, stamping his feet.

"I wonder what it's like, in there," Cully says, nodding

towards the brightly-lit house.

"Whatever it's like, it's not going to be as bloody cold as out here, that's for sure," Stride complains, blowing upon his finger-ends.

And indeed, inside the Hartingtons' huge house everything is warmth and whiteness and wonderfulness. Ivory candles blaze in crystal glass chandeliers. Vines twine and twist around banisters and balustrades and mirrors. Tall Chinese vases of rare hothouse flowers scent the air.

The partitions of the two big downstairs rooms have been folded back, and the wooden floors are waxed and polished to a conker-bright shine ready for the dancing. In an anteroom, the great Mandolini is warming up her voice with some vocal exercises and a bottle of brandy.

It is indeed a far cry from Stride's freezing doorway. It is also a far cry from the small cramped Watch Box on the south side of Russell Square, where young Police Constable Tom "Taffy" Evans, newly recruited to the Force, is on duty.

Constable Evans has a dark-lantern, a rattle, a whistle, a copy of the latest *Police Gazette* and a candle to keep him company. The latter is being currently used to help compose a letter back home to his sweetheart Megan, in service in Cardiff. Literacy is a fine and wonderful thing, even when it involves a lot of perplexed head-scratching and pencil-licking to carry out.

Every now and then, Constable Evans raises his head and peers out of the narrow wooden aperture, but the Square continues to be totally deserted. The only people he's seen in the past two hours is a couple and their son out for a stroll. Big man, hat pulled down against the cold; young wife, well-shawled and bonneted, clinging to his ar;, boy with his face completely muffled in a warm scarf and cap.

They had bidden him a polite "Good evening" as they passed. A completely ordinary family. Nothing to mark them out as significant. Since then it has been as silent as the grave. Constable Evans shivers in his overcoat, and focuses his attention upon the tricky question of how to spell "carriage."

While he is puzzling this out, the completely ordinary family have made their way across the Square, until they come to a halt outside one of the houses. They mount the steps and ring the bell. When nobody answers, they have a brief discussion.

Then the man and the boy descend into the street, and vanish down the area steps. Shortly after this, the man reappears, alone, tucking something into his back pocket. He exchanges a few words with the young woman, before continuing on his own, whereupon the young woman also goes down the area steps. And once more, the Square is totally deserted and silent as the grave.

***

Back at the ball, Mrs Thorpe has retired temporarily to the ladies' dressing room with a problem. Resplendent in a puce silk hooped dress with puce and yellow fitted bodice and inserts, gold braid and white lace, she is having her ornate wig and hat readjusted as they have slipped sideways. Meanwhile, just emerging from one of the "retiring rooms" (a polite way of saying "lavatory") where she has vomited up her supper, is a perfect replica, complete in every detail.

"Ah there you are, Bella my love. Come sit by me," the Resplendent One orders, signalling with a puce-gloved hand.

Mother and daughter are wearing exactly the same outfit. Naturally, it is Mrs Thorpe's idea, born out of Isabella's complete indifference to the upcoming ball, and to the importance of making one's debut in aristocratic circles.

Mrs Thorpe, who has had to organise everything, wants the world to see how close she is to her beloved child. Why, they are almost like sisters. Thus Isabella's entrée is, by some strange osmotic process, her mother's also. Love my child, love me.

Except that nobody does love Isabella. She's been ignored by the upper-class young ladies of her own age, who all seem to recognise each other despite their wigs and masks. They have gathered by the supper table, and are excitedly comparing costumes and accessories.

Nobody has come across to talk to her. No young gentlemen have asked to be introduced to her, and more worryingly, there is no sign of George Osborne. This may well be because he is at this very moment swilling strong drink at one of his favourite watering-holes nearby, and is rapidly approaching that stage of inebriation when he will completely forget that he has an elsewhere he is supposed to be, and a future fiancée he is supposed to be squiring.

To add to her woes, Isabella knows that puce does not suit her at all: it makes her look even more wan and sickly. Also her heavy wig and mask are making her feel claustrophobic. Thus the urgent need to walk upstairs, and the hasty retreat to somewhere private, to be sick.

Mrs Thorpe, wig now straightened, takes Isabella by the reluctant arm and conducts her back to the reception room. She peers through her fancy feathered mask, a vulture sighting her prey, then heads straight for a group of elegantly-clad Venetian noblewomen.

In the quest to do the absolute best for her sulky uncooperative daughter, the words "pushy" and "parvenu" are not in her vocabulary. Besides, she has recognised the Honourable Mrs Osborne amongst the number, equally resplendent in Bordeaux damask and black lace.

"What a splendid party!" Mrs Thorpe effuses. "And does not my Lady Hartington look wonderful!"

Behind the ornate carnival masks, certain significant glances are exchanged. Most of the women present are on "Caroline" terms with the hostess. Some have known her since childhood, and address her as "Caro." Hearing her referred to as "my Lady Hartington" is a clear giveaway that this particular guest is a rank outsider.

Mrs Thorpe blunders on.

"I have been looking all around for dear George," she remarks. "Can you point him out to me? Isabella is **wild** to see what costume he is wearing are you not, my love?"

Unbeknown to Mrs Thorpe, her question to Mrs Osborne has touched upon a raw nerve. George's mother has been mentally asking it of herself for the past two hours, and is beginning to despair of coming up with a satisfactory answer. Her errant offspring has clearly chosen to ignore the parental three-line whip to turn up tonight and be seen in public with his future bride.

"I am sure he is here somewhere," she replies stiffly. "Perhaps you should seek him in the supper-room."

Whereupon the Honourable Mrs Osborne opens her feather fan and turns her back upon the hapless Mrs Thorpe, leaving her to make her way to the supper-room, accompanied by a reluctant Isabella.

But they are unlikely to locate young George there. He is currently lying in the lap of a young woman called Jenny (a young woman for whom the word "buxom" could have been invented), and bawling out the sort of song beloved of drunken young males everywhere, involving a May morning, a fair young maid and the outcome of their encounter.

George will soon fall asleep in Jenny's ample lap, waking a short while later to discover his head pillowed upon a hard wooden bench, and his wallet and fob watch missing.

He will not be pleased.

***

Meanwhile, Josephine and Oi are making their way along a basement corridor accompanied by a dark-lantern that is casting strange distorted shadows upon the walls.

"Smells rank, dunnit?" Oi remarks, sniffing the air. "It's like some animal's been livin' down here. Or maybe just died."

He is right, Josephine thinks. And the kitchen they have just passed through does not look as if it has been used for food preparation for a long time. Mrs Hudson's kitchen exudes smells of boiling and baking and tasty dinners. There are no dusty pots and pans, and no bowls of rank-looking water in one corner. In Mrs Hudson's kitchen, the tiled floor is scrubbed clean, and doesn't crunch when you walk on it.

However, she is not going to think about this. She is trying to stay in control of her feelings, or at least she is trying to act as if she is. Little tendrils of doubt are curling through her mind as to whether this was a good idea after all. Also she has noticed that there seem to be slightly more shadows on the wall than there should be, and she is not sure why.

Carrying the lantern, Oi climbs the creaky wooden stairs to the ground floor. He reaches the hallway and stands still, waiting for her to catch up. Then he heads straight for one of the closed doors and turns the handle.

"Oh my eye," he whispers over his shoulder. "Come and see this, Jo King. You won't believe wot I just found!"

She follows him into the room. The curtains are only half-drawn and a shaft of moonlight streams through the gap, illuminating everything with an eerily bright yellow glow. The room is dark-panelled with old-fashioned wooden sconces round the walls, some containing melted candles.

The prisms on the ceiling chandelier are wreathed in arabesques of cobwebs. Dust is everywhere, as well as the same strange decaying smell.

Oi suddenly gives a small moan.

"I don't like this place, Jo King. Let's go."

She tries to make her voice sound reassuring.

"We can't leave now. We have to find the diamond, remember. And then we'll have that big fish supper I promised you. Besides, Mr Candy is nearby, so nothing bad is going to happen."

The words are barely spoken when the door is suddenly slammed shut with great force. The sound echoes round the empty room. They freeze, staring at each other, reading the sheer terror upon the other's face.

Josephine tiptoes to the door, and turns the handle. It does not move. She bends down and looks through the keyhole. And feels the breath leave her body. There is an eye on the other side, looking straight back at her. A black, malevolent eye.

Next minute, two enormous blows are struck on the door, as if by an immensely powerful hand. There is a low gurgling chuckle, followed by peal upon peal of demonic laughter, followed by silence. She waits for a heartbeat. Then reapplies her eye to the keyhole. Nobody. Whoever – whatever – has been there is now gone. She grips the door handle. It still does not turn.

"I fort you said the place was empty," Oi whispers.

"I thought it was."

"So who the 'ell was that?"

She shakes her head, refusing to allow herself to contemplate the unthinkable.

"I don't know. But whoever it was, they've just locked us in."

***

Music plays sweetly, servants hover discreetly, rich foods and wines are displayed abundantly. Lilith Marks is getting up close and personal with the cream of London society. Formerly, she has only encountered it singly, horizontally, naked, and in the male version. It is amusing to notch up mentally how many of the Pantalones, Counts, and Dottor Balanzones she recognises from a former life. And how many of them fail to recognise her.

It is equally amusing to be politely ignored by their snooty womenfolk, when she could so easily let slip the sort of intimate details that would wipe the smug smiles from under their masks.

But that is not why she is here, she reminds herself. And so she crosses the floor and stations herself close to Lady Caroline

Hartington, magnificent in gold brocade with cream lace sleeves and gold gloves and hat. From here, she can also see Countess Elenore, standing in the conservatory with her back to the company.

The Countess has come as Madame Noir. Her dress is black silk velvet with black fringes and beads. Her full-face animal mask is overlaid by a black net veil sewn with hundreds of tiny diamonds. Diamonds glitter coldly in her elaborate black lace head-dress and her wig. Even though she is heavily masked and wigged, Lilith recognised her at once as the same woman from the Lily Lounge. The woman who bought the stolen bracelet from Ikey Solomon. The woman she saw fastening her shawl with Lilith's own brooch.

Lilith is struck by the way the Countess seems to inhabit her clothes rather than just wear them for public display. There is something dark and feral about her. It is as if she has been turned inside out for the evening, and what is on show is the real person.

Even the way she is staring with such intensity out of the French window reminds Lilith of a big black dog that used to roam the East End streets when she was growing up. She almost expects the Countess to go down on all fours and start howling, and pawing the glass to be let out.

Lilith's agile brain starts to make connections. Not for nothing was she once part of a twilight world where fact and fantasy intertwine, where surface and substance are not necessarily the same thing, and where gender boundaries blur. She goes back further, recalling a childhood filled with her Grandmother's tales of the *Golem* and the *vlkodlak*. Stories told to keep the dark things of the night at bay, to mask the fear and cloak the truth in fairytale.

She fixes her gaze upon the dark figure. Meanwhile, unaware that she is being so closely observed, the Countess remains absolutely motionless, her eyes fixed on the glass window. It does not look as if she is about to go anywhere for the time being, so Lilith decides to leave her where she is. She has not eaten a morsel all day, and her stomach is rumbling in a highly unladylike manner. Some food will perk her up.

Lilith makes her way to the supper room, and allows one of the powdered footmen to fill a plate, which she carries to a solitary spot by the door. From here she can eat and keep an eye on whoever passes along the corridor at the same time.

But she does not remain alone for long. Freed from her formal, high-necked business dress and starchy apron, Lilith's full swelling hips, magnificent white shoulders and sloping bust draw males like a magnet.

Soon she is the centre of attention of a group of masked, costumed men, who ply her with sweet wine, and keep her plate filled with the best delicacies on offer. Lilith sips the sweet wine, and basks in the even sweeter flattery, until she hears the announcement by the master of ceremonies that the dancing is about to begin. This brings her back to reality with a start.

She has taken her eye off the ball. Literally. She rises, and with a few hasty words of apology, makes her excuses and hurries away. A quick glance round the ballroom reveals no Countess anywhere in sight. She checks the anterooms. Also Countess-free. Growing ever more anxious, Lilith visits every room in the house, asking each servant she encounters whether they have seen Madame Noir. Nobody has.

Finally, she arrives back in the conservatory once more. She approaches the French door and pushes lightly against it. The door swings open with ominous ease. Heart sinking, Lilith faces the truth. She has failed. While she was letting the wine and attention go to her head, her quarry has escaped. Slipping out of the French door, she sets off in hot pursuit.

***

Meanwhile, still prisoners in the locked room in Number 55 Russell Square, Josephine and Oi have worn out their voices shouting and their fists banging upon the door. It seems to be growing darker by the minute, though this might be attributable to the clouds gathering in the sky, and temporarily blocking the moon

Finally it becomes clear that nobody can hear them. Nobody is coming to their aid. Wherever Pennyworth Candy is, he is not currently within earshot. They are on their own.

Except that they are not.

After what seems like an age, they hear footsteps in the corridor and see a sliver of light under the door growing brighter as the footsteps approach. At last, a key turns in the keyhole, and the door is flung back.

"So. What do we have here?" asks a deep female voice with a foreign accent.

The Countess steps into the room.

For a moment Josephine is confused. This cannot be a person, this black-clad, animal-faced thing walking upon its hind legs with a strange prancing stride. Then she remembers the Countess has come from a masked ball. What she is wearing must be her costume. What she is looking out of is a mask.

The Countess's eyes glitter strangely behind the mask.

"Ah, Miss Josephine King – I see it is you. Well, well, we meet at last. Though perhaps not under the normal circumstances. I will not ask why you have broken into the house, for I know full well exactly why you are here."

Josephine draws herself up to her full height.

"I have come to get back my diamond. The one that my uncle left me in his Will and that you stole from me."

The black mask emits a low hiss.

"But you see, Miss Josephine King, it is not your diamond. It is my diamond. The Eye of the Khan belongs to my family. It has always belonged to my family, even though it disappeared from our possession many years ago."

Josephine draws herself up, backboard-straight.

"I don't believe you," she says defiantly.

The Countess shrugs.

"No matter; it is the truth. And were it not for a chance meeting with your uncle, it would still be lost to us. It was a lucky day for me when your uncle and I were introduced to each other shortly after I arrived in London. I quickly realised here was a man with a roving eye, who liked the company of beautiful women." She laughs. "Soon after, I discovered he also liked nothing better than to brag about his exploits.

"One night he told me the story of the jewels, and how he had been given them as a gift for his noble deeds. As soon as he mentioned a diamond called the Eye of the Khan, I vowed to get it back. But your uncle was stubborn. He refused to hand it over."

"So you killed him."

"You have proof of this?"

"I have the letter you wrote to him on the day of his death asking him to meet you."

"I do not think that is proof enough," the Countess sneers.

"And I know you asked to see his Will. And I'm sure that my maid – my former maid – would identify you as the lady who called at my house pretending to be Lady Hartington. It was during your visit that the diamond went missing."

The Countess unbuttons her long evening gloves. Her eyes are dead coals come alive, hard and bright.

"Yes, you think you have been very clever, playing detective, Miss Josephine King," she says softly. "But I am afraid that now your cleverness ends."

"Wait – not so fast," Josephine says, trying to keep her voice from shaking. "For you see, I have brought this with me!" And she reaches into her pocket, and pulls out one of Mrs Hudson's kitchen knives.

The Countess stares at it incredulously, then she throws back her head and laughs. Her teeth shine ivory-white. The incisors are unusually long and sharp.

"*Is this a dagger I see before me*? You think this frightens me?

206

Do you not know, you stupid girl, that I cannot be killed by steel?"

"I don't believe you."

"She is quite correct," says a voice from the doorway.

They all turn as Lilith Marks steps coolly into the room.

"A *vlkodlak* can only be killed by something silver – isn't that true?"

The Countess bares her teeth in a snarl.

"You? I recognise you. Who do you think you are?"

Lilith brings out her hand from behind her back. She is holding a small pearl-handled pistol.

"I *think* I'm the one with a gun," she says, pointing it straight at the Countess's heart. "A gun that is loaded with silver bullets."

The Countess spits rage.

Lilith takes a few steps towards her, keeping the pistol level, then leans forward and tugs hard at the furry mask with her free hand. There is a ripping sound, and the mask drops to the ground, followed by the diamond-studded veil and black wig.

Josephine feels the breath leave her body. Instead of a human face beneath the mask, she sees a grey feral muzzle, sharp as a knife, two pointed ears, and two evil eyes that gleam cold and unnaturally green in the flickering lantern-light.

"Aha, I am right: you are a *vlkodlak* – a werewolf," Lilith says triumphantly.

"But ... " Josephine stutters, "there's no—"

"... such things as werewolves?" Lilith finishes her sentence. "Really? Are you quite sure about that? Then what do you see before you?" She gestures with the pistol. "Take a good look. Recall the face you saw in the moonlight .... do you recognise it? Recall the wolf that broke into your house ... the wolf that you told me was 'not afraid'? Do you recognise it?"

"That was my brother," snaps the Countess. "I believe you met him that day you called on me."

Josephine recalls the big grey man on the doorstep of the

house in Russell Square. She'd thought at the time that there was something familiar about him. But not this. Never this, not even in her most terrifying nightmares. Her mind struggles to take it in.

"I have thought about it, and realised that there was a full moon on the night you saw the strange apparition," Lilith continues. "Just like there must have been a full moon on the night Herbert died. That is when they turn into wolves. And tonight, there is a full moon once again."

As if in confirmation of her words, moonlight suddenly shafts whiteness into the room. It falls upon dark furred hands tipped with wicked curved claws. But before Josephine has time to respond, or Lilith to act, something completely unexpected happens. Oi, who has been crouching under the table almost stupefied with terror, decides to make a break for it.

As he rushes past her, the Countess reaches out almost lazily, picks him up with one clawed hand as if he were a thing made of feathers, and flings him across the room.

The crossing-sweeper's small body thuds into the opposite wall, slides down it, and lies still. The Countess turns and bounds out of the room, slamming the door shut behind her. They hear a key turning in the lock. A second later the dark-lantern splutters and dies, plunging them into pitch blackness.

For a moment the two stand motionless, locked into the shock of what has just happened. Then there is a low groan, followed by a feeble cough. Josephine makes her way across the room, trying to remember where the table is located, treading warily in the thick darkness.

Eventually she reaches Oi and crouches down beside him.

"Are you all right?"

The crossing-sweeper slowly levers himself upright, and is immediately very sick.

"My head 'urts, Jo King," he whimpers.

Meanwhile, Lilith has slid back the glass panel of the lantern and re-lit it.

"That's better," she says. She regards Oi thoughtfully. "Who is this boy? I didn't notice him before."

"He's my friend," Josephine says. "He helped me break into the house."

Lilith runs her hands expertly across the crossing-sweeper's shoulders, then down his bony arms and legs.

"Nothing seems broken. Can you stand, boy?"

Shakily, and with a lot of coaxing, Oi staggers to his feet. He leans against the wall for support.

"I don't feel too good," he murmurs.

"You are lucky," Lilith tells him. "A fall like that could've broken your back."

"Well, I ain't feelin' very lucky, lady," he mutters.

"So what are we going to do now?" Josephine asks.

"We are going to get out of here," Lilith says.

"How?"

Lilith regards her levelly.

"By the only way we can."

She walks over to the pistol, which she has set down upon the floor.

"Cover your ears, both of you," she says. "This might be a little noisy."

***

While these events are taking place inside the house, on the opposite side of the Square Police Constable Evans has made as good a fist as he can of his letter home. Now his feet are so cold he can barely feel them, and his backside is numb with sitting. It is time to leave his Watch Box and indulge in a bit of what his boss back at the police station calls "proceeding."

He is proceeding in a southerly direction across the square when he hears the hoarse sound of men shouting. It appears to be coming from outside one of the big houses. Drunks, he thinks. Then he notices something curious. There is a tiny light in the upstairs window of the house, as if somebody has lit a candle. But the downstairs is in complete darkness. This is odd, he thinks, as surely a person would have had to light the hall lights first to see their way upstairs.

Police Constable Evans approaches the house in a cautious and careful manner, exactly as he has been taught. He notices that the shouting seems to have stopped. The next thing he notices (aurally) is the sound of footsteps making off along the pavement in the opposite direction. He proceeds a little further – and almost falls over an enormous grey man in a heavily-gold-braided grey uniform, lying face down on pavement.

Blood pools from the man's nose, which appears to be broken, and from his mouth, and there are a couple of huge, wolf-like teeth lying on the ground next to him. His hands and feet are tied together with rope. There is something else very wrong with the man, but PC Evans' simple Welsh brain can't deal with what his eyes are telling him he is looking at, so he just loosens the ropes, and steps away.

Now he notices a pale light flickering through a ground floor shutter of the house. He is just pondering on this new development, when the silence is shattered by a single gunshot. Without a shadow of doubt, some sort of a felony is taking place within.

PC Evans reviews his options. What should he do? On the one hand, he could view this as a Heaven-sent opportunity to single-handedly prove himself a hero. Although possibly, given the gunfire, the proof might end up being posthumous.

On the other hand, he is very young, and it is his first time in London, and – most importantly – he has not yet (to put it euphemistically) *joined giblets* with anybody.

PC Evans assesses the situation, and decides in the circumstances that there is only one acceptable course of action. He leaves the square, and goes to find back-up.

While he is gone, the man on the ground will return to consciousness, discover the ropes that bound him have been loosened, and will stagger off to lick his wounds in some dark corner of the city. Which is just as well, because nobody would ever have believed PC Evans anyway.

***

As PC Evans sets forth in search of help, another more frantic search is taking place. In the benighted silence of the shadowy house, Josephine and her companions are hunting the Countess. There is no logic to this decision. Logic screams that their proper course of action would be to get out as quickly as they can, and hand over to the forces of law and order. However, logic has been taken hostage by something darker and more primitive: a desire for confrontation and revenge.

And so, accompanied by a pistol, a kitchen knife, and a splitting headache, they progress from room to empty room, always keeping close to each other, and close to the flickering dark-lantern that now lights their way up the dark staircase to the next floor.

Entering the first chamber they come to, they spy an open-lidded trunk piled high with clothes. A four-poster canopied bed is strewn with silk sachets, hatboxes and jewel cases.

"It is as I thought," Lilith whispers. "She is preparing to leave. We have arrived just in time. Another day and she'd be gone."

Taking the diamond with her, Josephine thinks.

As if reading her thoughts, Lilith gestures towards one of the leather jewel cases. The top drawer has been flung open and is empty.

"Wherever she is hiding, she has the diamond with her."

"Then we must find her."

They search in the wardrobe and behind the curtains, and move cautiously on. But the Countess is not to be found. They are just on the point of giving up the search, when Lilith suddenly puts her finger to her lips. They freeze, ears straining.

211

Then the other two hear it also. A faint susurration, like silk being drawn along a wooden floor. It appears to be coming from somewhere above their heads. They look up.

The werewolf is standing on the upper landing, staring straight down at them. She is holding a massive, heavy, marble-topped washstand. Her eyes are the eyes of a beast of prey, nocturnal, red as an open wound. Next second she hurls the washstand over the banisters.

They cover their faces and cower back against the wall. The washstand hurtles to the ground with a deafening crash. Sharp pieces of wood and shards of shattered marble fly into the air.

When the dust has settled, they step forward cautiously. The upper landing is empty. They stare in dismay at the gaping hole in the floorboards, and the pile of debris.

"She could've killed us," Oi whimpers.

"But she didn't," Lilith says firmly, brushing powdered marble from her clothes. "She must be up in one of the servants' attics. Follow me. And take great care."

They clamber over pieces of shattered floorboard and chunks of broken marble, and resume the search.

***

There is a tavern in the town. It is a tavern where young men of a certain class go to drink beer and become acquainted with young women of a certain class (though not generally the same class, because we're talking about the sort of young women that the young men's parents would definitely disapprove of). Right now there is a fracas taking place at the tavern in the town, and the police have been summoned.

By sheer chance, Detective Sergeant Jack Cully happens to be in the immediate vicinity, having just enjoyed a nice hot tripe supper at an eating-house round the corner. A couple of local constables armed with truncheons are also in the neighbourhood. They all assemble on the pavement outside the tavern, where they enter into a brief discussion on tactics, before entering the tavern itself.

Inside the tavern, they find tables overturned and stools upended. People are cowering in corners and behind the long bar. The floor is awash with spilt beer and crunchy with broken glass. At the centre of the fracas is a young man wearing the unlikely costume of a Venetian nobleman. He is whirling about, waving a naked sword – not a good idea in a confined space, and with young women present.

The young man is yelling at the top of his voice about a certain purse full of guineas, and a gold fob-watch. Items he claims he had upon his person when he entered the tavern, and which he now no longer has about him.

The absence of these items is being blamed upon a young lady called Jenny Weaver. Cully is immediately informed by another young lady called Pearl, whose dress appears to be a couple of sizes too small, that Jenny is not in the tavern, was never in the tavern, and that she, Pearl, who has only just arrived in the tavern, has not seen Jenny for ... ooh, almost a week.

"Now then, my girl," Cully says briskly. "Enough of that gammon. You cut along sharpish, and tell your friend Jenny to bring the stolen articles down to the station toot sweet, and we'll say no more about it. All right?"

He gives Pearl a knowing look, whereupon Pearl shrugs and melts silently away into the crowd. Cully turns his attention to the young Venetian nobleman.

"Put the sword down. Please. Sir." Cully speaks in a polite-but-with-an-edge-of-menace tone.

But George Osborne (for indeed, it is he) ignores the request, and continues to wave the sword above his head, slicing several candles from their holders.

"Do you know who I am?" he demands angrily.

"No, Sir. Should I?"

"My father. My father owns a bank. That means I am an

important person."

Aren't they bloody all, Cully thinks wearily. As if it matters. As if he gives a damn.

"That means you cannot lay a finger on me. Not. A. Finger. Understand? None of you can lay a finger on me. Because if you do, my father will— nggh."

But Cully is never to know what George Osborne's father will do, because at this point George Osborne's head comes into sudden contact with one of the police constables' truncheons, and he drops like a stone. At some point in the future, this will be called police brutality, and will result in a prosecution being brought. But this is 1860, so it merely results in a loud cheer from the other occupants of the tavern.

George Osborne is dragged bodily out of the tavern by the two constables and thrown into a waiting horse-drawn police wagon, the floor and ripe air of which bear witness to long usage by equally-drunken men.

As the wagon trundles away, Detective Sergeant Cully is approached by another officer, this time from his own force. The officer is hot and sweaty, and out of breath.

"Sir," he gasps, "Detective Inspector Stride wants you to go to Russell Square as quickly as you can. Something has occurred."

***

Lilith, Josephine and Oi have reached the top of the house, where at last they find the Countess, crouched like an animal on the floor of an attic room. She is holding the diamond in her mouth. Even in darkness, the clear jewel glimmers softly. Ice-cold and pure and desirable.

The Countess sees them, gathers herself and leaps gracefully towards a skylight which bursts open at her touch. Before they can grab hold of her feet, she hauls herself up, and disappears.

Lilith fetches a chair, and places it under the skylight. They help each other to clamber out onto the roof. The vast scoop of sky is vertiginously high and clear, yawning like an abyss. The stars are a wild maze. The three of them stand gasping in the taut, biting cold. There is nothing between them and the infinity of space.

Casually, as if stepping upon the floor of some elegant society ballroom, the Countess glides over the flat surface until she reaches the edge. There she stops, studying the gap between the house and its nearest neighbour.

It is clear that she intends to leap across, and from thence make her way along the roof-line to the end of the row of houses. For a brief moment she stands precariously poised on the very edge, her weird hairy face framed in the moonlight, the diamond in her jaws glittering like the heart of winter.

Then suddenly and without warning, the flimsy parapet gives way. The Countess stretches out her furred hands as if trying to grip on to empty air. She utters a loud choking cry, and disappears over the edge. Josephine rushes forward, and sees her flying in the air, her long dark cloak billowing around her like black wings, as if in some terrifying dream.

Except that this is not a dream.

The Countess falls. Through the air, through the darkness, through every nightmare of the imagination, until she lands heavily upon the iron-tipped railings below. They all peer down. Skewered on the sharp spikes, the werewolf's body lies like a broken marionette. It does not move. The feral muzzle points upwards to the night sky, as if desperately seeking a last soundless gasp of life-giving breath.

Even from their rooftop vantage point, they can clearly see the sharp point of an iron spike pushing up from the centre of the black-clad chest. For a moment, the three stare in shocked disbelief.

Then Lilith pulls them back from the perilous edge.

"It is over," she says simply. "She has gone. And she has taken the diamond with her."

Josephine utters a great shuddering sigh.

"I don't care anymore about it," she says quietly. "It killed my uncle; it nearly killed me. I'm glad it's gone. Maybe now it has claimed its last victim."

"Brave girl," Lilith says, giving her a brief hug.

Oi gestures towards Lilith's pocket.

"Woz they really silver bullets in the shooter?"

"Of course they weren't."

He nods.

"Thought not. So what should we do now?"

Lilith smiles grimly.

"Not be here."

She takes him by the shoulders, and steers him gently towards the open skylight.

"Leg it out the back way. Detective Inspector Nosy and his pal have just arrived. We don't want them asking awkward questions. Like what are we doing here and how did we get in?"

Obediently Josephine and the crossing-sweeper swing themselves through the skylight, tumble down three flights of stairs, and race across the dark garden, fear of discovery almost giving their footsteps wings.

Only when they are beyond the garden gate, gasping and panting in the narrow alley at the back of the house, does Josephine suddenly realise they are on their own.

"Where's Lilith?"

"Dunno," Oi says. "And guess what? I ain't waiting around to find out."

And like a scrawny cat, he blurs into the shadows and disappears.

Meanwhile, out in the street, Detective Inspector Stride and Detective Sergeant Cully elbow their way through the usual crowd of gawping bystanders that never fails to materialise out of nowhere whenever something gruesome turns up.

They are both far too busy trying to impose their authority and create a semblance of order to notice the dark-haired woman wearing a velvet floor-length evening cloak, who steps casually up from the basement area of a house, and makes her way across the square in a northerly direction.

Had they noticed her, they might have wondered what exactly she was clutching so tightly in one hand, as if she'd never let go of it again. And why she was smiling.

***

London in 1860 is rebuilding itself. Carcasses of ragged houses, fragments of walls, and broken streets have ceded to giant cranes and scaffolding. Vast wildernesses of brick piles have moved in, as the new industrial landscape of rail and road drive relentlessly through old neighbourhoods, disquieting corpses and displacing populations on every side.

From the ruination of tenement lodgings, dank cellars and freezing alleyways, miserable wretches emerge each morning and stream towards the awakening city. Thousand upon thousand, they move in an endless stream. A treadmill of transitory souls. Food for factory, workhouse, or madhouse, or for charnel-house and the grave, they enter the great gaping maw of the monster, and are swallowed up and lost.

The crossing-sweeper is definitely lost. His pitch upon Westminster Bridge has been empty for days. His regular clients have had to make their way, at great personal inconvenience, across the icy, muck-encrusted street without his invaluable assistance. One or two have even gone so far as to ask the coffee stall holders if they know what has happened to the boy. Because really, it is a most unsatisfactory situation.

The coffee stall holders shrug their shoulders, shake their heads sadly and say they don't know nothing. He did mention that the building he lodged in had been recently flattened to make way for the railway. So he'll be sleeping rough. And the night-time temperature has dropped way below freezing. And he had that nasty cough, didn't he ... never mind.

217

No doubt they'll find the body, give it a pauper's funeral. Sad, but it happens all the time. Someone else'll take over his pitch soon enough. Meanwhile, how about a cuppa lovely hot coffee? Slice of bread-and-butter to go with it? Have a good day, sir. At least we'll still be here on your way home. You can be sure about that.

**

But can you really be sure about anything in this world of shifting reality? Bob Miller (who looks after the carriage- and riding-horses at a livery stables just off the Finchley Road) certainly thinks you can. He is telling his wife Rose (who looks after Bob) about the happenings of his day.

Supper has been eaten, and the cloth cleared. Now Bob is sitting back in his easy chair, with his feet on the fender and a pipe on the go, while Rose clatters the pots and pans.

"Green Ginger came back lame," Bob remarks. "Poor beast had cast a shoe. You'd think that stupid arsehole of a coachman would've noticed, but no. '*I am Lord Mauleverer's driver, not his farrier*' he says to me, all haughty like, when I pointed it out. So I says to him, '*Well, if you take out that poor beast again, I'll make it my business to tell Lord Mauleverer. Then you'll be his ex-driver.*' Didn't like that, I can tell you."

Bob Miller takes a good pull at his pipe, and chuckles at the recollection. The relationship between carriage staff and stable staff is always fraught with animosity, the former believing themselves to be vastly superior to the latter.

"Oh – and we might be setting on a new stable boy. Young lad turned up out of the blue first thing, said he was looking for work. Well, normally, I'd have sent him packing with a box round the ears for his cheek, but what with Tom Snape off with a fever, and that new family boarding four carriage horses and a riding hack, we're breaking our backs just to keep on top of the work.

"So I thought to meself, right, young feller, let's see if you're cut out for stable work. I gave him a broom and a shovel, and told him to muck out one of the boxes. The one where that horse has had a bad stomach upset. Shit up to your hoxters – if you'll excuse my language. Stank to high heaven too. We'd all been avoiding it. That'll soon sort you out, me laddo, I thought. You'll be off down the road in no time at all.

"But blow me down, if he didn't have the place all swept clean and tidy in a jiffy. Never seen anyone handle a broom like that. And then he says to me: *'You want to mix more bran in that nag's mash, gov'nor. It'll settle her guts.'* Could have knocked me down with a feather. So I says to him: *'Well, you certainly know about horses,'* and he says to me, *'I should do, I've worked with them all my life.'*"

Bob Miller grins. He leans back and folds his arms behind his head.

"You want to be careful, Bob," Rose says, wiping her wet arms on the towel. "You shouldn't let yourself be taken advantage of. After all, who is this boy? Maybe he's part of a gang or summat. Them horses is valuable, ain't they."

Bob gives her an affectionate women-what-do-they-know? glance.

"Ah love, I got a feeling for people, you know that. I can tell a good'un from a bad'un. And the lad's fine. Honest blue eyes. Looked me straight in the face, no flinching. William, that was his name. Just moved into the area, he said. So I said to him: *'William, my lad, you be here bright and early first thing in the morning as well, and maybe we'll see about taking you on.'*"

And bright and early first thing in the morning here is young William, in a pair of clean corduroy trousers, a warm jacket, muffler, stout boots and a tweed cloth cap that is slightly too big for him. He leans against the harness-room door, sucking a straw contentedly.

"Mornin' gov'nor," he greets the ostler. "Cold 'un, innit."

And as the day progresses, it looks as if Bob Miller is right.

219

William is indeed a good 'un. Without a word of complaint, he runs errands, mucks out stables, swills down the yard, and polishes tack.

Whenever he gets a rare break between jobs, he chats to the other grooms, asking questions about the horses and their owners. A bright lad with a bright future, Bob Miller thinks to himself. Young William could be a real asset to the yard, if he settles to it.

Then just before the dinner hour, something else happens. An unexpected visitor arrives. A redheaded young woman, snugly dressed against the cold, walks bold as brass into the yard, and asks to see William.

Slightly taken aback by her unexpected appearance, and by her confident manner, Bob makes a clumsy remark about young Will being a bit young for sweethearts, but is informed crisply by the visitor that she is in fact not his sweetheart, but his sister.

Bob locates William, and conveys the news of her arrival.

Brother and sister greet each other most affectionately. Bob and some of the grooms watch them. It is always interesting to observe other people's nearest and dearest. And it provides a welcome break from their labour.

"This is my sister wot I lives with," William announces proudly.

"I have brought you a pie, William," the sister says, in a voice that is, oddly, several classes higher than her brother's. "Veal and ham. I hope that is satisfactory."

"Veal and 'am is good, sis," William nods.

"Have you come far, miss?" Bob inquires.

The sister gives him a brief half-smile.

"Not too far, thank you."

Bob's glance moves from brother to sister.

"Well, anybody can see you're related," he says happily.

"They can?" The sister's eyebrows shoot up.

"Ho yes indeed! Def'nite family resemblance."

He claps young William round the shoulder in a friendly way.

"You go and 'ave your pie with your sister, young Will. You've earned your break."

Bob watches them walk out of the yard, side by side. It is nice to see such a devoted family. Warms the cockles of your heart. He thinks of Rose, and the dinner she is probably preparing for him right now. Oh yes, you can't beat family. Family is worth more than all the silver, gold and precious stones in the world. It is indeed.

***

But only where there is also love. And there is precious little of that nowadays in the Thorpe household, where the prospective nuptial plans of Isabella Thorpe continue to run on apace, though seemingly with very little input from the future bride herself. The union of the house of Thorpe to the house of Osborne seems to be bypassing her altogether.

Not that her Mama has noticed, for she is far too busy broadcasting the happy tidings to all and sundry, fussing over venues, drawing up guest lists, and trying to outdo the Honourable Mrs Osborne in veiled unpleasanteries.

Things cannot go on like this.

And indeed, they don't.

One icy night, as darkness settles on the topmost ridges of the Heath, and the view of the city has sunk into a black gulf, a thin female figure makes her solitary way along the deserted and unlit high road. Isabella Thorpe has reached breaking point, and is finally initiating an exit strategy.

It is a downhill journey from the heights of Hampstead to the streets of the city below. Downhill geographically, symbolically, and in so many other ways too, for London is not a safe place for a physically frail and emotionally naïve young lady out on her own. Especially at night. Will Isabella make it safely to her destination? Or will she be sucked into the teeming, vice-ridden metropolis, never to be seen again? Who knows?

Maybe the answer will become apparent at the next spring exhibition to be held at the Royal Academy, where visitors are going to be shocked by a painting entitled *The Princess's Dream* by the (up until then) little-known Pre-Raphaelite artist Henry Papperdelli. The picture depicts a young woman gazing with rapt delight out of a window at some peacocks and pomegranate trees. She holds a single lily stem in one hand. It is a very pretty picturesque scene.

The scandal however, lies in the languorous curve of the woman's parted mouth, the vacant, half-closed, pebble-grey eyes, the lock of curled chestnut hair straying wantonly across her bare shoulder, and the faint half-flush on her cheek, all suggesting that something other than peacocks and pomegranates has recently been giving her pleasure.

When questioned, Papperdelli will insist that the painting came out of his imagination. Shortly after the exhibition ends, he will quit Number 17 Red Lion Square for the even less salubrious artistic quarter of Paris. He will be accompanied by a pale young woman with chestnut ringlets, who is not his wife.

The Princess's Dream is going to be bought by a rich Hampstead businessman who will add it to his personal art collection and hang it in his private study. Sometimes his wife, who has taken to wearing full mourning, will be found there, staring at it with a slightly puzzled expression on her face.

***

But all this is yet to be. Returning to the present, Detective Inspector Stride sits in his office finishing the last sentence of his report. He places a triumphant full stop at the end, then lays down his pen with a satisfied sigh. His expression is that of a cat on the day it rained mice.

A knock at the door admits Jack Cully, carrying a piece of paper.

"The police surgeon's report on the body has just arrived."

"Excellent timing, Jack. I've just finished mine."

Stride takes the report, adds it to the back of his own, and straightens all the pieces of paper together. He glances up.

"Well, we did it. We finally recovered the Meadows emeralds."

"Yes sir."

"Which have now been returned to their grateful owners. And we discovered the real identity of that 'gigantic hound'."

Stride pauses, shaking his head in disbelief.

"Who'd have thought it – a werewolf! Here in London in 1860. Attending parties, mixing with high society. Robbing, and killing innocent citizenry. It beggars belief! No wonder Herbert King and the poor Snellgrove maid were terrified out of their wits. The sight of that ... thing ... would be enough to scare the stoutest of hearts."

"Indeed," Cully murmurs. The memory of what he saw impaled on those railings is still giving him nightmares.

"I thought Miss King received the news very bravely, in the circumstances," he observes.

"She did, Jack. Most impressive behaviour in a young woman. I had thought she might have a fit of the vapours or ... whatever it is young women have."

A fleeting vision of Josephine King rises before Stride's eyes, standing utterly still, her back ramrod-straight, her eyes fixed upon some point on the far wall. She had not shown a flicker of emotion when he and Cully had called to inform her that her uncle's murderer had finally been found, but due to certain circumstances beyond their control (and barely within their comprehension) the individual concerned would not be standing trial.

Instead, she had merely thanked them politely for bringing her the news. Then, after an awkward silence in which she did not faint dead away on the hearthrug, she had rung for the maidservant (a different girl from the one they had seen on previous visits), who had shown them out into the street.

Stride gestures towards a pile of morning newspapers.

"Have you seen the papers today? The bloody hacks love us. Even Dandy Dick thinks we smell of roses."

He shows Cully a copy of the *Inquirer*. The huge banner headline reads:

DARING DETECTIVES CATCH CRIMINAL COUNTESS!!

"What a shame that the editor has only one front page,"Cully observes drily.

Stride clips the two reports together with a flourish.

"There. Done and dusted. I'll just get someone to run this across to the Home Office, and that'll finally be an end to the whole affair."

Jack Cully shifts awkwardly from one foot to the other, then clears his throat. "Ah ... perhaps not quite."

Stride glances up.

"What do you mean?"

Cully feels around inside his pocket, and pulls out something, which he sets carefully down upon the desk.

Stride's eyes widen.

"My God! Is that what I think it is?"

Cully nods.

"A bloody great diamond. Look at the size of it!" Stride breathes in wonderment. "Where on earth did that come from?"

"It was lodged in her ... its throat. The surgeon says that if the fall hadn't killed her, this would. It was completely blocking her windpipe."

"Well, well," Stride muses. "What a beauty. It must be worth a fortune."

The diamond glints and sparkles in the dim office light.

"What are we going to do with it?" Cully asks. "It might have belonged to her ... it, or it might not. Either way, we can't very well place an advert in the papers asking the rightful owner or anybody who has information about it to come forward. We'd have every Tom, Dick and Sarah in London beating a path to our door claiming it was theirs."

Stride stares thoughtfully at the diamond.

"Who knows about this?"

"You, me and the police surgeon."

Stride scratches his head with the end of the pen.

"Right," he says slowly. "Leave it with me, Jack. I'll deal with it."

"You will? How will you?"

"In due course," Stride says obliquely. "Oh – and I wouldn't go mentioning this to anybody outside this office. As you say: we don't want word getting out."

Cully regards him speculatively, but Stride refuses to be drawn. He fiddles with the report and rearranges things on the desk, until eventually Cully gets fed up of waiting to be enlightened, and takes himself off to find a welcome mug of tea.

As soon as he has gone, Stride moves swiftly. He unclips the police surgeon's report and slides it under his blotter. Then he places his own report in an envelope, which he addresses to the Home Secretary. He gets up and reaches for his coat and hat. Just before leaving the office, he slips the diamond and the *Inquirer* into his inside pocket.

***

Robert Garrard of R & S Garrard & Co, Royal and Crown Jewellers, has closed the shutters of his Panton Street shop. He has locked the shop door, and drawn down the blind to keep the passing world away. He has given the staff a half-holiday. Now he sits in the deserted workroom, waiting for the waves of dizziness to pass over him.

He still cannot fathom how it occurred. The shop was busy. He remembers that. It is always busy in the run-up to Christmas. People like to buy expensive jewellery for their nearest and dearest. Or maybe just for their dearest, who can say. Whatever, the shop was busy, and at some point, a small newspaper-wrapped parcel was placed, or left, on the counter.

He remembers the last time he was this close to the jewel. The feeling of breathlessness, as if all the air had suddenly been sucked out of the room. The rising desire to scream with delight. He did not think he would ever feel the same way again. He did not dream that he would see it once more. And now it is as if a fault in time has opened, and the diamond has dropped through into his lap.

Garrard grips his hands together so tightly that his knuckles go bone-blue white, and his nails form red crescents in the palms. Of course he knows that the diamond is technically not his: it belongs to the young woman with red hair, but he does not know who she is, or where she lives. If, indeed, she still lives. People move on. Accidents happen.

So by default, he reasons to himself as his eyes devour its radiant perfection, the diamond has left her and has now come to him. For a while longer he sits and worships. But he is above all a man of business. A stone of this magnificence cannot be wasted. It is a jewel fit for a queen. And so it is to a queen that it must be offered.

Thus a few days later, Robert Garrard, wearing his best black suit, follows a footman along a rather threadbare carpet towards the private quarters of the most important and powerful woman in the kingdom, nay in the whole world, mentally noting as he goes that despite her global importance, her palace still smells of sewage.

He is shown into her private sitting-room, a place stuffed with sofas and chairs and writing-desks. The walls are full of paintings of horses, family pets and children, and, despite modern advances, the room is still being lit by candles.

Garrard has met Victoria on many occasions, but once again as he bows low, he is struck by how this woman, who rules over nearly a quarter of the earth, looks just like a child in a woman's dress.

She is so tiny, and there is a twist in her top lip, like a kind of deformity. She has china-blue eyes, heavy-lidded and protuberant. Diamonds wink and glitter upon her neck, in her shell-small ears. Rings adorn every finger, and both thumbs. He knows that she loves fine jewellery almost as much as he does.

"Mr Garrard. You have brought something special to show me?"

Her voice is beautiful. Low and bell-sweet, like that of a singer. The voice of a queen. He offers her a velvet bag, corded at the top. She takes it and opens it up eagerly, like a little girl on her birthday. Next minute, the diamond sits in her hand, winking up at her.

"Oh, a *fine* diamond, Mr Garrard! Very fine indeed. How did you come by it?"

He tells a tale. A French émigré, impoverished, washed up in London and in desperate circumstances came into his shop one day. Victoria listens eagerly. She has a child's delight in stories.

"I thought that, when properly cut, the stone might furnish the centrepiece for a new crown," he suggests.

She sets the diamond down and claps her podgy beringed hands together in glee.

"Oh yes. A new crown for a future jubilee. That would be wonderful. We are delighted to accept this precious gift. Thank you, Mr Garrard."

She replaces the diamond in the bag. He receives it, bows low and departs. The diamond will be cut and polished in his workroom.

And less than a year after accepting the gift, Victoria will be a widow, mourning the death of her beloved husband Prince Albert, struck down in his prime at the age of forty-two.

Typhoid fever, supposedly.

***

But now it is almost Christmas Eve, and there is snow in London. Snow lines the tops of trees, railings, and roofs. Snow sits on gravestones, settles upon the heads and shoulders of statues. In the streets, snow is churned with ash, soot, dung and mud. In places it has been swept into grey pyramids. Elsewhere, the press of traffic has cleared erratic paths through it.

In Regent Street the gaslit shops glitter with a superabundance of tempting festive goods. Bronze kid boots, silks, velvets, point-lace, hats, parasols, mantles, glass perfume bottles, fancy stationery and feather-fans pass by in an endless dazzling procession of visual desire.

Eventually the shops give way to quiet streets, a green space, a dairy, a canal, until finally we find ourselves back in the familiar territory of St John's Wood, with its fashionable and shabby-chic villas.

The curtains of one particular villa have not yet been drawn to keep out the early evening chill. There is a bright fire crackling in the front room grate, warm and welcoming. A Christmas tree stands in the window, lighted with thin wax tapers, and decorated with bonbons and nuts.

In the dining-room, the table is laid for supper with the good silver cutlery, newly shined. Guests are expected, for five places have been set. In the basement kitchen Mrs Hudson, assisted by her niece, is adding the final touches to the meal.

Roast mutton, peas, and potatoes will be followed by currant tart and cheese. A veritable feast. And after supper, there will be Christmas plans and preparations to discuss round the fire.

Look more closely. The first of the guests is just about to arrive. Lilith Marks comes round the corner and walks briskly towards the house. She holds a round parcel wrapped in festive paper. One of her legendary Christmas cakes. She mounts the

228

steps, and rings the bell.

She is followed a few minutes later by a tall broad-shouldered man who approaches the house from the opposite direction. He wears a cloth cap pulled low, and woollen pea-coat. It is Pennyworth Candy. Under one arm, he carries a bottle of wine. A brief hesitation while he checks he has the right address. Then he too rings and is admitted. Finally, the last guest arrives on the doorstep: a thin young man with a pale bony face, and a pale bony nose and a very shiny top hat. Trafalgar Moggs is let into the house.

And now the curtains have been drawn; the front door locked against the outside world. Family and friends are gathering in the dining-room, where supper is just about to be served. There is nothing more to see, and little reason to linger out here in the frost-crisped air where darkness is falling fast.

A cab has recently drawn up at the end of the road. Why not let it bear you away towards the teeming night-time city, with its seductive labyrinth of gas-lit streets where all is dazzlement, music and dancing.

Who knows what adventures await?

Finis

Fantastic Books
Great Authors

Meet our authors and discover our exciting range:

- Gripping Thrillers
- Cosy Mysteries
- Romantic Chick-Lit
- Fascinating Historicals
- Exciting Fantasy
- Young Adult and Children's Adventures

Visit us at:
www.crookedcatbooks.com

Join us on facebook:
www.facebook.com/crookedcatpublishing

BC	8/14
BB	6/16

Lightning Source UK Ltd.
Milton Keynes UK
UKOW05f0810160714

235200UK00001B/2/P